WEST OF IRELAND

C. P. HOFF

Danika

Thanks so much for
coming and making the
afternoon so wonderful
Connie

THE PICARESQUE NARRATIVES

BOOK ONE

Away in the Northwest, Mrs. John Anderson, 169-170, an Irish immigrant to Canada and author's Great-Great-Grandmother

Except of three lines from "'Tis a Fearful Thing": 1075-1141 Yehuda Halevi

Editor Adrienne Kerr

Copy editor Elizabeth McLachlan

Cover design Stuart Bache

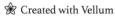 Created with Vellum

Jack
For a happy marriage

CONTENTS

Dear Reader   xi

Chapter 1   1
Chapter 2   8
Chapter 3   11
Chapter 4   16
Chapter 5   21
Chapter 6   24
Chapter 7   31
Chapter 8   36
Chapter 9   46
Chapter 10   51
Chapter 11   55
Chapter 12   62
Chapter 13   65
Chapter 14   71
Chapter 15   75
Chapter 16   78
Chapter 17   87
Chapter 18   93
Chapter 19   96
Chapter 20   102
Chapter 21   107
Chapter 22   113
Chapter 23   118
Chapter 24   124
Chapter 25   127
Chapter 26   132
Chapter 27   137
Chapter 28   140
Chapter 29   144
Chapter 30   149
Chapter 31   154

Chapter 32	158
Chapter 33	161
Chapter 34	165
Chapter 35	171
Chapter 36	174
Chapter 37	180
Chapter 38	183
Chapter 39	186
Chapter 40	189
Chapter 41	192
Chapter 42	195
Chapter 43	201
Chapter 44	206
Chapter 45	208
Chapter 46	215
Chapter 47	217
Chapter 48	223
Chapter 49	227
Chapter 50	234
Chapter 51	238
Chapter 52	244
Chapter 53	248
Chapter 54	252
Chapter 55	259
Chapter 56	262
Chapter 57	266
Chapter 58	270
Chapter 59	272
Chapter 60	277
Chapter 61	279
Chapter 62	284
Chapter 63	287
Chapter 64	289
Chapter 65	295
Chapter 66	297
Chapter 67	304
Chapter 68	306
Chapter 69	310

Chapter 70	314
Chapter 71	317
Epilogue	320
Dear Reader	323
A Town Called Forget	325
Chapter 1	327

If you like this book, tell a friend; if not, forget you read it.
  Black Crow Books

1

MRS. O'BRIEN

Mrs. O'Brien hummed as she pushed open the door to the kitchen. A spot of tea was what she was after, something just hot enough to ward off the early morning chill. It was what she told herself every morning in spring. In winter, tea eased the ache in her bones, in summer it steeled her up against the heat, and in autumn, it cradled her soul and prepared her for the dark months ahead. In her mind, tea was the answer to all ills, real or imagined.

Upon entering the kitchen though, she found the cook distracted, forgoing the expected greeting. The girl's eyes barely fluttered in Mrs. O'Brien's direction. As mistress of the house, she bristled. This was not the way to greet one's betters; it was dismissive. After a pause and the tap of her foot, Mrs. O'Brien cleared her throat. Mae's attention remained on task, pounding the hapless bread dough on the countertop.

Mrs. O'Brien considered the cook. Mae was new to the household and bland. Mr. O'Brien had insisted on her. He said she looked like a turnip, her face a patchwork of purple and cream, making her suitable for the kitchen. "After all, if a turnip can't cook a good meal, then what's this world coming to?" Mrs. O'Brien wasn't so sure anymore. A young girl with an uneven temper was liable to upset the household, even a household as unencumbered by formalities as the O'Briens.

"She's not forgotten her place," came an unwelcome voice from an unlit corner. "She knows you're here. No use wasting a good curtsy."

Mrs. O'Brien winced as she squinted toward the shadows. She'd know that stench anywhere: Sister Mary-Frances, her infernal sister-in-law. Now she understood Mae's lack of response. It was a warning, an omen, a harbinger of doom. Fighting to regain some of her former composure, Mrs. O'Brien readied herself to speak. She'd prepared for this moment, studied with regularity for hours, in front of the mirror. She'd squared her shoulders, lifted her head, and jutted out her chin, exuding defiance, resilience, steadfastness; shoulders too high and she'd look anxious, too low and she'd look cowed. Mrs. O'Brien closed her eyes as she raised and lowered her shoulders trying to reproduce the practiced sensation.

"What are you doing? Dancing with the fairies?"

Mrs. O'Brien took a breath and opened her eyes. "Never mind that now. To what do I owe this privilege?"

"In this house, my presence has never been a privilege. So, don't pretend it is now. You'll remember that my brother and I were raised in this house long before you ever darkened our door." The nun rose and stepped into the light. "And I think we both know what you owe me."

Mrs. O'Brien flung open a cabinet door to avoid looking at her, and took out a china teacup and saucer; it didn't occur to her to offer one to her guest. "Whatever do you mean?"

"My good woman, don't play the fool with me. I'm not in the mood."

Mrs. O'Brien faced her sister-in-law. Even in her habit, Sister

Mary-Frances had few feminine traits. Her broad shoulders and height matched that of Mrs. O'Brien's husband, and the nun's baritone voice rivalled any man's in Tnúth, but that's not what intimidated Mrs. O'Brien the most. It was the vow, that blasted pledge, and the weight of her sister-in-law's expectation. For two decades it had done nothing but gather dust. The curse of any good Catholic was to be fruitful and multiply, then promise one of the little fruits to the church. A human tithe. It had been little more than the breathless promise of a newlywed, but now, after time had revealed its realities, Mrs. O'Brien regretted it; she hadn't any fruit to spare. She could feel the weight of that vow in the old nun's stare.

Sister Mary-Frances casually brushed the top of the sideboard. Not two minutes in the same room and the judgment began. Mrs. O'Brien narrowed her eyes, but the gesture was ineffectual. Mae's head had already snapped to attention.

"You will not be doing that in me kitchen," she said. "Not a crumb is out of place here, I promise you that."

The nun withdrew her hand. "Old habits die hard. Once the mistress of a house..." Her words faded away, but her sneer didn't.

The cook snorted and went back to beating her dough, while the two O'Brien women stared each other down. At last, Mrs. O'Brien broke the silence. "The past is dead and buried. I should know, I carried the shovel. Don't be digging it up now."

"Who's digging? I've just come for what was promised me."

"I promised you nothing."

"True. How very true." The nun tapped the heavy cross that hung over her black habit and stepped closer. "You promised God."

Mrs. O'Brien tried to take a casual drink from her empty teacup. "That's right," she said. The cup clattered in the well of the saucer as she set them down.

"And as you know, the church represents God, and I represent the church. Besides, what will Mary-Kate say when she hears of it?"

"Leave my daughter out of this. She's the only one I have left, and you know it."

With the tip of one knobby finger, the nun jabbed Mrs. O'Brien just below her collarbone. "Oh, I don't think that's likely to happen. After all, she's in the thick of it, isn't she?"

"I suppose she is." Mrs. O'Brien stepped back and rubbed the spot. "But need I remind you she is standing in the shelter of her father? That man guards his young like no other; he'll be hard to get around."

"I've gotten around him before."

Mrs. O'Brien didn't know what possessed her, it might have been the nun's smugness or the fact that Mae stood close by, paring knife in hand, but whatever it was, Mrs. O'Brien lifted her chin and asked, "Is that why I'm here and you're in the convent?"

As soon as the words were out of her mouth, she regretted them. Sister Mary-Frances spread her arms wide like a great winged bird preparing to pluck out her eyes. Mrs. O'Brien recoiled at the thought and screwed them shut; even so, she felt the shadow envelop her, hover, and press down, before it lifted, dissipated and was gone.

———

Mrs. O'Brien stood in the kitchen for some time after her sister-in-law left. She felt too unsteady to move. She didn't trust her body or her heart. Mae glanced up at her between her duties, shaking her head and wiping her hands on her apron.

"Stop that," Mrs. O'Brien said.

"What ma'am?"

"Fussing over me."

"I'm not, ma'am." Mae peeked under the dishtowel at the rising dough. "But did you see the size of that woman? She could join a circus that one, with all that stubble; as large as her brother, she is." She clicked her tongue and resumed her tasks. "Never been so close to her before, gave me a fright."

"I'm well aware of her size." Mrs. O'Brien picked up her teacup and saucer and, forgetting the cup was empty, endeavoured to take another sip. "You mustn't tell anyone what just happened."

Mae was solemn. "I won't Ma'am. I can promise you that. Me mam says that I should be deaf and dumb about the goings-on of the house, but in me work, I should always act smartly."

"Good." Mrs. O'Brien patted the back of the cook's hand. She wanted to express gratitude for the girl's loyalty, but in her present state, she feared she might insult her. Having Mr. O'Brien's turnip cook quit before he bragged about her abilities to his rivals? She might as well set the kitchen alight.

More than that, how would she tell him of his sister's visit? There was no easy way around it; he would have to be told, in spite of how it might affect his health. She'd have to be the one to put the tremor back into his hands. That dastardly thing that caused him to retire early, forcing him to leave his affairs in the care of others, overseeing them with nothing more than a cursory glance. She tapped her nails together. Perhaps not today though, she could spare him for just one more day. "Have you seen him?" she asked.

"Who, Ma'am?"

Daft girl. "Mr. O'Brien."

"Haven't seen him, he rarely comes in here, but I heard him. He was going on about electric lights and motorcars."

Mrs. O'Brien gave a tired smile. "I'm sure there hasn't been a soul in Tnúth that hasn't heard him do that. The way he rumbles around fretting, some days that man is beyond me."

"No disrespect, Ma'am, but me ma says there must've been a fever on the boat when his people came over. She heard it from a reliable source, her sister's neighbour's cousin's father."

"You can't get much more reliable than that." Mrs. O'Brien rolled her eyes and took a breath that did nothing to hide her exasperation. "I don't doubt there was a fever, Mae. So many died."

"Oh, not that kind of fever, Ma'am. She meant one that addles the brain." The cook lowered her voice. "And their children's too. If you don't believe me read it for yourself. It was all there in *The Freeman*, the St. John's newspaper. Arthur and Daniel Bannister were hanged for murder."

"What's that got to do with the price of rice in China?"

"Their great-gran came over on the *Triumph*, the same ship as your mister's kin. The lot landed in Halifax, walked down the same gangplank, but not one was as fit as a flea." Mae's head tilted to one side. "And neither were the poor wee sots. The affliction passed from parent to child. 'Twould explain that brute of a nun and some of your man's strange ways."

Mrs. O'Brien grimaced as she turned towards the cook. "We may come from the same side of the tracks, young lady, but this is far too familiar. Talking about my family as if we were part of some sordid tea time gossip? Are you trying to provoke me?"

"No ma'am. 'Tis not me place to provoke." Mae straightened and placed one hand over her heart. "On me word, I was just informing you."

"Informing me or not, that's the most ridiculous thing I've ever heard. Came over on the same ship as Mr. O'Brien's kin. Claptrap."

"Aye that may well be, but there's no use getting cross with me for it. 'Twas me mam who said it."

Mrs. O'Brien took her empty teacup and saucer and jabbed them towards Mae. "In my younger days I'd have pummelled you for saying such a thing, but I'm refined now so I'll let you off with a warning. There is a compost pile in the back, and if you don't hold your tongue, my little vegetable look-alike, you'll find yourself under it."

Mr. O'Brien banged his walking stick against the side of the banister and called up the stairs, "Don't be troubling yourself, Mary-Kate O'Brien. It's not like I don't have all day."

There was no response from the upstairs bedroom, and Mr. O'Brien could feel his temper rise. "Can't a man see his own daughter's shining face in the morning? Is that too much to ask? I feed you, I clothe you for nigh twenty years, and my pocketbook has grown rather light because of it. To relieve me suffering, I've asked around and there is not a soul in the world willing to take you off me hands. Yet you don't hear me complaining, do you?"

The sound of his daughter opening and closing her dresser drawers drifted down to him. It was as if he spoke to the wind. All Mr. O'Brien wanted was for Mary-Kate to hurry her pace, skip down the stairs and merrily link her arm in his. However, Mary-Kate never skipped, and arm-linking was something she seemed to have an aversion to. The last time he insisted she take his arm, Mary-Kate went limp at the knees, and he ended up dragging her down the street. The great oaf and his rag doll.

He closed his eyes and leaned against the banister. She was up to something; he was convinced of it. The thought of not knowing what mischief she was entertaining irritated him like nothing else. If there was mischief to be had, it should be had together. It had been that way since she was a babe, and he saw no sense in changing their ways now. It was what steadied their rudder, kept them from going adrift when storms threatened. Pulled him back when he forgot his place and lost sight of the one he chose to be tethered to.

"Are you well?"

Mr. O'Brien opened his eyes. His wife stood in front of him with a cup and saucer in hand. As fetching a woman as he could have hoped for, she even rivalled some that plied their trade on the street. Though he'd never found an opportune time for telling her so. His Mary-Kate had inherited her mother's mass of red hair and, sadly, much of her attitude. "Why would you ask me such a thing?" he frowned, puffing out his chest. "Am I not as robust this morning as I was last evening?"

"Keep your voice down," Mrs. O'Brien snapped, roses blooming on her cheeks. "Or you'll not see the inside of me bedroom for a month."

"Oh, I don't have to see the inside of yours, you could cross the hall to mine." Mr. O'Brien stepped into his wife. He looked down at her and waited for her to lean her ample waist against him. Her breathing changed, but Mr. O'Brien wasn't sure if she were inclined or annoyed. He gave her a seductive wink, or it would have been, had an eyelash not worked itself free and blurred his vision.

A look of disgust crossed his wife's face. "You're making a nuisance of yourself, Mr. O'Brien," she said thumping him in the chest with her free hand.

Ah, now he knew. She was annoyed. The thump was too hard; there might even be a bruise. The morning was not going as he hoped. There was no tenderness in it, no cooperation. "What'd you do that for?"

Mrs. O'Brien turned her face away. But before she did, he caught a flicker of something unfamiliar in her visage, in the corner of her eye, the shape of her mouth. He wasn't sure what it was, but there was a darkness to it. "In all our years together, you've not done such a thing to me," he said rubbing his chest. "What's got into you?"

Instead of answering his question, Mrs. O'Brien handed Mr. O'Brien her empty cup and saucer before heading up the stairs.

"What'll I be needing these for?" he asked looking down at the cup and saucer.

"For a happy marriage."

"A happy marriage? Never heard of such a thing."

"I heard that Mr. O'Brien," she said without turning around. "Don't be acting like I've given you a snake. Just take them to the kitchen."

"Don't be acting like I've given you a snake," Mr. O'Brien mimicked softly. He pulled back the leaves of a nearby fern and carefully set the dishes on top of those his wife had given him the day before. Forgetting his daughter, he picked up his bowler and stepped out the front door into the chilly April air.

3

MARY-KATE

It wasn't until Mary-Kate was outside the library on Goose Lane that her plan began to go awry. Her goal that morning was to exchange a book and avoid her father, or at least give him the impression she was avoiding him. Returning the book was easy, eluding her father was another matter. He was leaning against a sandstone buttress smoking his pipe when she exited the building.

"Saw you through The Donnybrook's window," he said, without turning to face her. His voice was sunny and hopeful as the day. "Was just about to order meself a pint, and low and behold, there is me own daughter. I says to me mates, I say, 'Look, there is me Mary-Kate.' 'What's a girl like her be needing books for?' says one. 'Not sure,' says I. 'You better go see what she's up to before she gets ideas in that head of hers,' says another. So here I stand, waiting on me lass, to find out why she is strutting about, bold as brass, like she doesn't have a care in the world."

Mary-Kate pulled her new novel to her chest and tried not to smile. "I don't strut," she said, "and as for the ideas in my head, they're my own."

"That may well be, but you *are* as bold as brass. I know that for a fact, you came from the same forge as I." Mr. O'Brien drew hard on his pipe before letting the smoke billow from his nose. He lifted his chin, showing his full face to the sun. "As for the other, don't even ask."

Her father was baiting her. He was always wanting her to ask about whatever nonsensical thing she wasn't supposed to ask about. It was part of the thrust and parry between them. But he wouldn't have his way today, she would make sure of that. And with that firm conviction, she restrained herself all the way to the bottom step. There, she lost her agency. Her mouth twitched. She stopped and turned. "Ask what?"

Mr. O'Brien tapped his pipe on the heel of his shoe before returning it to his inside jacket pocket. "I knew you couldn't resist. You never have. Ever since you were a small child with a little soft-soap and coaxing, I could drag almost anything out of you." In a couple of strides, he covered the distance that separated them. Looking down at her he squinted his eyes and touched the tip of her nose with his forefinger. "And as for what you are not to ask, it's how I knew it was you without turning to glimpse. It's elementary my dear Mary-Kate, I deduced it." His voice changed timbre. "The sound of your step, the very smell of you. You drifted down to me in a way no other can. With me eyes closed, I could pick you out in a crowd of thousands. You're an O'Brien through and through. Would know that sound and that scent anywhere."

Despite her father's pronouncement the only words that Mary-Kate heard were *elementary* and *deduced*. There'd been a betrayal. She turned and fixed her gaze on the door of The Donnybrook. "Have you seen Father Connelly this morning?"

"I may have."

"And did that little imp of a man tell you the last book of stories I read?"

Mr. O'Brien frowned. "He may have."

"May have? He either did, or he didn't." Mary-Kate liked it when they sparred. The way her father would nonchalantly lift one shoulder when he was about to be more of a rogue than usual. She waited and lo, there it was.

Mr. O'Brien shifted. "The poor Father couldn't help himself. Thought you were quite clever with your Author Conan Doyle. Following me around town, unbeknownst to me, making notes of all me goings-on and then pretending that you deduced them at the dinner table, claiming it was evident by a hair on me lapel, a pebble in the tread of me shoe. I just thought I would beat you to the punch."

"So, you couldn't tell it was me by the sound of my steps or my scent?"

"No, and I'm a little sorry for it. Accosted five others before it was you. And some were a little indignant. Didn't appreciate me commenting on their odour."

"You've commented on worse."

"That may well be, but I only want to spend some time with you, lass. Me one and only sweet lamb." With the tip of a finger he pushed up the brim of his bowler exposing his unruly brow.

"What about your pint? The one you were going to order before you've wiped the sleep from your eyes?" She reached up and brushed off what had evaded the morning washcloth.

"Oh that?" Mr. O'Brien licked his lips at the mention of the ale. "Was not a morning indulgence, I promise you that. It was an act of commiseration."

"Commiseration?"

"Aye. A solemn act if ever there was one. Father Connelly received some disturbing news from the diocese. It seems that Father Browne has been waylaid and has postponed his visit."

Mary-Kate rolled her eyes. "And you have to commiserate over that?"

"Why wouldn't we? The lot of us have been looking forward to it for more than a fortnight. Been preparing too." He waved his hand through the air. "But enough of that for now. Let's go for a bit of a stroll while the light is still good."

"It's hardly half past ten in the morning. Most of the good light is still ahead of us."

"Aye, that it is, but the best light is now." He extended the crook of his arm towards her.

Mary-Kate hesitated. It wasn't the stroll she objected to — it was the conversation. The last time they went for a turn, he asked almost every man they came across if he was in need of a wife. Whenever the gentleman answered in the affirmative, her father suggested he consider her. He said she came from good sturdy stock and anyone with an ounce of wit would take him up on his offer. It was not an ordeal Mary-Kate wished to endure again in their little corner of New Brunswick.

It wasn't just the matchmaking that made her hesitant. All the gents in The Donnybrook would have their noses pressed against the window pane and be laying bets on what she would do next. She was sure of it. Her father regaled her mother and herself with tales of their unorthodox wagers around the dinner table all the time. How many steps it would take Father Connelly to dodge a spring puddle. How long it would take Mr. Finnegan Donavan to realize his trousers weren't wholly fastened. But in spite of her misgivings, she relented. "All right," she said. "I'll take a stroll with you." She slipped her hand through the loop of his arm. "But you have to give me your word that you won't try to pawn me off on the first eligible male we come across. I know you want me to marry and give you grand-children, but not today. Can it just be a stroll this one time?"

"Is that all you want?" Mr. O'Brien patted her hand. "It was only to tease you, lass, no use making a fuss."

"No use making a fuss? You asked Mr. Sullivan, and he is in his nineties. I felt like a cow on the auction block."

"Anything to bring a smile to the old man's face. He isn't long for this world and watching him light up, for maybe the last time, is the least we could do." His tone softened, and he lowered his face, so it was a hair's breadth away from his daughter's. "When the time comes for you to pass from me arm to another's, it will be to someone far more suitable than any man who treads these streets. Besides," he motioned towards the pub, "it cost me a pretty penny to go on this stroll with you. Before I stepped out of The Donnybrook, I bet against you. Thought you were sure to turn me down." He leaned his head towards hers, affectionately. "But 'tis money well spent, me girl."

4

Mrs. O'Brien finished her afternoon tea and stared into her cup. "Well that's enough to make a preacher swear," she said, examining the tea leaves. No matter how she tipped the cup, she couldn't read anything in their dregs. It was as if they were deliberately goading her.

"Excuse me Ma'am," said the upstairs maid. At least, Mrs. O'Brien thought she was the upstairs maid; the girl was one of a set of Irish twins.

"What is it, Rose?"

"I'm not Rose, Ma'am. Rose is the upstairs maid. I'm Daisy, the downstairs maid."

"Well?"

"Did you want me to get Rose, Ma'am?"

"Oh, for the love of God, not this again." Mrs. O'Brien pressed a palm against her forehead. "I don't need you to fetch Rose. I need you to ask your question."

"There is someone at the door." Daisy twisted her apron between her fingers looking more timid than usual.

"That's not a question, Daisy. That's a statement." Mrs.

O'Brien tipped her cup once more and looked back at the leaves. "And the answer is the same as always, let them in. How many times do I have to tell you that?"

"I can't, Ma'am. Mr. O'Brien is blocking the entrance."

"Don't be ridiculous. Why on earth would he do that?"

"Don't know, Ma'am, but he's shouting, 'You shall not pass' and striking the floor with his walking stick."

Mrs. O'Brien set down her cup harder than she intended; she was sure she heard it crack. "Hasn't that woman done enough damage for one day?" She looked at the maid as if she expected an answer, but Daisy could only add one more twist to the apron. "For some nuns, the wafer isn't enough, they have to take the cake as well."

"No, Ma'am," came the wincing words. "Not the nun, 'tis your ma. Mr. O'Brien says she still has that new widow smell about her."

"Herself!" Mrs. O'Brien's eyes narrowed. Her mother wasn't due for a visit. In fact, Mrs. O'Brien was sure it was quite the opposite. Her father's funeral was but two weeks past, and she distinctly remembered standing overtop his open grave casting lots with her sisters to see which one would have the misfortune of taking the old crone home. She had never been her mother's favourite daughter, and her husband was her least favourite son-in-law, so on the day of the funeral, chance was on Mrs. O'Brien's side. Today, though, with the dark-hearted nun's early visit and her mother demanding entrance, chance seemed to have deserted her. Two bad omens in a row did not bode well, and Mrs. O'Brien knew the significance of it.

Mrs. O'Brien stood, smoothed her skirt and pushed past the maid. She wasn't in the mood for any of the old woman's shenanigans, dead husband or no. Unlike her morning caller, this intruder she would make short work of. She quickened her pace; she was almost looking forward to the opportunity. It would make up for the weak-kneed debacle earlier.

She heard the commotion long before she clapped eyes on the pair: her husband's bellows were not quite able to drown out her mother's squall. It was as if the wreck of the Hesperus was upon them.

"What on earth is going on?" Mrs. O'Brien demanded.

"You promised me that the old bat would never darken our step." Mr. O'Brien yelled over his shoulder, refusing to give her mother any ground. "Your sisters gave their word, which I bought and paid for I might add, and now I open me own door and find she hasn't just darkened it — Herself demands entrance."

Mrs. O'Brien sucked her teeth. She was tempted to tell him to shut the door. The old hag would go away eventually. But there was something a little too unfeeling in the response, and she couldn't bring herself to speak it aloud. It was almost a relief that entrance was all her mother was demanding. After the morning's events, she took snippets of comfort where she could find them. "Let her in. She's barely buried her husband. Besides, what will the neighbours think?"

"They'll think I'm a man who knows how to put me foot down," Mr. O'Brien said, stepping aside.

It didn't take long for Mrs. O'Brien to regret her decision. Her mother and husband continued where they'd left off at the funeral. Mr. O'Brien called her mother Our Lady of Blessed Misery, and her mother called him a great lout and demanded he collect her things from the verandah. Mrs. O'Brien sat in the nearest chair. "Why did I even get out of bed?" She sunk her elbows into her thighs, rested her chin in her palms and waited.

"Go ahead," Mr. O'Brien said following Herself around the sitting room. "Make yourself at home. Count the silver, test the crystal. While you're at it pocket me best china."

"Pocketing china never ends well, God knows I've tried." The newly-minted widow rubbed her backside. "Puts splinters in me arse when I sit on them."

Mrs. O'Brien could have stepped in between them, but they were bound to wear each other out. They always did. She looked at the mantel clock and wondered if she held her breath and passed out, how long would they take to notice.

"If you're finished taking inventory," Mr. O'Brien said, grabbing his bowler from the hat rack and jamming it on his head, "I'm off to the pub." He bellowed as if he were calling from the next room. "Check her pockets before she leaves."

"Don't I always?" Mrs. O'Brien got up from her post and handed him a walking stick. Her husband muttered something she didn't want to understand before disappearing out the front door and down the walk. She shook her head as she watched him go. If only she could get rid of her mother as easily.

"You're not checking me pockets," the old woman said, crouching down like a cat eyeing a mouse.

"Have I ever?" She motioned for her mother to sit. "I just tell him what he needs to hear to keep the peace."

Herself sniffed as she made a beeline for the best chair in the room. "Tell him what you like, he's your husband," she said fluffing a cushion with her fist. "I, meself, preferred an honest marriage."

The clipped tone brought Mrs. O'Brien back to her childhood, reduced to a four-year-old with scabby knees, an aching belly, and few words. It boggled her mind. Her husband said it was a gift, the way her mother could alienate all five daughters with a single breath. But she could do nothing about that now. Instead, she forced herself to ask the question she didn't want answered. "Why are you here, Mother?"

"I've come to stay."

"Here? That would be a fine kettle of fish. I'm sure one of my sisters would suit you better."

"Suit me better? What kind of foolish notion is that? The lot of them should be locked up, I tell you that. Not one of them has shown me the kindness I deserve." She ran a finger along the edge of the velvet cushion on which she sat. "Never thought one of mine would climb so high. If I had I'd have dug my nails in deeper, but there's no use getting into that now, water under the bridge." Herself looked her daughter over. "No chimney sweep for you, is it, Miss High and Mighty? I must have done something right."

Mrs. O'Brien took a deep breath, pushing down the deluge of emotions that threatened to spill forth, untethered. "I'm sure after a good night's sleep you'll rethink the matter."

"Rethink the matter? You'll be shovelling dirt on me grave first."

"That can be arranged," whispered Mrs. O'Brien. "There's a spade by the compost pile. If the Turnip doesn't start behaving, you can join her."

It was decided that Herself, Our Lady of Blessed Misery, Mrs. O'Brien's widowed mother, should inhabit the Deadman's room. Mr. O'Brien made the proclamation when he returned home from the pub. The Deadman's room was set aside for the dead and dying. Notwithstanding its name, it was pleasant enough. Twelve-foot ceilings, velvet curtains, and walnut furnishing boasting cabriole legs and padded feet, pieces that rivalled any fashioned in the Queen Anne style. But despite all its attributes, the room was the most dreaded in the household. Rose and Daisy, the upstairs and downstairs maids, refused to cross its threshold.

Mrs. O'Brien rubbed her palms against her temples as she looked up at her husband. "Don't be putting her there."

"And where would you have me put her?" Mr. O'Brien eyebrows knit together. "Closer to you? Mary-Kate? Would you prefer that?"

Mrs. O'Brien shook her head and looked back towards the intruder, the hollow-boned creature at her elbow.

Her husband's blue eyes twinkled. "How about the servants' quarters? Wouldn't persecuting them make life all the sweeter?"

The thought of her mother taking residence below stairs, strolling the hall and inspecting her unwilling subjects, made Mrs. O'Brien cringe. How could she consider such a thing? How could her husband propose it? Those poor girls would be at her mother's mercy. "All right," Mrs. O'Brien conceded, "but step lightly, or you're liable to poke fate in the eye."

Mr. O'Brien stuck a thumb through a buttonhole in his vest and rocked back on his heels. "Fate has two eyes, just like everyone else. He'll survive well enough with one."

Her husband did have a point, but it wasn't fate's conundrum that concerned Mrs. O'Brien most. It was how to keep the old girl happy. If all five of her sisters had failed, she didn't imagine she would fare any better.

The trio trod up the stairs, not a word exchanged or uttered. A deadman's march. Mr. O'Brien lugged a trunk, while Mrs. O'Brien flanked her mother like a dutiful daughter. The very idea made her feel like a fraud. How could duty hold within its frame such guilt and trepidation? Not even a whiff of pride or loyalty. There was a whiff of something though, something that allowed her mother to weasel her way through the front door.

At the top of the stairs, Mr. O'Brien turned and set down the dresser trunk, placed his hands on his knees and caught his breath. "You're not the first of the four horsemen to have visited us," he said, running the back of his hand across his brow. "And we will survive you as we survived them."

"Oh, for the love of God, you barely survived carting me belongings up the stairs. I doubt it would take much more than a plug on its last legs to do you in."

"It's not a regular trunk," Mr. O'Brien thumped the top of it before crossing himself. "This monstrosity could sink the Empress of Ireland."

"That is cold, even coming from you. The dead, what they

could find of them, are hardly in the ground, and you don't give a tinker's cuss."

"Don't be telling me what I give a tinker's cuss about."

"Enough." Mrs. O'Brien put up her hand and stepped between them. "The bat's not even in the belfry yet and the bickering's begun."

"What bickering?" Mr. O'Brien turned on her, his eyes speckled with ice. "I just want her to know I'm not lugging her belongings as a show of hospitality. I want to make sure they make it to their rightful destination, for I'll not abide her anywhere else."

"And where are you planning to abide me?" Herself pulled back her weeping veil. There was a tremble in her voice, and Mrs. O'Brien wasn't sure if it was a sign of defiance or subjugation.

"In the Deadman's room." Mr. O'Brien leaned in, "And as a good Catholic, I'm not encouraging you to go the way of the long-ago departed, but neither am I discouraging you. You've already made old bones, no use pausing now."

Herself slumped, her clothing shifting like a pile of leaves in the wind. "In a fortnight, I've slept with dogs, screeching children, and under a kitchen table on the floor. To sleep in a room for the dead or dying would be a godsend."

Mr. O'Brien turned to his wife. "I don't like her tone."

MARY-KATE

Mary-Kate lay prostrate on her bedroom floor, her head tilted ever-so-slightly to hear the commotion that drifted under the door. "Oh, hurry up," she whispered. "I want to get there before evening vespers." It was just a matter of the uproar in the hallway subsiding, but the back and forths between her father and gran went unabated. When Mary-Kate thought they were making progress, she would hear her father turn on her gran with some new witticism. "And if you care to take notice the number of steps between the top of the stairs and the Deadman's room is thirty. Did you hear me? Thirty. The number of Judas."

Mary-Kate imagined her gran's expression, eyes narrowed, brow lines doubled. "Showing off your counting, are you? Wouldn't be so proud of it, if I were you."

There was a thump and some sort of kerfuffle. Mary-Kate imagined her father dropping the trunk, like the ceremonial dropping of the glove. She closed her eyes and tried to visualize every allegro, every pirouette of the duel.

"Did you not hear me woman?" her father yelled overtop her gran. "I said Judas. Now his number is yours."

"Oh you cheap bugger, givin' away deadman's numbers and acting like you've done something grand," her gran shouted back.

The more the two squabbled, the more Mary-Kate was torn. Her father's and gran's lifelong feud was entertaining, but she was missing out on the full grandeur of it. It was all that she could do to keep herself silent. If she had her druthers, she'd fling open the door, step out into the hallway and join in the mayhem. Even the smell of it was invigorating. Yet she lay inert and out of sight, for as her gran would say, there were bigger fish to fry. Fish she had become aware of after her return from her morning stroll. Until she knew what had been caught in the net, she thought it best to keep herself to herself.

When Mary-Kate returned home from her library amble, she was pleased there hadn't been a single unsolicited marriage proposal. Her father had kept his end of the bargain, even though she saw his lips twitch each time they passed an unaccompanied male. But now, with the brawl in the hallway and the conversation she'd overheard between the maids and cook, the walk didn't feel so triumphant. While she'd been traipsing around town mocking neighbours and irritating her father's rivals, there had been a mystery brewing under her own roof. And she might have missed the whole thing if she hadn't stumbled upon the hired help in the servant's stairwell.

It was only by happenstance that she overheard. She had been practicing silently descending the stairs, the way Sherlock Holmes would if he was sneaking up on an adversary, when she heard the posy sisters and the turnip cook knee-deep in an illicit conversation; something about her aunt, Sister Mary-Frances. That in itself was monumental. It had been years since the nun had visited — a relief to her parents; neither her mother nor her father could countenance the woman. She'd made appearances, but Mary-Kate was hard-pressed to remember the last time it had happened. Mary-Kate took care to balance her weight and incline an ear.

Her first observation: the trio weren't natural allies; more than once Mary-Kate had seen the twins skirt the edges of the corridors to avoid contact, as if the cook's blotchy skin was contagious. But the duo now stood within striking distance. Furthermore, Rose had neglected to dislodge a twig that had caught in her slightly disheveled bun. Mary-Kate tapped a finger on her chin: a vestige of a rendezvous in the lilacs with the young man who delivered the milk? Rose was his Tuesday girl, while Daisy stood in on Thursdays. Mary-Kate found the whole situation quite distasteful, but in their favour, the sisters were rather good dusters. Her baseboards were spotless.

The clipped whisper of the trio reinforced Mary-Kate's first deduction, there was trouble afoot, and the trouble, she soon discovered, was with her mother.

Mae: "I was there minding me own business when that foul creature rose from the corner looking like she could devour the Mrs. That old nun was spoiling for a fight, and when she said Miss Mary-Kate's name, I thought the Mrs. was going to die on the spot. She'd been going on about shovels and burying things, but Miss Mary-Kate's name brought her round. Never seen anything like it in me life. 'Twas like she'd been slapped." Mae lowered her voice, so Mary-Kate could barely make out what she said. "And I can tell you what, we were both glad to see the back of that one."

Mary-Kate wanted to scream, "The back of what one? The nun or me?"

"Me being the good Catholic that I am, I tried to comfort the Mrs. but she'd have none of it. Told me I'd forgotten me place. Me not knowing me place! It's her who's forgotten hers. And her threatening to skin me alive and throw me bones on the compost heap."

The sisters gasped.

Taking a breath, Mae continued. "Stood there in me own kitchen foaming at the mouth, lips curled back to show a row of jagged teeth, like she sharpens them in her spare time."

Rose brought a hand to her throat. "An ill wind. I felt it when I was getting dressed this morning, didn't I, Daisy? Said there was an unnatural chill in the air."

"She did. I said she should have warned someone."

Mae looked directly at Rose. "You should have. I'll keep it to meself this time, but you better not let it happen again." The look on Mae's face was almost haughty.

Mary-Kate shifted her weight, causing the step to creak. The three malcontents scattered, not once glancing upwards to see who might have overheard them.

Mary-Kate ran back upstairs to her room, her heart pounding. She was offended by the familiarity of the hired help who spoke of her mother as if she were common, but she hadn't slipped down the servant's stairs to scold them, or to eavesdrop. She closed her eyes and let out a breath. She was a student of the great detective, detached and objective. When she looked at the evidence laid before her there was only one conclusion. Her mother was keeping something from her. Something dreadful enough to make the turnip cook tremble. Her mother, a woman who kept her confidences under lock and key and never made idle threats, had a secret.

Mary-Kate only caught glimpses of her mother's true nature when she was tired or caught unaware. Though she was generally good-natured, she had a tendency to be peevish when Mary-Kate's father pushed her too far. She was almost certain now would be no different: her mother would withdraw into a world of her own upon the merest inquiry. Her father would be no help, he was oblivious to the underpinnings of the household. Therefore, against Mary-Kate's better judgement, she knew what she had to do: go to the convent and sidle up to her aunt. The thought of it made her shudder. She had to remind herself she was a student of the great Sherlock Holmes and built of sturdier stuff. Even if her abilities were mediocre, surely she could gleam a modicum of truth. Her aunt wouldn't be expecting a visit and would be caught off guard.

As soon as she was sure she heard the Deadman's door close, Mary-Kate got up from the floor and brushed herself off. She cracked open her door and listened. Nothing. Crossing her fingers, she ducked out of her room, down the stairs and out the front door.

No sooner had she crossed the veranda and slipped down the walk toward the front gate than the local priest, Father Connelly, whistling and twirling his rosary, greeted her. "Good evening, Mary-Kate." He paused long enough to swing open the gate and bend slightly at the waist.

Mary-Kate returned the bow before she stepped through. "And to you, Father."

"Come to collect your Da." The priest swung his rosary, narrowly missing Mary-Kate's bosom. "'Twould be a shame if he didn't tip a pint." Spreading his short arms wide he sniffed the air. "Birds twittering and the breeze dancing across the tip of me nose. Have you ever seen an evening as fine as this one?"

"Oh, that depends on who you're asking, Father. And I think if that someone is my da, he'll want a lot more than a pint to tip."

"And why is that?" Concern entered Father Connelly's voice as he followed her gaze back towards the house.

Mary-Kate hesitated, remembering the priest's earlier betrayal. To look at him now she could find no guile. Besides, his size hardly gave him room for the necessities, let alone guile. Mary-Kate towered over him. "My gran has taken up residence. I think he has his hands full."

"Claimed sanctuary has she? Thought she might." Dancing breezes and twittering birds seemed to evaporate with his words. "I've been up to my elbows in confessions. Your mother's sisters are a fiery crew. The way they talk, it would make your head spin."

Mary-Kate didn't have a relation that couldn't be described as fiery. From their first wail to their last breath each one of them could spit a mouth full of nails if needed. "And you didn't warn my da? He'll have your ears for that."

"He'll never know. It would be breaking the bonds of the confessional to tell him."

"Then why tell me?"

"Was thinking out loud, that's all. You can forgive an old priest for that, can't you? Besides, it's eavesdropping that's the sin. I'd be worried about me own eternal soul if I was you." He tucked his rosary into his cossack pocket. "Have to reconsider me whole evening. Wouldn't want to disturb your da when he is dealing with the cat o' nine tails. Might not live to regret it." He smiled at Mary-Kate before swinging closed the gate and offering her his arm.

"I think that's wise," she said accepting the offer.

"And where are you off to all by your lonesome?"

"Where any good Catholic girl would be off to. The convent."

"I'm headed that way meself. But not to the convent mind you. Sister Mary-Frances is taking stock of the communion wine. I'm afraid she might come up short when she tries to balance the account."

"So, it's not the best time for a visit?" Mary-Kate felt a palpable relief. Curious or no, it didn't dawn on her until that moment it was Sister Mary-Frances she had to confront and ask about the encounter in the kitchen that morning. Not just the thought of her, but the reality of her.

"Perhaps not, but you can join me, lass," he winked. "Some-one's been switching the grave markers again, and I need to make sure that your aunt has set them right this time. She appreciates me checking on her work. She may not say so, but I know she does all the same."

7

MRS. O'BRIEN

Mrs. O'Brien shivered in the hallway. Her thin nightdress hung loosely around her, but she wasn't particularly cold; she was anxious. Now that her mother had taken up residence, it was only a matter of time before the crepey creature ferreted out her secret and exposed it to the whole world. Mrs. O'Brien knew she had to tell her husband quickly, before he found out from someone else. But even if it came from her, she wasn't sure how she could couch it in a way that wouldn't cause an upheaval. Her husband would be horrified — he loathed his sister to the degree that he adored his only daughter. Mary-Kate, she was sure, would feel unwanted, and abandoned by her old, foolish promise. As for Herself, although she'd want more for her granddaughter than a dusty cell, she'd revel in her son-in-law's sorrow. It didn't matter how Mrs. O'Brien envisioned it, no good could come of this particular secret.

Reaching out, she touched the dark wood of her husband's bedroom door. It was slightly ajar; she could hear him snoring. The sound of a man at peace. The rhythmic sound reassured her, but not enough to steady the brass candlestick in her hand.

She pushed open the door and glided across the room. Once she snuffed out the candle, she slid into bed beside her husband. His snoring remained even and undisturbed. Now was her chance to tell him. She would whisper in his ear. If later, he claimed to be ignorant of the matter, she would click her tongue and declare that he never listened to her. It had worked before.

"When we were first married," she began, her lips brushing her husband's earlobe, "and life sprang so easily and quickly inside of me, I promised one of our wee ones to the church." Mrs. O'Brien paused and listened for an interruption in his breathing; there wasn't one. She continued. "We were so full of promise back then, we were so hopeful. But nothing turned out the way we planned, and now your cow of a sister has come to claim the only child we have left. She thinks Mary-Kate should be a nun."

Mr. O'Brien's snoring abruptly stopped, and he sat straight up in bed. "I knew it," he bellowed. "I knew there was something afoot! It's been niggling at me for years, and now you'll not be denying it."

Mrs. O'Brien fell back onto the pillow. "I thought you were asleep," she gasped.

"Perhaps I was," he said, a finger punctuating the air. "But you've been hovering outside me door for the better part of an hour. All the sighing and fussing, it was enough to wake the dead. I had to do something to make you stop."

"So, you pretended to be asleep?"

"Aye, don't act like I've betrayed you. You're the one that threatened to lock me out of your bedroom."

Mrs. O'Brien shook her head. "No," her voice dropped. "You've not betrayed me."

"Good." Mr. O'Brien's voice contained a note of glee. He laid back down, and his feet began to thrash beneath the blankets.

She rolled her eyes and propped herself up on her elbows. "For heaven's sake, what are you doing now?"

"A bed jig."

"A bed jig?"

"Aye, a bed jig." His head bobbed to an unheard tune. "All these years you've been telling me that I'm not mindful of the things you say. And now I find out that you come into me room, in the dead of night no less, and whisper in me ear. How do you expect me to be mindful of that? I'm a finer husband than you give me credit for, I haven't even gotten mad at you for it." Mr. O'Brien finished his jig and rolled into his wife, planting a kiss upon her lips. "Am I not a fine husband?"

Mrs. O'Brien thumped him in the chest for the second time that day. "Why do I even bother? You haven't heard a word I've said. What about Mary-Kate?"

The glee disappeared from Mr. O'Brien's face.

Mr. and Mrs. O'Brien lay side by side in the dark, staring in silence at the ceiling. Her fingers interwoven in his. How many nights had they lain like this? Mrs. O'Brien couldn't remember. It was their unspoken vigil. At times, she could feel him melt into her, so close that she could barely breathe; at others, they were two stones as far apart as they were together.

Mary-Kate was not their only child, but she was the only one who had survived — the last to come. Three boys and five girls buried one after the other in the churchyard, none living long enough to open their eyes to see, or their mouths to cry. Those babies didn't live long enough for Mrs. O'Brien to feel the weight of them in her hands, to bring them to her breast. She had been denied it all, and now she was expected to give away the one precious child she had left. The thought crumpled her.

When Mary-Kate was little, she and Mrs. O'Brien would take gifts to the graveyard. Not just for birthdays and Christmas, but for all the things they should have celebrated in between. She tried to make Mary-Kate feel like they were going on a grand adventure. "You remember all their names, don't you?" she would ask as she looked in the mirror to straighten her hat.

Mary-Kate nodded solemnly.

"And the dates of their births?"

Another nod.

"Good. It wouldn't do if you didn't know your own brothers and sisters." Mrs. O'Brien reached down and gently cupped Mary-Kate's chin. "You're not going to cry this time, are you lass? Remember that we Irish have suffered worse. Your own Great-granddad O'Brien was the only one of his kin who made it over. The rest died on the ship, God rest their souls, making your poor great-granddad an orphan. We're the lucky ones, Mary-Kate, because we have each other."

The little girl trembled in front of her mother, her big eyes filled with tears.

"You'll be fine, me girl. Don't you know that I couldn't have imagined a better child than you? Not a finer one under the sun. I'm afraid that I love you best of all and have favoured you terribly. How would that have made the others feel?"

Mary-Kate shrugged.

Mr. O'Brien disapproved of these 'shenanigans' and tried to put an end to their visits. "I'll not have it," he said. "The two of you traipsing around, buying gifts for dead babies, then planting them in the graves as if they were daisies."

"Don't take that tone with me, Mr. O'Brien!"

"I'll take any tone I like."

Mrs. O'Brien pulled a hankie from her sleeve and dabbed at her eyes. "They're your children too, or have you forgotten?"

"Aye, they are. And I was there the day each and every one of them was buried." His voice softened as he touched her face. "Said me goodbyes then. It's time you do the same."

Mrs. O'Brien could feel her lips tighten, almost disappearing. "You can ask anything of me, but not that."

"I'll not ask it then. I'll demand it."

Although Mr. O'Brien curtailed the frequency of the graveyard visits, he was unable to stop her from buying gifts. It was the unspoken fissure in their marriage. Mr. O'Brien stopped coming home for meals and visiting his wife's bed. Once, when Mrs. O'Brien passed him in the hall, she caught a faint whiff of a woman's perfume. It wasn't hers. She wasn't inclined to cheap things.

Now as then, the silence bore down on her, a weight on her chest. She drew a slow breath, but she couldn't find peace or sleep.

"I did listen," Mr. O'Brien nuzzled into her, grasping her fingers. "I promise you that, me sweet girl. I've never stopped."

M r. O'Brien rubbed the palms of his hands together. In his mind, there was no better time of day, no better place on God's green Earth, than dusk at The Donnybrook. And considering the week he was having, with his wife's daft promise to Mary-Frances and the invasion of his mother-in-law, if any man needed sanctuary in such a place, it was him. The pub had a rhythm about it, its very own heartbeat, one that Mr. O'Brien heard louder than his own. Whenever he approached it, he felt like Ali Baba seeking solace in Jabal Al Gara's den of forty thieves. Solace came with turning of the doorknob and stepping over the threshold; it was a sacred act if ever there was one.

"How's the men?" Mr. O'Brien said as soon as his eyes adjusted to the smoky light. A mixture of unintelligible cheers rose in the din. When he heard the reply, he inclined his head towards Callum, the bartender. "I've got a throat on me."

Callum nodded and pulled back the tap. "Those words, Mr. O'Brien, are like a prayer.'

"Amen to that." Mr. O'Brien took his pint. He stretched to his full height and craned his neck to scan the room. There at his table under a grimy window, as he expected, sat his own little brood: Father Connelly and Patrick Fitzpatrick. Mr. O'Brien gave a little wave, but the duo were too engrossed in conversation to notice. "Nothing good can come of that." He sucked in his ample midriff and began wading through the array of tweed-clad men, some doffing newsboy's caps, others bowlers. No matter how hard he pushed in, the dense crowd did not give with the ease to which he was accustomed. Mr. O'Brien cleared his throat and raised his pint in the air as a rapier. "I'm not crossing the blasted Rubicon," he bellowed. "To the seat of my beseeching." The words echoed off the rough-hewn timbers of the room.

In response, bodies shuffled and chairs scraped the floor as young and old made way. Mr. O'Brien passed some with a nod, others he patted on the back. When he passed Finnegan Donavan, he leaned over, picked up the other's pint and stole a sip. "That'll teach ya," he said wiping his mouth with the back of his hand, "for letting me catch ya unaware."

"For the love of God, keep your hands to yourself," Donavan protested before he turned to see who he was dealing with.

Mr. O'Brien guffawed. "And who are ya to speak of the love of God? I ask ya that!" He brought his hand down squarely atop Finnegan's bowler, flattening it to his skull. "Look at the state of ya! Ya look like something the cat dragged in. I'm surprised your ma let ya out and about."

Slack-jawed, Donavan fumbled with his misshapen bowler.

"Never mind that now though," Mr. O'Brien said slipping by Donavan and heading toward Father Connelly, who was frantically waving him over. "I'm needed."

Holding court at The Donnybrook was a daily occurrence for Mr. O'Brien, with or without a gavel. As the wealthiest patron, it was easy for him to elicit deference. In business he'd been a master of speculation, buying and selling when most opportune — at times by instinct, others by dumb luck, but who was he to quibble over the difference? It gave him status and that's all that mattered. The little table under the window was an island unto itself; there, he held court out of affection.

"Glad you made it, O'Brien," said the priest when he got within earshot. "Paddy here and I have been discussing who has the worse fate."

Paddy kicked out a chair from under the table and Mr. O'Brien took his seat. "And to make the fight fair," Patty said, "the good Father promised to leave the Saints and Blessed Virgin out of it."

"Aye." The priest scratched his neck and shifted on the apple box fixed atop his chair. "They always win. You can't be a saint these days unless ya've been drawn and quartered first. No use conceding before we even get an oar in."

Mr. O'Brien agreed. This wasn't the first evening they'd matched woes and been trumped by the Church. It was the trick the priest pulled from his robes anytime his title of martyrdom wasn't as tattered as the next man's. "Well, if there's a fair contest to be had," Mr. O'Brien said leaning into the table, "I'm afraid I'll trounce the both of ya. No use even getting started."

Paddy leaned back in his chair, balancing it on two legs. "And what could be troubling a man as rich as the pope?"

With a bit of a nudge, Mr. O'Brien reckoned he could send the boy flying. He restrained himself for the moment, thinking he'd keep the act for a more opportune time. "I'd tell ya, I would, but I promised me wife I'd not mention it in public."

"If ya're not to mention it, how will we know ya've trounced us?"

A look of exasperation crossed Mr. O'Brien's face. "Do I have to go through this again? I'll give you me word just like every other time I've trounced ya. Besides, if the Mrs. hears I've been airing me troubles, she'll have me guts for garters."

"Before pinning on your own medals, I'll wager you can't

guess Paddy's predicament," Father Connelly said waving his hand in the air. "Stumped me for near an hour."

"I'll take your wager," said Mr. O'Brien turning to examine Paddy. On first pass, there was nothing amiss in his physicality. He was not a bad-looking boy. His brow was dark and heavy, and his hair still twisted and curled at will. Mr. O'Brien fancied that, thirty or more years back, he himself might have looked similar. High cheekbones and a sharp jawline. The lad's face wanted to be remembered. Mr. O'Brien's heart softened with fondness for the boy. "Well, ya don't look any the worse for wear to me. Your clothes are as rough and patched as they were the last time I laid eyes on ya."

"Oh, it's not poverty that he's laying claim to," said the priest almost twitching in his seat.

With renewed purpose, Mr. O'Brien kept examining Paddy like a fortune teller from a summer fair. "Something different about your eyes. They don't carry the usual amount of mischief. Have ya lost something, son?"

"Wrong again," Father Connelly interjected an octave higher. "It's his ma that has got his nose out of joint. She wants him to get a job. Thinks the life of deceiving and thieving has run its course."

Mr. O'Brien took a sip from his pint. "It was bound to happen. But ya won't need to worry about that lad; women are fickle. She'll change her mind."

"That's what I told the boy." Father Connelly plumped up like a rooster on his roost. "That woman will never give up your scams, not in a month of Sundays. It's in her blood! The pope himself doesn't have enough holy water to wash it from her veins."

"Aye," agreed Mr. O'Brien. "The streets wouldn't be the same if ya two weren't pickin' pockets and swindling the newcomers. Besides, there's nothing more unpredictable than a woman. One day she wants ya to get a job, and the next she says that ya're not spending enough time at home." Mr. O'Brien leaned in and lowered his voice. "My advice to ya would be to just pretend to listen. They never know the difference."

"'Tis true," said Father Connelly. "That's how I run me confessions. It has saved me many a sleepless night."

"I hope so," Paddy said. "It would be a shame, givin' up our —," he cleared his throat, "unconventional pastime." Paddy brought his chair back down on all four legs, placing his hands on the table, palm side up. "Look at me hands. Not a blister has graced me palms. That's the mark of a true Fitzpatrick."

Mr. O'Brien and Father Connelly leaned over and examined Paddy's hands. "'Tis a thing of beauty," Father Connelly said. "Like they've been tucked away under the armpits of Jesus."

Paddy pulled back. "But I still think I've beaten the good Father. He thinks he leaves this fine establishment no better off than when he came in. That our fine company and sparkling conversation don't provide enough fodder for his sermons of Catholic hellfire. And that there's not enough breathing room between saint and sinner." Paddy ran his tongue over his teeth. "In case there be any doubt, Father Connelly be the saint and we the sinners."

"When ya put it that way," Father Connelly reddened, "it makes no sense whatsoever." He turned from Patty to Mr. O'Brien, a look of concern crossed his face. "It's just that the sisters need a little something to still their wagging tongues. A spicy confession that might slip from me lips, unaware mind ya, when having me afternoon nap in the vestibule. If I don't give the sisters some good gossip soon, I'm sunk, lads. Your mother, Paddy, and your mother-in-law, O'Brien, are no match for the Sisters of Mercy."

Mr. O'Brien's little finger twisted in his ear, he must have heard wrong. "And break the sanctity of the confessional?"

"Not the confessional," Father Connelly touched his collar. "The sanctity of the pub. I don't mind doing that."

"And tell me, Father Connelly, what's the difference?" Paddy asked.

The priest dipped his fingertips into his beer and flicked Paddy. "It's not anymore sacrosanct here than that was a blessing." Father Connelly turned back to Mr. O'Brien. "And to top it all off, Sister Mary-Frances doesn't think I'm enough like our blessed saviour. She says I'm cavorting too much with the drunks. I keep telling her a well-lubricated tongue makes for the best confessions, but she maintains that a well-lubricated ear isn't worth the bother." He paused and scraped a fingernail along the bevelled edge of the table. "If I'm cavorting too much with the drunks, she must be thinking I'm neglecting the prostitutes."

"Paddy here doesn't neglect anything." Mr. O'Brien looked at the boy like a proud parent. "He's the one who should be heading to the confessional, I tell ya that. He hasn't chased a skirt that didn't yield."

"True," Paddy said, in a sombre tone. "But I swear on me honour that I haven't enjoyed a moment of it."

The priest grunted and tapped his collar. "Need I remind ya that I'm a man of the cloth?"

Paddy and Mr. O'Brien shook their heads in unison.

"Ya don't. And we hold ya in the highest regard, isn't that so, Paddy?"

"'Tis so, even when ya be in a stupor."

Father Connelly snorted. "Asleep ya may have seen me, but in a stupor? Never."

"Father, ya forget yourself." Paddy inclined his head. "There's not been a man who can swagger under the drink as well as ya."

"Swagger! I'll box the next man who says it square in the nose. See what he'll be seeing then."

"Ya're right, Father," Paddy said. "Forgive me, I wouldn't want ya to bear me hard feelings. Just wanted to give ya something to feed to the penguins. My exploits and your sturdiness should do the trick."

Mr. O'Brien slapped the top of the table. "See what that dried up old prune has to say then. My sister doesn't understand the ways of men. Never has, never will. Not even when we were boys. Remember the time the good Father put a toad down the back of her frock and she acted as if he'd done her an injustice?"

Father Connelly's shoulders slumped. "'Twas an early birthday present. Took me a week to catch the thing."

"That's why you're The Donnybrook's unofficial mascot," Paddy said. "We'd paste your image on the front door if the church allowed it."

Father Connelly looked forlorn. "The church is too finicky for such things; the bishop was a bit miffed when I mentioned it."

"No use crying over spilt milk." Mr. O'Brien patted the back of the priest's hand. "If the old nun had an ounce of compassion she'd understand how hard life is for each and every one of us men. Then she'd be pouring our pints herself."

Father Connelly brightened. "She does encourage communion."

"Well, she's halfway there then."

Father Connelly shrugged and nodded as if the statement was a foregone conclusion, something that skirted the edges of his fingertips, too slippery to grab. He stared deep into his pint.

Mr. O'Brien snuck a glance at Paddy; he'd soon be asking what O'Brien's dilemma was. And he'd pick and pick at it, trying to unravel it like an old sweater. It was best to distract him. Pursing his lips and twisting them this way and that, Mr. O'Brien looked around the room. His beetle-brow rose when he found his mark. "'I've got a wager for ya, lad," he said as he placed two bits on the table and pushed them towards Paddy. "Convince Donavan that ya've lost your hearing, and they're yours."

"That shouldn't be too much of a challenge, me boy," said Father Connelly, a smile springing to his eyes. "Donavan thinks he can predict the future by placing his hand on his wife's goiter."

"Now if I were going to be predicting the future," said Mr. O'Brien, "it wouldn't be me wife's goiter I'd be placing me hand on."

Paddy didn't bite; the boy eyed the coin like it was already fleeced. "I admire ya," he said. "I can say that much. Leading us down the garden path without even a whiff of what ails you, Mr. O'Brien. But I won't be so easily led today. I'll be hearing about your sorry state of affairs, so that we can settle this present wager."

"I wasn't fixing to lead ya anywhere, lad."

"I'm not so sure," Paddy said laying his hand over the coin. "I was willing to play along until ya brought up your wife and where you might lay your hand. Seemed a bait and switch if ever I saw one. And if I were to take the bait, I might have said that I've not paid much mind to your wife," Paddy winked. "But if she's anything like your daughter..."

"Hold it right there." Father Connelly put both hands in the air. "Nothing good is going to come from this, I can tell you that. And I'm far too tired to get between the two of ya."

Mr. O'Brien tightened his hand around his pint glass and stared hard at Paddy. "I'll hold me temper, but next time, Mr. Fitzpatrick, ya'll not be getting off so lucky."

Paddy perked up. "Your daughter? Is that what lays so heavily on ya? The very mention of her stirs ya. That must be it! I meant no disrespect, Sir, not a bit. Never so much as said a word to your girl. I swear I've not even got close enough for me shadow to cross hers."

"Ya keep it that way," said Mr. O'Brien. "I like ya, lad. Always have. Haven't I, Father?"

"Aye, ya have, like the rest of us. We have a fondness for ya, boy."

"That's right," continued Mr. O'Brien. "But a fondness can change quickly if certain lines are crossed."

Paddy considered Mr. O'Brien in a way that made the latter feel uncomfortable. How a young man's gaze could penetrate him with such little effort rankled him. But it was the manner in which he spoke that galled him most of all.

"I appreciate the warning, O'Brien. I do. It was good of you to give it, but it puts me of the mind to take a closer gander in your daughter's direction. After all, the blood on her mother's side comes from the same side o' the tracks as mine. No use letting her think she's grander than she ought."

Mr. O'Brien reached forward to grab Paddy around the throat, but before his hand found its mark, Paddy darted in among the other patrons.

"Let him go," Father Connelly soothed Mr. O'Brien. "We all know your Mary-Kate would never look at the likes of him."

"And why is that Father?"

"He's the most annoying parts of you."

"Aye," said Mr. O'Brien settling back down in his chair. "He is, isn't he?" The very thought relieved him. "Good riddance to Patrick Fitzpatrick," he yelled as Paddy made his way to the door.

"Aye," the priest said looking down at the table. "To Paddy and to your coin."

————

THAT NIGHT, when Mr. O'Brien got home, he pulled his

daughter out of her bed and tried to toss her in the air. The toss was successful, but the catch was not.

"You've been drinking," stammered Mary-Kate as she got up from the floor, her white cotton nightdress billowed about her.

"I have and ain't it grand? Judge me girl and judge me hard. I've never been prouder of you. Because we are so much alike, he'll never be able to lay a finger on you." Mr. O'Brien laughed and did a little jig. "Wish me luck, lass. I'm off to wake your mother."

9

PADDY

Patrick Fitzpatrick climbed atop his hovel of a home, a frayed ball of yarn in one hand. It mattered little whether his day started at dawn or noon, the soliloquy was the same. Today though, the conversation of the night before wove its way through his thoughts. Paddy was beginning to regret his rash words. What started in jest had become more of a challenge. He had gotten carried away with the wager, the task to unearth O'Brien's sorry state. His only regret was that he might have. Perhaps not all the details of it, just the fringes - the ones, if drawn back, would reveal O'Brien's most guarded vulnerability. On the other hand, Father Connelly's tribulations didn't worry him much. The church had survived worse woes than a lack of entertaining gossip to distract the nuns from Father Connelly's daily ministrations at The Donnybrook.

Paddy plucked harder at the ball. O'Brien wasn't a man who forgave those who saw his underbelly, but there was no use fussing about that now. He shook his head and refocused. He had climbed onto the roof for the sake of tradition, not to chase from his thoughts a girl and her father. They should have been forgotten in passing; disappeared with the next swallow from his pint. But there they lay, tempting him to step forward and raise his sight to something forbidden.

Paddy closed his eyes and pushed back the conversation. When he re-opened them, he focused on the discoloured yarn. The exact hue of the ball was long forgotten, faded and hidden by decades of grime and fondling. In his mind, he envisioned one great-grandmother standing on Irish shores unrolling the fleece while another younger one aboard a ship wound it. The wool that prolonged a final departure. Who these women were, Paddy could only imagine. All that he knew was the winder didn't have it in her to fashion her prize into anything practical. As if doing such a thing closed a door.

For his part, Paddy faced east towards Ireland. He was sure he could almost smell the place, as if its essence was carried on the damp air. He blinked slowly towards the horizon and whispered the familiar mantra. The words held him together like the buttons on his clothes, the yarn in his hand, keeping what was Irish, Irish.

While me breath is easy, and me joints are young and free
I swear if ever you need me I'll come to thee at a whisper
I'll come along at a whisper
And when me breath does waver and me joints are tired and stiff
I swear if ever you need me I'll crawl to thee at a whisper
I'll crawl along at a whisper
And when I'm dead and buried and me bones have turned to dust
I swear if ever you need me
I'll rise for thee at a whisper. I'll fly to thee at a whisper.

The sound of a creaking door in the street below interrupted his repose. Instinctively, Paddy dropped. He lay flat on the roof and waited, out of sight. An impish grin crossed his face at the thought of how this silly game could make his heart race. His mother was trying to sneak out of the house and catch him unawares. The last time, to avoid the creaking door, she'd tried to crawl through the kitchen window but only succeeded in breaking what remained of the pane. It had been boarded up ever since.

Paddy inched his way across the roof to peer over its edge. There she was, in all her glory. His mother, Miss Brigid Fitzpatrick. She stood on the doorstep teetering on the heels of her mismatched shoes. Paddy lightened at the sight of her. Today she might win the argument of who was taller, especially if she rested her weight on her right shoe.

"Begging your pardon," Biddy said to Maggie who lived across the way. "Have you seen me brother?"

A smile curled at the edges of Paddy's lips. *Her brother my arse*, he thought. Maggie turned from the laundry she was hanging, fleetingly looked up to the roof and then shook her head no.

Paddy slipped back into the shadows, but he could imagine his mother rolling her eyes as she tilted her head back in an unnatural arc; as if she were trying to catch a glimpse of him. "Oh, the poor dear," he heard her say. "Probably after some skirt I tell you. Now that he thinks he's a man about town, he wanders off all on his own. Not so much as a word." Her voice was mournful, but Paddy knew her eyes would be sharp and merry. "He's lost to the church that one," she continued. "The nuns won't have him now, not for all the tea in China. Just last night I heard O'Brien chased him from The Donnybrook."

He inched back to the roof's edge, curious how his mother already knew his plight, and more than that, why she was engaging the neighbour. Usually, she greeted Maggie with a nod, a conversation between the two being scarce. Maggie, thinking Biddy was below her station now that her husband had installed a new clothesline, ignored Biddy as if she were no more than a shrub. Paddy reckoned it was a way of toying with the neighbour, nullifying the status of the new line. Biddy scratched her backside and jutted her chin towards Maggie.

"Come sniffing around you soon enough," she said. "Mark me words. No collar or leash will hold him now."

Maggie dropped the white shirt she was fixing to the line. Her hands flew to her hair, quickly re-pinning that which had fallen. "My husband won't approve."

"I don't think that boy will ask for his approval now, do you?"

As if on cue, Paddy slipped off the roof and landed with a thud by his mother. He gave Maggie a wry smile. She stammered and turned a bright shade of pink before abandoning her basket of laundry on the step and disappearing into her house.

"I take that as a challenge," Paddy called after her, handing his mother the ball of yarn before touching the brim of his cap.

Biddy jabbed him in the ribs with her elbow. "What did you do that for? You scared the poor thing. I'll never be able to borrow a cup of sugar now."

"We don't have a pot to pee in, what will ya need sugar for?" Paddy asked.

Biddy shrugged before she hooked her delicate chin over his shoulder, so that together they stared at Maggie's slammed door. Paddy could feel his heart slow. He loved it when she did that. He always had.

"You were on the roof again, weren't you?" she asked.

"Aye."

"Did you whisper the words for me?"

"I did," he said leaning his cheek against hers.

"Thank you." They stood on their doorstep a moment longer, breathing in each other's company. The morning sun melted into them, melding them.

"Brother..." Paddy said after a time. "Do ya have to call me that?"

His mother rubbed her cheek deeper into his. "You don't mind, do you?"

Paddy pulled away from her and turned to examine her face.

Disappointment had spilled out of every corner of their lives, yet he couldn't find it in her countenance. As a boy, Paddy had slept on a mat on the floor, while his mother had a cot in the corner. A sheet was drawn around the cot when she had company or Paddy was sent away. "Out with you," his gran would say, slipping a few coins from her pouch. "I've no time to be a nursemaid tonight." The stranger would stumble into the house, never seeming to care where Paddy was sent. Even if the cold night bit him before the door was closed behind him, no compassion was extended. Black-Hearted John with his rough hands and ragged greatcoat was in his mother's bed more nights than not. Paddy knew of his presence without ever having to see the man by the way his mother sobbed. He shook his head to rid himself of the image and bit his lip.

There were only thirteen years separating his mother and himself; it was hard to imagine how she managed. How could he possibly mind? They were poured from the same cup. He the warm pepper to her sustaining salt. "No," he said. "I don't mind."

10

SISTER MARY-FRANCES

Sister Mary-Frances looked at the paper piled high on her desk. It was unending. She sighed, took her seat, and pushed through it until she had cleared a significant spot. Light from the bevelled glass window across the room shone through the ragged stacks and speckled her desktop. When she was younger, she might have imagined the speckles as a ballet of fairies, but younger was so far away now she had forgotten the feel of it. She no longer noticed such things as dancing fairies or mischievous leprechauns, for they served no practical purpose.

The desk drawer twisted and turned as she pulled it open. She could feel her temper rising as it fought her, and she had to stop herself from cursing. The drawer needed to be added to the long list of things to be repaired. After taking out a fresh piece of parchment and her fountain pen, she banged it shut with the palm of her hand.

All morning the conversation with her sister-in-law had echoed in her mind. She didn't know why it bothered her now; more than a week had passed. She supposed it had been festering in the back of her thoughts like a sliver and was bound to come out. For the past ten years, Sister Mary-Frances had avoided the woman, but now she couldn't help it. The long line of O'Briens was coming to an end, and she wanted to make sure it finished with some dignity.

She stared at the paper as if it were a porthole to the abyss. Her pen felt unsteady in her hand. It couldn't be for lack of confidence, she wouldn't allow that. Why then? The old nun knew she was right. She never took a false step. Her life was as austere as the room in which she sat, in the shadow of a rough wooden cross. The starkness of it all seemed to make visitors uncomfortable. They twitched in their seats when she stood over them, and they quaked when she raised her voice. The room suited her. But this time something troubled her, something she couldn't put her finger on.

A tap at the door drew the nun's attention. "Yes?"

The door cracked opened just enough for Sister Benedict, a mousy contemplative, to squeeze her head through the opening. "Father Connelly here to see you."

Sister Mary-Frances sighed and rubbed her temples. "Tell him not today. I'm not in the mood to deal with his antics."

"You'll have to tell him yourself," the nun said, closing the door slowly until only her lips fit the space. "He is quite insistent."

Before Sister Mary-Frances could respond, Father Connelly had pushed the timid sister out of his way and strolled into the room. She looked at him over her paperwork. The top of his head was barely visible. "What can I do for you, Father?" she asked. Her tone was more grave than usual.

The priest's brows knitted, then disappeared as he took one of the chairs across from the desk. "Is there something troubling you, Sister? There is something in your voice that gives me reason to wonder."

The nun craned her neck just to be able to see the little man.

She knew his feet would be dangling a few inches above the floor. She'd insisted on the highest chairs in the convent for that very purpose. "I feel fine," she said. "Is that all you've come by for? Your concern about my happiness?"

"Nothing concerns me more than your happiness; not the sacraments, not the sanctity of the sanctuary, nor even the pope himself." Father Connelly made the sign of the cross and leaned towards her. "Many a sleepless night has been spent considering that very subject. I can promise you that. Until recently that is." His mouth twitched and his fists clenched. "But let's not get into that now. With you, it's all about the pining."

Sister Mary-Frances's face hardened. Listening to the little man set her teeth on edge. It had been that way since they were children. With all the toads and garter snakes he'd foisted on her, it was a wonder she hadn't opened a reptile exhibit. And now that they were both dodging the grave, he irritated her even more.

Father Connelly waved his hand dismissively. "But that's not why I have come here today. I wanted to talk to you about the new caretaker. You haven't hired one, have you?"

Sister Mary-Frances blanched slightly before looking at the sheets that flooded her desk. "Do I look like I've had time?"

"Are we playing now?" The priest's eyes widened. "A guessing game? Let me see, do you look like you have time." Father Connelly put a finger to his chin as he examined the room around him searching for a clue.

Slapping the top of her desk, the nun rose. "No, we are not playing a guessing game. And no, I did not hire a new caretaker."

"You shouldn't be teasing me like that. I'm always up for a good game. But, never you mind that now. To show that there are no hard feelings, *I'll* hire the new caretaker."

Sister Mary-Frances eased herself back into her chair. She

knew the grounds and buildings looked rather unkempt; there was only so much that the sisters could do. The last caretaker, although he was advanced in his years, had died of exhaustion tending to the vast grounds, she was sure of it. The thought of being relieved of this one burden appealed to her. "Thank you," she said softly.

The priest leaned forward in his seat and cupped a hand to his ear. "What's that you say?"

"Thank you."

"That's what I thought you said." The smile on Father Connelly's face was triumphant.

Sister Mary-Frances narrowed her eyes; she was no longer thankful. She wondered what game he was playing. Things hadn't changed since their youth. He tormented her then as he did now. He claimed it kept her spry and watchful, but it only made her more resentful. Now that it was his duty to hire a caretaker, his choice would be dubious at best. How could she have not seen through the veneer of his concern? He would be doing her no favours, but she would deal with that later. It wouldn't be the first time she had chased a man off the convent grounds. For the moment, she had more weighty things to think about. A promise to collect, and an empty bed to fill. The thought soothed her. She ran her tongue under her lip and furrowed her brow as another thought crossed her mind, that she had missed something, a throw away comment from the little priest. What was it now? That something happened recently? Something that made him twitch. She'd have to investigate.

Mr. O'Brien sat on the porch steps waiting for his daughter. She was bound to come out sooner or later. A little patience was all that was required. Being patient was not Mr. O'Brien's strong suit, and Mary-Kate seemed to prefer being later to being sooner. She was late to her own birth and had been running behind every day since.

He consoled himself with the prospect of intimidating a neighbour if one should happen to pass by. His grandfather had constructed the three-story stone monstrosity in which Mr. O'Brien now resided for that purpose alone, he was sure. It pleased him knowing the house loomed in the background, turrets and watchtowers daring attack. The only thing it needed was a moat, and he could have easily dug it in the time it took for his daughter to make an appearance. He peered down the length of his block, not a victim in sight.

From his vantage point on the porch, Mr. O'Brien had spent many an hour keeping watch. He had witnessed Tnúth spring into a city before most had even known it was a town. At times, the changes overwhelmed him. He shook his head and looked beyond the rooftops; it was a sight he never tired of. Everything was built on a craggy slope, edging as close to the water as land would allow. It was an engineering marvel. The most beguiling place in New Brunswick, if not in Canada.

There was hardly a level place for a body to stand, save one. The Flats. They were as smooth as the top of a table and held all that was dear: churches, graveyards, schools, and of course, pubs.

When the door finally opened and Mary-Kate stepped out into the sun, Mr. O'Brien frowned. His daughter was dressed neatly enough. A practical frock and hat, an old shawl he was sure he had seen his wife wear, and gloves. But something was amiss. At first, he couldn't put his finger on it, then it came to him. She was dressed like the Turnip! Bland and unpalatable, outfitted as much for foul weather as despair. "Good Gawd, girl," he said. "You can't go out looking like that. We'll be a laughing stock. And since your gran arrived, we're tiptoeing on the edge of that as it is."

Mary-Kate looked down at her dress with a flat expression. "You don't approve?"

"Jasus, Mary and Joseph, I'd sooner approve of a potato sack."

"I don't have a potato sack, but I promise as soon as I have time I'll go to the market and fetch one."

Mary-Kate curtsied and leapt off the step beyond his reach. She sped down the walk as if she were on spider legs. Mr. O'Brien cracked his walking stick against the side of the step. "Mary-Kate O'Brien, have I not told you to lighten your step?"

His daughter didn't even pause before she turned the corner and disappeared out of sight. Mr. O'Brien rose to his feet and spat. He had spent the better part of his life amassing a greater fortune than his predecessor, and to have his daughter dart through the neighbourhood without even the slightest swagger or gloat infuriated him. He tucked his walking stick under his arm and readied himself to give chase.

His long strides caught hers before she had reached The Flats. Mr. O'Brien thought they must look an odd sight, with his broad shoulders and imposing frame compared to her — a wisp of a thing. If it wasn't for that mass of red hair holding her down, he was sure she'd be airborne as soon as the first breeze hit her skirts.

Ahead of them stood the church and convent. They looked like forgotten castles, places of solitude where even the wicked could find rest. The convent was recessed to accommodate an old cemetery. The building stood like a brave headstone at the head of an ancient tomb, with the noble church meeting it at its corner. The two faithfully flanked the top and side of the grave-yard like old friends refusing to give up on the dead. The only sign of life on their stark exteriors were the vines that fingered the stone walls. It was a sight that always gave him pause and left him slightly breathless.

But Mr. O'Brien was not looking towards the convent now, he was looking at his daughter beside him. Her nostrils flared, and she quickened her pace. Not to be outdone, he matched it. Even at his age, it was easy for him to keep up with her. At her full height, she barely reached his shoulder. Soon the two broke from their brisk walk into a dead run toward the church. It wasn't the first time they had made this journey, but it was the first time they'd raced. Since his wife had told him about her careless promise, Mr. O'Brien insisted on accompanying his daughter to confession. He wanted to hear of at least one indiscretion, something juicy, that would prove the girl was a hot-blooded O'Brien, not clay for some dried-up old nun to fashion in her own image. Just the thought of it stirred his blood with unseemly pride. His lovely daughter was not going to be cloistered by his miserable sister.

"You'd better not be wasting the priest's time," said Mr. O'Brien as he opened St. Augustine's heavy oak door and allowed his daughter to pass in front of him. "'Tis becoming embarrassing." The massive door swung back hard on its hinges, and Mary-Kate breathed solemnly and made the sign of the cross.

"Don't ignore me, child."

"I'm not ignoring you; I'm just pretending you're not here."

"Oh, is that what you'll be doing then?" Mr. O'Brien turned his eyes towards the heavens, and his voice rose as if he were speaking to God himself. "Whatever happened to honour thy father and mother? I ask you that?"

Mary-Kate gave her father no notice and forged on. As of late, the more time he spent accompanying his daughter, the further apart they seemed to grow. To him, it seemed counterintuitive. He didn't think he was any less charming than usual. He'd have to ask the lads at The Donnybrook about it.

The ceiling curved its spine as it beckoned them forward. They passed splendid pillars and elegant wood carvings depicting the Stations of the Cross, and the stained-glass windows dappled the sanctuary floor with coloured sunlight. Mary-Kate covered her head with the shawl. Mr. O'Brien cursed under his breath. "You're not pretending that you're the Virgin Mary again, are you? 'Tis a stupid game." He flicked her in the head with his finger. "I heard you tell Father Connelly about it in your last confession, how you're being taken before the Pharisees for a trumped-up transgression."

A crocodile tear rolled down Mary-Kate's cheek.

"and your only friends are lepers." He reached over and pulled down her shawl. Mary-Kate turned to him and narrowed her eyes. He could almost hear the words rising to her lips, but she was silent, as if yelling at him before confession would somehow give him satisfaction, and more to confess. "Jasus, just say it. Would it kill you?"

"Mr. O'Brien," came a deep voice from the other side of the confessional. "We will not be having that kind of talk within this sanctuary."

"Sorry Father, I didn't know you were awake." Mr. O'Brien took off his bowler and ran a hankie over his brow. "It's just that the girl confounds me. Today she breathes, and I'm annoyed. Looks like she's been sucking lemons."

Mary-Kate thrust her nose in the air. "Maybe I have."

"Maybe I have," Mr. O'Brien mimicked. "I can't spend all day looking at a face like that. Look at her, Father."

Father Connelly shuffled behind the confessional curtain. When he emerged, Mr. O'Brien was amazed anew how a body could be so much smaller than its voice. He had to stop himself from ruffling the old priest's hair. He probably would have if it weren't for his annoyance with his daughter.

Father Connelly squinted his eyes as he examined Mary-Kate. "Come, Mr. O'Brien, it's not that bad. I've seen worse. The look on Mrs. Donavan's face when she was saying her vows, for instance. Now that was something to behold. That woman had been sucking more than lemons." Reaching up, he slapped the large man on the back. "Think yourself lucky. Remember poor St. Patrick? Did he not drive the snakes out of our sacred homeland? And what did he get for it? A crust of bread? A bowl of stew? No, I tell you. He got an 's' and a 't'. Can you believe it? A sainthood. It burns me bum just saying it. Calling him St. Patrick now does him no good at all. The poor man's not even around to enjoy it."

"I've never thought about it that way."

"Not many have." The priest pulled another rosary from his pocket. Mr. O'Brien noticed that lately, when he accompanied his daughter to confession, Father Connelly usually held one in each hand. The priest nodded and motioned to Mary-Kate. She made the sign of the cross as she and the priest disappeared on either side of the confessional, leaving Mr. O'Brien to pace alone.

"Bless me, Father, for I have sinned," Mary-Kate said, speaking loud enough for both the priest and her father to hear.

"When was the last time you were to confession, me daughter?" the priest asked.

"Don't you remember, Father? Just ask the lurking intruder. He should know. It was two days ago. Wasn't it, Da?"

"How am I supposed to know? I'm just your loving father, not your social calendar."

Father Connelly thumped the inside of the confessional. "Am I going to have to call Sister Mary-Frances? She'll clear this church faster than you can say Jack Robinson."

"Sorry," said the O'Briens in unison.

"Go on, Mary-Kate."

"I kept a button that fell off of one of my gran's old sweaters. Is that a sin?"

"Did you steal it?"

"No, Father. It was being thrown out."

"Then, it's not a sin."

"What if she wants to use it in a séance?" shouted Mr. O'Brien, slamming his fist into his open hand.

"Mr. O'Brien!"

"Well, 'twould be a sin, wouldn't it?"

"Are you going to use it for a séance, Mary-Kate?" asked the priest.

"No, Father."

Mr. O'Brien groaned. "And why not? Your Great-grandmother O'Brien did. She held them so tight that the dead couldn't help but listen. 'Tis in your blood."

"I have more buttons," Mary-Kate continued, as if her father hadn't spoken. "Years ago, Sister Mary-Frances gave them to me. She said they were to remind me of all the good O'Briens who've come before me. All but my father, that is. Sister Mary-Frances said there is no reason to remind me of that one."

"You'd think she'd be pleased, me marrying and letting her go to join the penguins," yelled Mr. O'Brien. "She could leg-wrestle the lot and come away with all the drippings, just like she used to at home. The woman should be in her glory."

The priest cleared his throat. "Mr. O'Brien, how many times do I have to tell you that you cannot be part of Mary-Kate's confession?"

"I know, Father, but it's been like this all me life. Why aren't me buttons worthy?"

"We will deal with your buttons later. For now, let me get through this confession."

"Sorry, Father."

"I've written away for more buttons from my Irish cousins," said Mary-Kate. "They're still in Ireland," she added. "Is that a sin?"

By the time Mary-Kate had gone through her long list of possible improprieties, the priest had dozed off and Mr. O'Brien was frustrated and bored. To wake the priest, he blustered and howled, "Forgive her, Father. She has not sinned. No imagination in that one, and it's beginning to make me doubt her paternity!"

He stormed out of the church letting the massive door slam shut behind him.

Mary-Kate smiled and trotted after her father. "See you soon Father Connelly," she called to the priest. "I'll be back for my real confession later."

Father Connelly pulled out his pocket watch. "I have time now, lass."

"I'm not going to give a confession in *this*." Mary-Kate grimaced and pulled at her drab dress. "I look dreadful."

"You O'Briens will be the death of me."

"I won't, but my father will." She blew a kiss before following her father out the door. Confession was starting to feel more like treading the boards than a religious experience, and to be honest, Mary-Kate could not say which she preferred.

Standing on the church steps, she had a good view of her quarry. He had crossed the narrow street and was now in a strip of a park that separated the church from The Donnybrook. From what she could tell, his gait was neither a stroll nor a strut. It was a stomp.

Oblivious to the blooming violets and budding catchflies, he flapped his hands and muttered curses. She could imagine the conversation he was having with himself. That probably wasn't going well either. She didn't know why it should be so, but irritating her father brought her pleasure. Her father had pestered her mercilessly throughout her childhood, and now it was her turn. Her mother said it was because they were so much alike, but Mary-Kate wasn't so sure. Irritating him now made up for the fact that everyone seemed to know a secret, something they whispered behind her back when they thought she was out of earshot. What bothered her most was the pervasive feeling that the secret was about her.

She waited until her father had weaved his way around the clumps of dogwoods and willows before she called to him. "Do you want me to join you?"

"What's that?" brayed her father, coming to a halt and turning to face her. "Did you say something?"

"Did you want me to join you? It will give me something to talk about during confession. A woman in The Donnybrook will set tongues wagging. There's only so much one can say about buttons," she said as she descended the steps and crossed over to the park.

"Jasus, Mary, and Joseph! Mary-Kate O'Brien, you try me like no other."

Mary-Kate stretched out her arms and did her best imitation of Father Connelly. "It's just that it's such a beautiful day. The birds be singing, and the spring breezes be dancing 'cross our noses. "Twould be a great day to go for a stroll."

O'Brien pulled his bowler down around his ears. "What are you playing at?" he yelled. "I'm just minding me own business and enjoying this little park before making me way to that little establishment standing forlorn on the other side."

People were stepping out of nearby shops to find out what the commotion was about.

"By the little establishment do you mean The Donnybrook?"

"Aye. And what's that to you?"

"I just thought I'd join you. We could talk about," she tapped her chin, "the whispers in the hallway, or perhaps the visit from your sister. If you don't want to talk about those things, we could delve into why you've been slipping in and out of my mother's bedroom in the middle of the day."

Mr. O'Brien reddened. "Keep your voice down." He stepped closer. "What have you heard?"

"So, you have been whispering in the hall!" Mary-Kate jabbed a finger towards her father. "I thought as much." As soon as she made the proclamation, she knew she'd said too much. Overplayed the hand before she'd even picked up her cards. Holmes would be so disappointed.

"Playing silly buggers with me, are you? You know you'll never win. I've been playing before you were a gleam in me eye." Mr. O'Brien paused and looked her up and down. "And as for the other, you joining me for a pint, O'Brien or no, there has never been one of your kind step foot in The Donnybrook, and there won't be one today. A man has to have his principles."

"So, your principles are more valuable than your daughter?" Mary-Kate was on her tiptoes now, as if being taller would make her more persuasive.

"For the love of Gawd, Mary-Kate. Do you have to wreck everything?"

"No, just some things."

Turning his back on his daughter, Mr. O'Brien continued his trek to the pub. "By the way," he snapped over his shoulder. "Keep an eye out for your mother, will you? You know how she hates it when you stand around like some common trollop."

Mary-Kate blushed. Her lips twisted into a tight little knot.

"Don't pucker up, lass," he said without turning to look at her. "There's not a soul in sight would want to be kissing you."

"Is that what you think? That I want to be kissed?"

"No, but it annoys you that I said it."

When both O'Briens returned home later that day, neither was in the mood for conversation. Mary-Kate retreated immediately to her room muttering about wasted confessions and insufferable fathers. Mr. O'Brien arrived several hours later, mumbling about buttons, to find refuge in his study. As mistress of the house, Mrs. O'Brien greeted each at the door, and at each, in turn, she shook her head.

Mary-Kate had passed her with hardly a word. She took the stairs two at a time. Mrs. O'Brien knew why her daughter was so eager: her confessions never went well, at least they hadn't since her husband started attending. Now Mary-Kate would ignore them both and bolt herself in her room. Mrs. O'Brien didn't like the separation that was growing between them, but what was worse, she didn't know how to prevent it. Mr. O'Brien was trying to prove her unsuitable for the convent, but he was humiliating her tender feelings in the process.

The whole situation only proved what Mrs. O'Brien's mother had always said, that bad luck came in threes. Sister Mary-Frances calling in her debt, the arrival of Herself, and those damned buttons. Mrs. O'Brien knew Mary-Kate had probably talked about the buttons in confession to irritate her father. Of late it seemed to be her irritant of choice, and it always ignited him without much effort. How a jar full of buttons could bring so much strife escaped her.

Sister Mary-Frances had given the empty jar to Mary-Kate when she was just a wee child. With each subsequent encounter she'd given her a button with a story attached. Mrs. O'Brien had added a few of her own. She thought it sweet how, when Mary-Kate was small, she played with the buttons like dolls, giving them the names of their departed owners and memorizing their stories. At first, it seemed harmless enough, a way of passing down oral history, but when Mary-Kate started bringing them to the dinner table and talking about them as if they had never died, Mr. O'Brien put his foot down. The buttons were locked away in a drawer. He said obsession with the dead ran too strong in the family.

Mrs. O'Brien often paused when passing the drawer. A button from each of her babies dwelled there, cut from something she had knit or sewn, as an act of hope — except for Mary-Kate, the one babe who'd lived when all Mrs. O'Brien's hope had dried up.

Until recently it was in the drawer that the buttons remained, out of sight and out of mind. But then Mr. O'Brien started to attend confession, and Mary-Kate retrieved the jar out of what Mrs. O'Brien assumed was spite. From then on, Mary-Kate's attachment to the buttons seemed to grow stronger, and she turned to them whenever she was upset. It was as if she were rekindling childhood friendships, oblivious of her father's wrath. A thought struck Mrs. O'Brien. "I could bring you more comfort," she whispered in the silence.

When Mr. O'Brien came home, Mrs. O'Brien was sitting on the bottom step of the staircase, pondering the situation. She could imagine his mood. "One is consoled by buttons, and the other..." She shook her head and stood, holding out her hands.

"You're a sight for sore eyes." She ran her gaze over the tall, broad length of him. The effect was the same as when she'd been a girl, trotting after him, picking up his things when she came to clean with her mother. And despite all the years, all the heartache, that feeling never left her, not even when he shared another's bed. The thought made her tighten her lips; it would not get the best of her today.

Mr. O'Brien grunted. "Where's Mary-Kate?"

"In her room."

"With her damn buttons?"

"Aye. They bring her comfort."

"They don't bring comfort to anyone else." Mr. O'Brien brushed past his wife and into his study, slamming the door behind him. He banged and knocked around until the whole place shook. Mrs. O'Brien waited patiently outside the door, hoping for a lull so she could interrupt him. It never came. She considered breaking the hall mirror and risking seven years' bad luck but decided against it. She didn't want the posy sisters to bleed to death cleaning it up.

"Mr. O'Brien," she called through the heavy oak door. "You come out here this instant, or I'll set The Donnybrook alight."

"You'll do no such thing," he scoffed.

"Aye, but me ma will."

Mr. O'Brien flew out of his study more out-of-sorts than when he'd gone in. "Why the hell would you get that old bat involved?"

"For a happy marriage. Besides, it was the only way I could get your attention."

"Jasus, Mary, and Joseph, woman. You are as strange as your daughter."

"I'd watch meself, Mr. O'Brien! You're treading a thin line. It's you that's hounding her, not the other way round. Following her to confession like you are going to a spring fair." Mrs. O'Brien put a hand to her lips. Her voice had cracked, betraying her emotion.

Mr. O'Brien grabbed the newspaper off the hall table and stomped into the parlour. Regaining her composure, she followed, picked up her embroidery and sat on the settee across from him. On such occasions, when his anger exceeded what Mrs. O'Brien felt she could appease, she allowed him to smoke his pipe indoors. Otherwise, she said the habit was distasteful, a sign of poor breeding. Mr. O'Brien sat in their best parlour chair, crossed his legs and tapped his pipe on the heel of his shoe before refilling and lighting it.

Mrs. O'Brien raised an eyebrow. "I trust Mary-Kate's confession didn't go well," she said, pulling out a misplaced stitch.

Sucking hard on the pipe, Mr. O'Brien snapped the newspaper. "Has it ever gone well? It's like listening to a blasted saint."

"That's too bad. I know how you'd hoped for the worst."

"Confounded woman. I hoped for nothing. I just want to hear something that would keep her close to me." He laid the newspaper in his lap. His voice grew soft and mournful. "And far away from me sister."

"She is young, darling. Give her time. She'll find her feet."

"Find her feet? She never lost them. They've been in the same place since the day she was born. What else can I do? When I find the right man, I'll hand her off, I promise you that. Far be it from me to keep her underfoot. I've never been the controlling sort, never will be." He scratched his head. "But the lass is beyond me."

The two looked past one another. Mary-Kate came to them late in life and Mrs. O'Brien knew she was more than either of them could have envisioned, that just the bounce of her curls made him smile. But since Mrs. O'Brien's promise had come to light, made before she knew only one of her babies would survive the cradle, he no longer noticed the bounce. Worry furrowed his brow, banged his walking stick, and halted his fingertips at night when he touched her.

Father and daughter had become a mystery to each other. Their playful antics were now cloaked in ulterior motives. What used to make Mary-Kate unique, being singular and bookish and not paying attention to any of the young men in town, frightened Mr. O'Brien now. It made her vulnerable to Mary-Frances.

"It's enough to drive a man to drink," Mr. O'Brien complained to his wife.

"Oh, come dear, you drank long before Mary-Kate came along."

"Aye, but I was never driven to do so before, although Herself tried. Wouldn't be surprised if that woman didn't put me sister up to it. Reminding her of your ridiculous pledge."

Mrs. O'Brien stiffened. "I never told me mother. But if you insist on dredging up the past, I can dredge up a few things meself."

"I was stating facts, nothing more."

"Really?"

"Really."

Mrs. O'Brien sniffed. "Well if it's facts you want stated, I have some doozies."

"Keep them to yourself, woman. You're only making a difficult situation worse."

This was getting her nowhere. Mrs. O'Brien went back to her handiwork, jamming her needle through the fabric with unnecessary fervour.

"I can't believe that in the age of electric lights and motorcars, me own daughter prefers the company of buttons. If I'd known she'd want to carry on with the dead, I wouldn't have wasted all that money burying them."

Mrs. O'Brien set down her embroidery and let it slip to the floor. "Don't say such things. You'll bring us bad luck."

"Oh, bad luck is ours all right. She lives in the Deadman's room. Treading our halls and poking her nose into every nook and cranny. If someone should be banished to the convent it should be Herself."

Mrs. O'Brien's gaze shifted to the ceiling. Herself pattering amongst the penguins — that would be a sight to behold. She smiled, and a new plan began to percolate.

14

MARY-KATE

Mary-Kate plopped her mason jar of buttons down on the breakfast table, more for effect than anything else. Her father didn't look past the newspaper he was reading. She plopped it down again, determined to irritate him as much as he did her at confession. What had got into him as of late, she couldn't imagine, but whatever it was, she was determined to deter him at every turn.

"You'll not get his goat that way," Herself said, her weeping veil rumpled and askew as if she had slept in it. "I've tried to get it all morning." The old woman threw a piece of toast at the stiff newspaper only to have it fall to the white linen tablecloth, near two others. "See? He doesn't so much as bat an eye. Had to butter meself three different pieces of toasts and have yet to take a bite."

"Well, at least your morning hasn't been a total waste. Plenty of buttered bread to feed the birds." Mary-Kate patted the back of her gran's hand. "I just wanted to know if he's coming with me to confession this morning. I'm thinking about talking about my preference in lady's hosiery."

"Oh, lady's hosiery! Would accompany you meself if me bursitis weren't acting up."

Mr. O'Brien snapped his newspaper but gave no response.

"I think it's Morse code." Herself flung another toast.

The light in the breakfast room seemed a little brighter to Mary-Kate, now that her gran had come to stay. She had always preferred the smaller, informal space to the dining room. Its round-windowed edges housed her mother's many plants. Mary-Kate was energized by the soft light and spurred on by her grandmother's barbed tongue.

"When I was younger," the older said, "I cleaned this house. I wager you didn't know that?"

Mary-Kate shook her head. Herself rarely talked about her early years, and she definitely didn't talk about anything to do with Mary-Kate's father. To admit she was his subordinate was unheard of.

"And your ma, well, let me tell you, she was something. That one could turn heads without even trying. But the only head that mattered to her was your da's. Most days he walked past her as if she wasn't even there. Too busy apple-polishing his own kind." She licked her butter knife. "It wasn't until she caught Fergus Connelly's eye that your da took notice."

Mary-Kate needed a moment to realize Fergus Connelly and Father Connelly were one and the same. She knew the priest and her father had been childhood friends, but she hadn't heard anyone use his Christian name before. It seemed odd to think of him as a regular person —someone who had courted girls and danced until the wee hours before choosing the priesthood. The thought felt somehow threatening; for the life of her, Mary-Kate couldn't figure out why.

"But as soon as that man took notice," Herself continued, "your ma's life changed. No more scrubbing and dusting for her.

No. Too good for service. Leaving the rest of us bowing and scraping just to get by." Herself narrowed her eyes at the front page of Mr. O'Brien's newspaper. "And before I had a chance to put my oar in, they eloped, hardly a month after he stood down-wind of her. Never did figure out why the hurry."

Mary-Kate leaned on to the table. It was the first time she'd heard of her parents' courtship, what little there was of it, and she almost tingled with excitement. There must have been a scandal: wealthy upscale family opens door to working class girl. Neighbours whispering behind hedges, ladies drinking their tea through clenched teeth. No one had ever spoken of it in her hearing before, though she wagered no one who knew had forgotten either.

Herself threw another toast. "Your da was thinner then, but not by far. And his ma was less dead, though she always had a peculiar smell about her." Herself paused and looked towards the newspaper as if expecting a heated response, but Mr. O'Brien stayed on his page.

"They were an odd bunch, the O'Briens. Always prancing around like they owned the place."

"But they did own it, didn't they?"

"Aye, but the prancing got on me last nerve."

The paper snapped again, and when Mr. O'Brien flipped down the top corner, Mary-Kate was surprised to see hurt in her father's eyes. As if he'd reached out but had his hand slapped away.

"I took you in for me love of your daughter. Me love of your daughter, not her love for you," he said to his mother-in-law, his voice void of guile. "And you," he turned to Mary-Kate. "I'd walk on hot coals for you. If you can't see that by now, you need to give your head a shake."

Herself rolled her eyes and scoffed. "You'll not be making me regret a word I've said. Sitting there all wounded and mournful, as if I'd be taken in by that. It must be hard being indignant at your own behaviour."

Mr. O'Brien narrowed his eyes, picked up a toast and aimed.

Herself smiled. "Pass the jam, Mary-Kate."

15

MR. O'BRIEN

Mr. O'Brien hummed as he made his way home. He ventured there wasn't a man around as happy as he. Spending an afternoon at the pub usually had that effect on him, but this was more than that. He'd been paid the highest compliment an Irishman could be paid. The boys at The Donnybrook had called him a Seanachie, a revered story-teller. The day was his. It made him want to click his heels in celebration. After the first attempt, however, he brushed himself off and decided the day was not entirely his — just the better part of it.

It had been two days since Mary-Kate's last confession and their kerfuffle at the breakfast table. If he set aside his irritation, he had to admire that when he pressed her she didn't bow or cave. She resisted, like a true O'Brien. He closed his eyes and thought of how she'd accosted him outside the church, and fashioned her confessions to enrage him. The girl was showing a fair amount of wit, more than any son he'd hoped for. As for Paddy and their little disagreement, he could only laugh. There was no use staying mad at him. The lad gave him all his best stories.

When Mr. O'Brien rounded the corner to his house, his pace quickened and his whistle pierced the air, shrill as any bird's. He was announcing his arrival, and he expected his wife to be ready. When he opened the front door, she wasn't there. He raised his voice and called. "Mrs. O'Brien, where are you hiding yourself? What kind of wife doesn't greet her husband? Come to me now, and I won't make you answer for it later."

There was no response. Mr. O'Brien scratched his head. Any other time he lumbered through the door demanding an audience, she was there squelching his fire faster than water on a flame, mostly to prevent the ire of Our Lady of Blessed Misery. But even Herself was nowhere about. Mr. O'Brien felt a hint of disappointment. "Are you ill, woman?" he yelled. No answer. His humour began to evaporate. "Mary-Kate, are you anywhere about? Is there no one in this household who will greet a man at the door?"

Mae came tottering down the hall holding a dishrag. Mr. O'Brien scowled at her turnip face. "Good Gawd, woman, I didn't mean you."

He found his wife upstairs, sitting on the edge of Mary-Kate's bed. The blind was down, and there was not a light to brighten the place. "What are you doing sitting in the dark? I've been looking all over for you. Haven't you heard me calling?"

"Sorry," said his wife. "I've other things on me mind."

"Forget that now." Mr. O'Brien pulled his wife to her feet and kissed her hard on the cheek. "My love, I've been called a Seanachie. Have you heard of anything grander? A Seanachie."

Mrs. O'Brien pulled back from her husband. "You've also been called a liar and a thief."

Mr. O'Brien let go of his wife. "Jasus, Mary and Joseph, woman. What are you going on about?"

"This letter. Mary-Kate found it." She waved a crumpled

sheet of paper in the air. "She went through the mail before I got a chance to throw it out. It's from Mary-Frances."

"Not that woman."

"Aye, that woman. The day isn't so bright now is it?"

Mr. O'Brien crossed himself, took the sheet from his wife's hand, made his way to the window, and drew the blind. "It was bound to happen," he said. "But why did it have to happen today of all days?"

My dearest Mary-Kate,

I am writing this letter in the hope that it will find its way into your hands. If my brother has his way, it never will. I've written to you at least a dozen times, and I have yet to receive a response. I would speak to you myself, but I've been forbidden to see you. Father Connelly won't even pass on my messages during your daily confessions. Does your father interfere with every aspect of your life, intercept all your correspondence? It must be hard to live under such a heavy hand.

Remember what we talked about when you were little? How, when you got older we could spend more time together? Wouldn't that be lovely? You and I sitting around sharing stories and secrets. Your father would be fit to be tied. I'm sure we both would rather enjoy seeing that.

Well, I think the day has come. I would love for you to come and see me as I have missed you so. There is so much to tell you.

I'll be waiting.

Aunt Mary-Frances

Mr. O'Brien crumpled the paper in his fist. "Where is our daughter now?"

"I don't know. Why'd you think I'm sitting here in the dark with me head in me hands?"

"Damn that withered prune to hell!" The crumpled letter fell to the floor, where he ground it under the heel of his boot. "I should have put a stop to her years ago."

16

It wasn't the first evening Paddy had walked by The Donnybrook, but it was the first time in a week that he ventured inside. The place was full, and Paddy had to squeeze in just to make it past the door. Standing on his tiptoes, he scanned the room as best he could. O'Brien wasn't there. Paddy couldn't hear his booming voice, and the place had a heavy feel to it as if something horrible was about to happen. That wasn't something O'Brien allowed. He always said, "If ya can't leave your troubles at the door, then ya have no business being here."

From what Paddy could tell, there were many worries in the smoky air, but he, at the moment, ignored his. In addition to avoiding O'Brien, he was avoiding his mother too, with all her talk about being more respectable and stepping away from the life. The first time she mentioned it, he took Father Connelly's and Mr. O'Brien's advice and ignored her. After days of her insisting, he began to dodge her; if she went hither he went thither, and if she wised up and gave chase, he outran her. He'd never put on as many miles outrunning the constabulary.

Even if his mother did track him down, she would never set

so much as a toe inside The Donnybrook. If she did, they'd throw her out. This was a gentlemen's club, and if a lady was mistaken enough to believe she was welcome, then she wasn't much of a lady and was treated accordingly. Paddy himself blocked a lass or two, but only if she had the right look about her — a girl who was a little green and pleasing to the eye, but most importantly, in need of comfort. And as for O'Brien, if he should happen by, Paddy was fairly sure he could slide like an eel through a crowd this thick.

Paddy took off his coat and hung it on a hook by the door. When he turned around, he saw Callum, the bartender, motioning him over. "Glad to see you made it," he said, bouncing on the balls of his feet while he polished a glass with a cloth. "The boys thought you might be too busy patching things up with your ma to make it by."

Paddy scowled and asked for a pint. "There is no patching with that woman. She's bound and determined to have her way and I'm bound and determined that she not."

"Glad to hear it. Wouldn't want Tnúth to lose its welcoming committee."

Leaning an elbow on the bar, Paddy turned and regarded the room. "He's not here then?"

"Who?"

"O'Brien."

Callum pointed towards the back of the pub. "Don't you have eyes in your head? He's been sitting at his table all evening. If you'd looked, you'd have seen him through the window."

Paddy pushed his cap back and stood on his toes. "Aye, you're right. Couldn't see for looking."

Putting down his towel, Callum shook his head. "Don't know what's wrong with him, lad. He's a different man than when he left this afternoon. He was fit as a man half his age, now he looks like he's been dragged through the gutter. Go over if you like."

There were no truer words, thought Paddy. Mr. O'Brien did appear different. He was hunched into a ball and looked a fraction his former size. But even so, he towered over Father Connelly who sat across from him. The sight made Paddy shake his head. "It's not that I don't care," he said. "That I do, but I don't think I'm the man to be talking to him. Been avoiding him for a week. He was a bit troubled at our last encounter."

"I think you're wrong. He's been asking for you. Even paid a lad to go fetch you."

"I'd like to take your word for that, but me cowardly knees aren't so easily convinced."

Callum shrugged and turned to another customer.

Paddy jostled between the men. The crowd gave him ample cover from which to watch O'Brien. He was the only gent Paddy knew who seemed to have just one name. Never heard a man older or younger call him anything else. Even Mrs. O'Brien, from what Paddy understood, kept to formalities. Once, he heard a stranger ask O'Brien about it. "What is your Christian name?" the man asked. "The one your ma gave you when you were nothing more than a wee suckling?" O'Brien only answered with his eyes — a warning it was best not to ask again.

Only a stranger wouldn't know the old Irish wisdom that prevented O'Brien from speaking his Christian name. A name was power, and giving anyone that power was unwise. As things stood now, Paddy didn't think there was enough fire left in the man for a stranger to notice him, much less care what his name was.

From Paddy's vantage point, it seemed Father Connelly was pleading with Mr. O'Brien, who held his head in his hands and refused to look up. The priest's thunderous voice filled the room with his concern.

"Remember your health, man. Nothing is worth this much grief."

O'Brien's great shoulders shook in response. Around him, The Donnybrook got an itchy feeling about it. Paddy curled his back like a cat trying to shake it, but it didn't work. O'Brien was The Donnybrook, and The Donnybrook was O'Brien. If one crumbled so did the other.

Keen and Keenan, a set of freckled twins, watched Mr. O'Brien carefully and then began comparing observations. They leaned into their table, their noses almost brushing. Paddy sat with them, hoping to educate himself.

"I've heard he's been thrown out," said Keen, his voice so low Paddy strained to hear it. "His wife's cold heart finally got the best of her."

"Not so," Keenan returned. "Her heart's as good as gold. Seen her with me own eyes. She adores the man. 'Tis his daughter has caused him so much misery. Wouldn't put it past the girl to put a dagger in his very heart."

"Is that so? Didn't think she had it in her. We'll have to drink to that boys, to encourage the old man." Keen turned. "Join us, Paddy?"

Paddy nodded. "I'll tip me glass with ya, lads, but I'll not stand. Don't want to draw the old gent's attention me way."

"Do as you please," said Keen. The brothers stood, clinked their pints and toasted Mr. O'Brien. "May we never be as forlorn as the chap sitting before us and may his sorrow last no longer than the wink of a butterfly's eye."

"Beautiful," said Keenan. "Never knew me brother was such a poet."

"I am. And the more you drink the better I get."

"Here's to your improvement." Keenan downed his glass and called for another.

"There is nothing like the support of a dear brother but let us not forget why we are drinking. Tonight, 'tis for the misery of

Mr. O'Brien." The men sat, turned, and looked his way. "The man is lost. Never thought I'd see the great oak bend."

On most nights the pub had a sound about it as sweet as any songbird's. Tonight, Paddy couldn't hear the song. Almost every man owed something to O'Brien. They or their fathers had all worked for him at one time or another, and he was friend to all. Paddy was the only one who came of his own accord.

He and all the others kept a close watch on the table in the corner, quieting at every sound, straining to see any movement. There were many occasions for sorrow in their small world, but usually it was for things that were lost — a babe in arms, a job, a girl run off. This was different. O'Brien suffered none of these misfortunes. Paddy figured his sadness was the anticipatory variety.

Father Connelly placed his hands on those of his friend. "Letter or no, I'm not sure I can be of much use. A priest is not in the habit of banning girls from the convent. Besides, how much does a young girl want to read anyway?"

The room hushed. "Did you hear that?" Keen said, a bit too loud. "Being banned from the convent. His daughter isn't even fit to be a nun. Would throw her out if I were him. Mr. O'Brien is too good to her."

Mr. O'Brien banged his head against the table. "Ya won't be talking about me Mary-Kate like that. She's fit to be a nun if she wants to be. Even the pope wouldn't deny her that."

Keen blanched. "Excuse me, sir. Never meant no harm. Will hold me tongue next time."

"Ya do that." O'Brien lifted his head and glared in their direction. "Or ya won't have a tongue to hold." Instead of returning to his former despair, however, his gaze locked with Paddy's and his voice lightened. "When did ya get here, lad? Did anyone tell ya I was expecting ya?"

"Aye, they did. But I wasn't sure I wanted to be expected."

"Nonsense, me boy. Come have a seat."

Drawing himself to his full height, Paddy picked up his glass with one hand and plucked the pipe from Keen's mouth with the other. He knew O'Brien had a fondness for pipes, and right now he felt that any fondness worked in his favour. He waded through the men. "Troubles with your daughter?"

"Oh, you've heard."

"Only just. Want to assure ya I'm not the cause."

Mr. O'Brien coughed. "Why would ya think ya were? Didn't ya give me your word that ya'd never even crossed her shadow?"

"That I did. That I did."

"Behind these doors, that's good enough for me." He relieved Paddy of the pipe. "It's times like these a man needs those who are closest to him, those he can depend on."

Paddy nodded and felt a knot in his neck untwist a little.

Within The Donnybrook there wasn't a man not taken at his word. Gaining entrance to the pub guaranteed him that. To become a member was near impossible to do. A stranger could make it through the doors but not without every head turned to face him. In the dim light, only the pipe smoke would move, drifting up towards the rafters. The warm puffs were all that received an outsider. If that didn't drive him away, the sheer silence did. When a stranger entered their midst, neither a word was spoken, nor a drop was drunk.

Only the men who came on someone else's recommendation were received. Every gent was someone's son, brother or nephew, and if one faltered, the lot had to go. It was a significant risk for a man to vouch for another, and a high price if the gamble failed.

Paddy had no kin to vouch for him. He'd first braved the doors when he was no more than six. The curiosity of the situation made the men forget their common practice, and they spoke to the boy.

"Looking for someone?" Callum asked.

"Nay," said Paddy, taking a stool. "Getting away from someone I am. Me gran. Ya wouldn't let her in here would ya?"

The bartender looked out the window at an odd-looking woman wearing a monocle and a brown duster. "Wouldn't let her in. Seen her with Black-Hearted John. You poor lad. She can't be much of a gran if she's spending time with that vile creature." He pointed to the end of the bar. "Named the spittoon after him."

Paddy reached for a half-empty glass. "That was kind of ya." He downed the drink and wiped his mouth on his sleeve.

"Not really," Callum said without taking his eyes off the boy. "It's filled with bile. Where'd you learn to drink like that? Not even a sputter."

"Not sure."

"Who's boy are you?" another asked. "Black-Hearted John's?"

"My ma says I'm too good to be his. But she's not sure. Maybe it's one of ya."

The men looked at their feet. "We don't talk about such things here, lad. You best ask your ma."

"She won't speak of it. Only cries when I ask."

"No use making a good woman weep, best leave it be."

Paddy shrugged and jumped down from the stool. "It's been grand, gents," he said with a slight bow as he slipped a hand into the closest jacket pocket.

Mr. O'Brien stood, and with a couple of long strides beat Paddy to the door. "That's no way to treat grown men." He tried to stifle his smile. "Or ya'll not be allowed back."

"Ya saw that did ya?"

"I did, and ya better return his change purse, or the next time it won't be half a pint ya down."

"I'll remember that."

"Ya do," said Mr. O'Brien tossing the boy a coin. "Any lad

with that much pluck and a little less lip is welcome here anytime."

Paddy nodded, opened the door and, after checking to see if his gran was gone, disappeared.

Father Connelly snatched the pipe out of O'Brien's hand and drew Paddy out of his reverie. "The lad knows the lay of the land," Father Connelly sucked hard on the bit. "Don't ya, boy?"

Paddy nodded, a little unsure of what the conversation was about.

"Besides," continued the priest, "I think we've spent enough time on this tittle-tattle. A man can only endure so much kitchen gossip before he gives up the ghost."

Mr. O'Brien rapped his fingers on the table. "If talking about me precious Mary-Kate is beneath you Father, lead the way."

"Glad to see we're of the same mind." Father Connelly cleared his throat. "I have an announcement to make: Tnúth is getting a new priest."

"Ya interrupt me musing about me wee lass for this malarkey? Me sister's been threatening that for years."

"Not malarkey this time." Father Connelly pulled an envelope from his pocket. "Got it this morning from the diocese."

"Ya leaving us Father?" Paddy asked.

"Not likely." Mr. O'Brien plucked the pipe from between the Father's lips. "We're the only parish that will have him."

"And consider yourself lucky for it," Father Connelly snapped. "Sister Mary-Frances, that lovely lummox, has been writing the bishop for as long as I can remember. Complaining about me inadequacies and asking for help."

"Ya don't need help with being inadequate."

"Exactly. He's but an auxiliary." Father Connelly rose on his apple box and waved the letter in the air. "For me it's like falling out of bed. But the worst part is that the fraud is English."

"English," Paddy gasped. "They might as well have used the Lord's name in vain."

"Oh, believe me I have," spat Father Connelly. "But it has brought precious little comfort."

Mr. O'Brien handed the pipe back to the priest. "Ya'll be needing this more than me."

Mary-Kate paced the length of her room trying to bring her mind into focus. When she first discovered the letter, she slipped down to the cellar and hid amongst the crates and cobwebs, shivering and blubbering. She knew her parents would make a frantic search but never consider the bowels of their own home. She felt a little foolish, but it was the first place that came to mind. When she slipped back up to her room, she looked like an overdressed chimney sweep. And she didn't feel any more equipped to deal with the letter now than when she'd chanced upon it.

"Come on, come on," she said, chiding herself for her lack of agency. If she became this muddled over one letter, a few paragraphs that were more of an invitation than a threat, what was to become of her? A stiff wind or bit of drizzle could do her in. It wasn't the suggested visit that unnerved her — although that was troubling enough — it was the mention of sharing secrets, underlined.

Her thoughts flitted about like a bird not trusting itself to land. She had no choice; she turned towards the window. Not that long ago, if she'd been told she'd seek out her aunt, of her own free will, she'd tell the bearer they were either drunk or mad. That no such thing would happen, could happen, when she was in control of her faculties. But now the shoe was on the other foot, she couldn't see past not going. The blasted letter made sure of that.

She paced the room once more, this time to drown out her parents bickering downstairs. As far back as she could remember the pair never squabbled. Her father would do or say some asinine thing, her mother would feign displeasure, and then they'd fawn and fuss over each other like love-sick idiots. Mary-Kate found the whole thing distasteful. But since her aunt's visit and her grandmother taking up residence, her parents weren't themselves. The two of them were going at it hammer and tongs, oblivious to the tittle-tattle it would create below stairs. Mary-Kate wanted to yell back at them through her closed door but knew it would do no good. Her plea for peace would go by unnoticed.

Destroying correspondence seemed like such a foolish thing to do. She couldn't fathom how Sister Mary-Frances had frightened her father into such an act. They could have discussed it at the dinner table — unless it was the secrets her aunt alluded to that prevented them? Mary-Kate's hands balled into fists. This mystery was too much for her.

If truth be told, her aunt had always frightened and repulsed her. Her first memory of the woman was at a Christmas dinner. While the tree lights twinkled merrily, the nun and her father sprawled under the dining room table fighting over the turkey gizzard. With her habit askew and her skirts hiked up to show ample leg hair, her aunt's ferocity had frightened Mary-Kate. When a table leg snapped and the Christmas china came crashing to the floor, her mother had howled bloody murder. After that, Mary-Kate found the brawling sweat-ball a bit much to take. If it hadn't been for the allure of the buttons her aunt brought with each visit, Mary-Kate would have screamed at the very sight of her. The thought of those mammoth arms pulling her close in some show of affection made her want to shrink and disappear.

Pursing her lips, Mary-Kate gazed out her bedroom window, beyond the barren rosebushes, at something unseen. Out of the emptiness, a thought wiggled its way into her consciousness. The letters were linked with her father's intense interest of late, and the appearance of her aunt in her mother's kitchen some time back — the encounter the maids were prattling about on the back stairs. They had to be connected; it was the only thing that made sense.

Mary-Kate considered her options. She couldn't ask her father for information, he'd deliver some twisted Irish diatribe. Only yesterday he'd told her the very air in Ireland was richer, and that the children's laughter was full and bright enough to waken the dead and keep them up. As for her mother, she was liable to turn on her father and blame him for encouraging Mary-Kate to read. It would serve her better not to say anything, to leave the house without letting anyone know where she was going or when she would return. She'd suss out the details on her own, leaving her parents as oblivious of her actions as she was of theirs. She would be like Holmes stalking the streets of London, finding clues where others found nothing.

The thought brought a smile to her face. She grabbed a wrap, jutted out her chin, and slipped out of her bedroom door, down the stairs and out of the house without so much as a whisper of enquiry.

Escaping the house unmolested was an accomplishment. With her head down, she forged through the streets of Tnúth with purpose. Shadows lengthened and shortened, and she walked on, her mind flitting from the past to the present, never settling on either place very long.

It wasn't until a weariness possessed her that she looked up and realized she was in unfamiliar territory. She stopped to examine her surroundings: boarded-up windows, missing planks on the walkway, battered doors. The young men hanging about in the middle of the day gave the place an air of despair. Her father would have scolded them, called them shiftless. It was the first time Mary-Kate could remember feeling unsafe — that is, if she discounted Sister Mary-Frances hanging about or her mother's graveyard visits. She'd read about neighbourhoods such as this one in Dickens, dilapidated and inhospitable, but never considered there was such a place in her beloved Tnúth. A street right out of a penny dreadful if ever there was one.

"Lost your way, Miss?" a dusty man asked, tipping back his cap to have a better view. "Cause if you have, I'll be the one to help you."

The tone of his voice made Mary-Kate draw into herself. His approach was more of a slither than a walk, and she felt sure she would collapse. No one had spoken to her in that way before, and she couldn't find her voice to protest. To her horror, a second man joined the first. He slipped up from behind and patted her backside.

"No need to be coy with us, Miss," said the second man. The smell of hard liquor accompanied his words. "We know what you be looking for."

The two men were so close that Mary-Kate couldn't have run even if she wanted to. One licked his lips while the other sniffed her hair. "Aren't you pretty as a picture?" said the one with the cap. The words stuck to her skin, made her stomach flip with nausea. The dirt-encrusted fingernails of the second man traced a line from her waist to her hip. She said nothing, but her body stiffened. It was as if she was hovering somewhere overhead, unable to defend herself. The men continued their circling, saying things she could no longer hear.

"Aren't ya lads brave?"

Mary-Kate searched for the new voice. It was somewhere behind her, but she couldn't bring herself to look.

The men who were giving her such a careful examination stopped, and one spoke to the newcomer.

"What's it to you, Fitzpatrick?"

"Nothing. Nothing, at all," said the man as he strolled into Mary-Kate's sightline and leaned on a nearby pole. He paused and examined his fingernails. "It's just that, I thought I should tell ya, that's O'Brien's lass."

The two men stood dumbfounded, but even then it didn't occur to them to slip back into the shadows. "You want to get me killed? Is that what you be wanting?" said the second man to the first.

"You're the one that be groping the poor dear in the light of day." The man with the cap pulled it down over his eyes as if trying to hide his identity.

"I was not groping. I promise you that. I was brushing away a spider."

The one called Fitzpatrick pulled on Mary-Kate's arm, leading her away from the bickering layabouts. "It will be all downhill from here," he said. "Best be on our way before someone starts swinging."

Mary-Kate nodded, but she couldn't take her eyes off the pair pummelling each other in the dirt. "Are they always like that, accosting women in the street?"

"Not always. Most women around here would have beaten them to a pulp. They've never had one stand still for them before."

Mary-Kate looked at the foreign surroundings, so close yet so far from her own. "Oh. I didn't realize that was the custom here."

"I'll take ya to Father Connelly. He'll have ya fixed up in a jiffy with a quick blessing and a little holy water."

Mary-Kate nodded and dutifully followed her new acquaintance through a maze of darkened buildings with boarded-up windows — and that stale, desperate air.

18

MR. O'BRIEN

I n the drizzle of the late April evening, he didn't see her coming. She was upon him before he heard her cries, accosting him before he had a chance to enter his precious Donnybrook.

"What do you mean you've never seen me before? I'm carrying your child."

Mr. O'Brien turned towards the commotion, to see what fool was being confronted in the street, only to discover it was himself. "Miss Fitzpatrick," he said to the petite woman who stood so close the rain dripped from his bowler directly onto her skirts. "You make a fine pregnant wench." He dipped his head slightly, allowing whatever moisture that remained in the brim of his hat to pour out.

Biddy stepped back, avoiding the small deluge. "So you do know who I am."

"That I do. Your reputation precedes you."

Biddy curtsied, fanning herself with a tattered glove. Her hat was pelted flat to her head, her hair, void of any style, hung in lumps. Her dress had been darkened by the wet, masking whatever hue it once was. "I've been using that line for as long as I can remember. It's amazing what a baffled soul can dig out of his pockets when push comes to shove."

Mr. O'Brien shifted with impatience. The weather had taken a turn, and he wanted refuge. In an evening that was more accommodating, he might engage her in a longer conversation, pick her brain on the ins and outs of thievery, but this night held no such pleasantries. "And you seek me out?"

"I do." Biddy brushed the hair out of her eyes and got to the point. "Not to pick your pockets mind you." She poked him in the ribs with her elbow. "Though I bet there's a treasure trove there."

Mr. O'Brien took a step towards the door of The Donnybrook and Biddy picked up her pace. "You see it's like this," she said. "I asked me Paddy, that's me son Paddy, to find himself employment. I quite insisted upon it. Telling him that no man worth his salt lived the life of a wastrel. Whiling away his days thinking of his latest swindle. Laid it on rather thick, if I say so meself."

Mr. O'Brien nodded. "I've heard."

"I thought you might have." Biddy paused, and half closed one eye as if considering carefully what she would say next. "The thing is, I didn't mean a word of it."

"The working of a woman's mind eludes me," he said trying to keep the irritation out of his voice. "Why on Earth would you say something like that if you didn't mean it?"

"To give him his freedom." Biddy stepped closer, so her face was directly under Mr. O'Brien's. "Paddy's freedom. Doing what we do is a vocation, a calling, and if Paddy doesn't hear it, or feel it, how could I ask him to live a life like that?"

"Why are you telling me this now?"

"He's avoiding me. If I go left, he goes right." Her voice cracked. "I just want you to tell him to come home."

"I'll tell him when he's ready to hear. The boy should be weaned by now, needs to be with the men more than he needs to be clinging to his mother's skirts like some milksop."

"Aye Mr. O'Brien. That's just what I was thinking meself. I raised him right, now you make him a man. "

19

I t wasn't until the following morning that Mary-Kate knew what she wanted to do. It was only a matter of searching her closet for the right thing to wear. For her confessions of late she had arrived at the convent looking as dull as dishwater, but that would be bad form today. Considering that in all likelihood she would end up cowering in a simpering heap before her prodigious aunt, at least she'd look good.

The closet was divided into two sections — garments that irritated her father, and attire that pleased her. Her father's section, a recent addition, was relatively small but most effective; it made going to her fake confessions quite enjoyable. Today she wanted to look her best, and show a little more ankle than usual. Flipping through the hangers she fell upon her Mary Pickford number — commanding yet feminine. She slipped it out of the closet, sliding her hand down the rose Messaline silk. If she felt intimidated wearing this, there was no hope. She might as well give up now.

A bang in the hallway drew her attention. Mary-Kate stifled a grunt, tightening her grip on the silk. How was she supposed to enjoy her pre-emptive triumph over her father and aunt, imaginary as it was, with Herself banging around? The sound of the old widow dragging her rocking chair about the house, up and down stairs, knocking in and out of doorways, was beginning to wear thin. Nicks and dints marked the old woman's daily paths on the rocker itself, but also upon door frames and furniture legs.

Mary-Kate's father claimed the exercise was for the good of The Blessed Lady of Misery's health and wouldn't allow anyone to assist. Herself didn't agree, arguing with him about it until all hours of the night. "If I'm already in the dead room," she'd wail, "give me some relief. You have help enough, going about dusting where there is no dust to be had. Toting me rocker would be a treat."

It was the only piece of furniture her gran brought with her, and she insisted on conveying it from room to room so she wouldn't have to put her bottom anywhere the great oaf had sat. For his part, the great oaf seemed relieved that his feathered cushions were spared.

Mary-Kate inclined her ear towards her bedroom door. From what she could make out, her gran had parked herself on the other side of it. The runners on her chair groaned rhythmically on the hall carpet.

"What's she up to now?" Mary-Kate whispered as she slipped on the silk dress. By the speed of the grinding, Mary-Kate presumed that Herself was not in the best of spirits. For that matter, neither were her parents. Their arguing filled the house and, she was sure, spilled over into the street as well. She couldn't understand what all the fuss was about. Her aunt wanted to spend more time together. Mary-Kate paused. It *was* a frightening thought. The two of them, seated across from each other, forcing smiles.

"I'll not have it," she heard her father yell through the floorboards.

"It's not your choice. She's a grown woman," her mother returned.

"Grown or not, she's still under me roof."

"If you keep yelling like that, she won't be for long."

Mary-Kate took a deep breath. She felt like a horse in the starting gate. Closing her eyes, she steadied herself; then, with a smooth motion she opened her bedroom door and ran past her grandmother. She felt the old woman's fingers grip her frock and release as she pulled free. Mary-Kate was past three others and out of the house before the voices stopped trailing her. She reached the convent in record time and was still panting when Sister Benedict greeted her at the door.

"Sister Mary-Frances will be with you shortly," said the nun, leading Mary-Kate into the old nun's office. "She and Father Connelly are discussing the stock of communion wine. It's his weekly come-to-Jesus moment. I think he does it just to spend time with her."

"Oh," said Mary-Kate. "Will it take long?"

"That depends on how long it takes for Father Connelly to admit that he's been putting the sacrament on his oatmeal."

The nun closed the door and left Mary-Kate to herself. She fidgeted in her seat. Voices travelled up and down the hallway and slipped under the door, but even with the distractions, her nerves had almost eaten her by the time her aunt arrived.

"Sorry for making you wait," Sister Mary-Frances said as she entered the room and shut the door. "I had an incident to deal with. I see one of the sisters let you in."

Mary-Kate nodded, not taking her gaze off the other as she took the seat across from her. "Mary-Kate." Sister Mary-Frances took her hand. "I might as well get to the point. You're a young woman now, with a mind of your own. I think it's high time you start using it instead of drifting. I would like you to come and join me here at the convent."

Mary-Kate flinched. Becoming a penguin had never occurred to her! Was this what all the fuss was about? She couldn't imagine spending her days fighting over offal and doing penance for it. For what else was there to do within these stony walls? Pray and collect alms for the poor? How long could she do that before she became mad and ripped out her own hair?

Mary-Frances eyed her carefully. "Don't you remember our talks when you were younger?"

"Yes, but I didn't think you were serious!"

"You think I was asking for the good of my health? If you do you are sorely mistaken. I meant every word of it." Sister Mary-Frances tapped her foot, waiting for a response. When none came, she continued. "Or did your father tell you I was a failed spinster and that you should indulge me?"

Mary-Kate's cheeks heated; her blush gave the answer. To sooth her aunt's growing fury she considered qualifying the silent reply. That her father only spoke of the failure with company or when he had put his feet up after a long day. It was more of a playful remembering than spite. But how to approach such a thing evaded her.

The nun's eyes widened. "I knew it! Let me tell you something. I have never failed at anything in my life, despite your father's protestations! And the only reason I'm approaching you now is because of your mother's solemn promise."

"What promise?"

"Hasn't she told you? And I thought the two of you were close. She promised you to the church before you were born."

The grip of the nun's hand on Mary-Kate's tightened, so that Mary-Kate flinched again. Sister Mary-Frances's face softened, and her voice almost slithered out of her mouth. "She made an oath to God."

Mary-Kate felt the world close in around her as if everything in her life had been confined to this one small room. "How could she do such a thing?"

"Dear girl, how could she not? She must have recognized even then that she was out of her depth when it came to raising children."

"But she's not out of her depth." Mary-Kate's gaze met her aunt's.

"Then why did you come here so quickly upon receiving my latest request? Did you even discuss it with your mother?"

Mary-Kate didn't answer.

"I thought as much. Besides," there was a cruelness in Sister Mary-Frances's voice, "it's kept you alive, hasn't it? All the others are dead."

Mary-Kate's heart constricted at her aunt's declaration, but she couldn't call it a lie. All the others *were* dead, and who was she to question Mary-Frances's assertion that her mother's promise has saved her life? Still, she knew her aunt had crossed a line. And her father, if he found out, would happily punt the old girl back to the other side.

Sister Mary-Frances stood, walked around her desk, opened the top desk drawer and pulled out a dog-eared datebook. "It's just a matter of picking a date." She flipped through the pages. "I want to be able to spend time with you, to help you adjust."

"Do I have to?" Mary-Kate's voice was barely above a whisper.

Her aunt snapped the book shut. "You are considering turning your back on God? Your mother made a promise, Mary-Kate. It needs to be taken seriously."

"I know, but I didn't."

"Didn't what?"

"Make a promise. My mother did. Before I was born."

Sister Mary-Frances's shoulders slackened. "You're right,"

she said. "The promise wasn't yours, but in the eyes of God, you're just as responsible for it."

Picking at a splinter on the corner of the desk, Mary-Kate tried to contain her rising panic. "I don't think I can do this, at least not yet."

"When, Mary-Kate? When will you be able to do this?"

Mary-Kate shrugged.

"All right. I'll give you a week, but I'm not going to tell your parents about the delay. Let them turn on a spit. Knowing about your reluctance would only make them happy, and that's the last thing I want to do."

Mrs. O'Brien looked at her hands and sighed. She hated when they turned black. It reminded her of the days she was not an O'Brien, days when the future was not so steady or bright. When working with newsprint, it couldn't be helped. "Take this," she said to her mother as she handed her an article she had just clipped.

Herself turned the clipping over and frowned. "That Tenpenny woman is something else. With all the things happening in the world, she wrote about your bridge game."

"I don't expect you to understand the workings of this kind of household," Mrs. O'Brien sniffed. "Not from where you come from."

"What's that supposed to mean?"

"If I have to explain it..."

Herself let out a puff of air, causing her weeping veil to flutter like curtains in a breeze. "Don't be troubling yourself. Wouldn't want a fine lady like you to break a sweat. What would Miss Tenpenny say? Oh, the scandal." She snatched the paper away from her daughter. "What about this piece, *The Rise and Fall of Tnúth's Finest.*"

"I love that column." Mrs. O'Brien leaned forward. "It only comes out twice a month, but when it does it is sure to cause a stir. The thing I like best is guessing who the fallen are."

"I hate guessing. We'll skip it." Herself licked a finger.

"Just read it, it won't kill you."

After a little more cajoling, Herself cleared her throat and began to read. "*Upstanding Citizen Accosted by Undesirable.*" She put the paper down. "That happened to me this very morning, at your breakfast table."

"Be serious."

"I am, but I didn't see the Tenpenny woman there. She must be a mind reader."

Mrs. O'Brien ignored her mother. "Keep reading."

Herself skimmed the article. "Says here that some prominent man, who often frequents The Donnybrook no less, was recently accused of impregnating an across-the-tracks girl. Says she came upon him in the rain and shouted it for all the world to hear. Sounds familiar doesn't it? Even I can guess who that is."

"Well I can't." Mrs. O'Brien reddened.

"Oh, you've heard this story before. Don't you remember? Though far be it from me to bring up anything from the prickly past."

Mrs. O'Brien blinked hard as she grabbed the paper back from her mother. "I didn't invite you down here to show off your reading," she said, tucking the offending piece under her bottom. She would peruse it later when she was away from prying eyes.

"And I wouldn't have come if I'd known you'd be working me to the bone. I'd have stayed in me bed."

"Honestly, it's just a bit of pasting. Let's not make a meal of it."

The two pursed their lips and narrowed their eyes, each unaware of the other's synchronization. When Mrs. O'Brien had asked her mother to help paste news stories into the scrapbook, she'd meant it as a way to ease the tension and pass the time while waiting for Mary-Kate.

"Is that your good brooch?"

Mrs. O'Brien touched the cameo that concealed the top button of her white blouse. "No, it's me every day one. Why?"

"Oh, I don't know." Herself twisted her mouth as she pasted. "It's just that I wouldn't be wearing such a piece meself. Looks like something from a dime store window."

"You gave it to me."

"Oh, so I did." Herself raised an eyebrow. "But there's no need to be churlish about it now, is there?"

Mrs. O'Brien set the scissors on the maple table, safer there than in her hand. She did not want to add homicide to her list of troubles. She chided herself for thinking that there could be some truce; the thought of easing tension seemed foolhardy now.

"It's just that everything else in this house seems to be bragging." Herself waved the paste brush in the air, and droplets of glue worked their way free from its bristles, leaving a spray in its wake. "Ceilings as high as the heavens, and fancy carved furnishings that could have belonged to Methuselah, dust and all." Her voice dropped. "Yet you're not grand at all, prouder than punch to be in your every day."

Mrs. O'Brien's lips parted, but she gave no reply. Her mother was never one to give up on a quarrel. If there was a sore spot Herself could poke with casual effort, she poked it.

Right from the start of Mrs. O'Brien's marriage, whispers had drifted up from the bowels of the house like sour notes, claiming Mrs. O'Brien was an unrefined trespasser. And every time a new staff member was hired, the whispers were stirred and fed. That was her sore spot, right there, at least the most obvious one. The others she tucked away and prayed Herself wouldn't smell their festering edges.

Granted, Mr. O'Brien's house was much grander than the home she was raised in. She was now one of the wealthiest women in New Brunswick, perhaps even in all of the Maritimes. In spite of this, and being married for more than thirty years, when she looked around her, Mrs. O'Brien still felt like an impostor — the impostor that her mother now called out of the shadows.

Mrs. O'Brien closed her eyes and imagined what her husband would say to her. He would chuck her chin and say she had more curves than straightaways and that any man worth his salt favoured the curves. In his primordial mind, nothing else seemed to matter.

"Well," Herself continued, "you know what they say. You can't make a silk purse out of a sow's ear, can you?"

Mrs. O'Brien picked up the pair of scissors and ran a finger along the blade. Who would blame her? Not anyone who spent any amount of time with Herself. "Oh, I don't think you're the one who should be talking about silk purses and sow's ears. I've seen you eat the pope's nose." Mrs. O'Brien crossed herself and shuddered.

"You've seen no such thing!"

"I have so. I have served it to you meself on me best china. And you gobbled it up with your own jowls a-swaying!"

Mrs. O'Brien saw by the look in her mother's eye that she was contemplating murder too. They were still embroiled in their talk of turkey parts and culinary refinements when, out of the corner of her eye, Mrs. O'Brien spotted Mary-Kate slumped in the doorway as if her bones had grown soft. Staring at not a living thing, the blankness about her reminded Mrs. O'Brien of the Deadman's room.

"Your gran and I are cutting and pasting. Care to join us?"

Mrs. O'Brien lightened her voice and pushed out a chair from under the table, narrowly missing the barley twist table leg. As if on cue, her mother ceased her bickering and drew her lips over her gums in a garish smile.

Mary-Kate gave no response before she turned and trudged up the stairs.

"That one," Herself said, wincing as she rubbed a varicose vein, "looks as if she's lost her moorings."

Mrs. O'Brien nodded. "Aye, she knows. All those years of tender care and it all comes to this, a misplaced promise."

Herself paused and raised a questioning eyebrow. "What promise?"

"The one I misplaced. Were you not listening?"

"This is unlike me." Mary-Kate blinked as she waited for her eyes to adjust.

"What's that?"

She sat back on her haunches. She had followed the Fitzpatrick person into the caraganas out of curiosity, not expecting to explain her actions. "Well," she said. "Not this. I usually don't crawl through bushes. In fact, I've never been in the bushes before." She brushed away a spider that dangled in front of her face, stifling a scream but unable to stop the shudder running through her.

"Yet, here ya are." Fitzpatrick pulled back the branches and looked towards the graveyard. The midday sun had warmed their hiding spot enough to chase away the chill, but not enough to dry the smell of damp.

"Yes, here I am." The words came out of her mouth and felt as foreign to her ears as they had saying them. That morning she couldn't have imagined doing such a thing.

He mumbled something and continued crawling, and Mary-Kate followed. "In for a penny, in for a pound."

The strip of shrubbery that separated the convent from the

graveyard had been of no particular interest to Mary-Kate
before. The seasons changed, and the birds came and went, and
she remained ignorant to the subtleties. Now she was worming
through dead leaves and dirt, and with a boy no less. She knew
how she got there, but whatever possessed her was a whole
different matter. It happened naturally, without conscious
thought, and it was too late to do anything about it now.

That morning, barely a breeze had greeted Mary-Kate on the
front step, but she did not notice. She'd left the house in such a
hurry that she was oblivious to her entire state of being, let
alone the state of the day. Without looking, she couldn't have
told anyone what she wore or how she chose to do her hair. It
was as if she'd dressed in the dark, paying more attention to the
sounds that drifted under her bedroom door than to her appearance. The clip of her mother's hard shoes pacing the hall all
night was like the sound of a ticking clock after an unwelcome
event. She assumed her mother and gran were taking shifts.
Each guarding her door, whispering, "It's not going to happen
today."

The escape was all that Mary-Kate had planned. She wasn't
sure how she would spend her morning, but she knew how she
wouldn't. Covering the distance between Germain Street and
the convent took less time than Mary-Kate anticipated. The tight
line that connected the two seemed to have shrunk, but it was
on that line that her life now teetered. How could she ask her
mother about the promise that, according to her aunt, saved her
life? How could she make her mother face all those dead babies
again? And for that matter, how could she sidle up to her ghastly
aunt and cleave to the bosom of an institution? She had no
place; she was living in purgatory.

As for her father, talking to him would be like beating a dead
horse. The man rarely gave a straight answer, and when pressed
disappeared into the doors of The Donnybrook. Between her

mother's despondency and her father's emotional ineptitude, she had nowhere to turn.

Outside the convent, she paused before she turned back in the direction of Germain Street. That was when she caught sight of the young man who had come to her aid in the alley. He had slipped into a strip of caraganas, quick as you please. She told herself it was curiosity that drew her to him, a simple reprieve from her current situation. It would be a relief to investigate something besides her own predicament.

When Fitzpatrick stopped crawling, Mary-Kate felt a wave of panic. She didn't know what to do next. Mary-Kate stuck out her hand. "We haven't been formally introduced. Mary-Kate O'Brien. You helped me a few days ago."

He turned and wiped his hand on his pants before taking hers. "I remember. Patrick Fitzpatrick."

"What are you doing?" she whispered, the excitement sparkling in her eyes.

"What makes ya think I'm doing anything?"

"I saw the way you skulked into the caraganas like a fox toward a hen house."

"I wasn't skulking."

"Then you certainly have a peculiar gait." She waved a hand through the air. "And I'm sure you're not in here for the good of your health."

"Not me health, but your aunt's." Paddy frowned at her. "Why are ya following me?"

"Curiosity. Why are you waiting for her? My aunt?" Mary-Kate broke off a twig that was jabbing her in the ribs, then settled down, tucking her knees, covered by her taut skirt, into her chest.

"I switched some of the wooden grave markers earlier this morning. Wanted to see how long it will take her to notice." Paddy took a jackknife from his pocket and cut away some of the branches to enlarge the spot where they were seated. "That's better," he said. "Now we can sit side by side."

"Who says I want to sit side by side?" Mary-Kate moved over. "It's a little presumptuous of you."

"Kissing ya would be presumptuous, lass. Making ya comfortable, that would be kindness."

Trying not to smile, Mary-Kate peered through the foliage towards the graveyard. She felt her heart race, and her pulse pounded in her ears. "This is the most exciting thing I've ever done."

Paddy turned to look at her. "Ya can't be serious. Where has your da been keeping ya? In a box?"

"He hasn't been keeping me anywhere. Where I come from, people don't do things like this."

Paddy leaned back on his elbows, a look of horror on his face. "I'd die before I'd come to a place like that. It's things like this that make ya feel alive."

Mary-Kate couldn't argue with him. She hugged her legs harder and stared at the graveyard. From where she sat, she didn't feel the same revulsion as she usually did at the sight of it. Perhaps it was due to being beyond the gate, beyond the call of any gaping hole in the ground.

It took the better part of an hour before Sister Mary-Frances emerged from the convent to inspect the grounds. Paddy's eyes shone, and Mary-Kate had to cover her mouth to prevent herself from squealing. He jutted out his chin toward The Donnybrook. "They'll be laying wagers now," he whispered under the rustling of the leaves. "Father Connelly being in the thick of it."

Mary-Kate shivered with delight and whispered back, "You've done this before?"

"Aye, for years."

"And always for sport?"

Paddy nodded. "The old girl has come down in her times,

but the fervour with which she completes the task, that's magical. We're not ready to retire her yet."

Mary-Kate was still a little puzzled. "But my aunt doesn't know about any of this? The challenge, the betting, Father Connelly's involvement?"

"Aye, and don't ya be telling her. We're going to race against a parish in the Midlands next month and don't want her catching wind of it now."

"There are priests in other parishes doing the same thing?"

"Some." Paddy made a face. "Others think it's beneath them."

"And Father Connelly approves?"

"Aye, he holds the stopwatch. He's our most reliable timekeeper."

Mary-Kate wasn't sure what to think. Her aunt rushed around the graveyard, her black robes billowing around her as she pulled a wooden cross from one spot and moved it to another. Now it made sense why Father Connelly insisted on wooden grave markers rather than granite. It wasn't because they were more humble and Christ-like. It was because they were portable.

"Does my father know?" she whispered.

"Does your da know?" Paddy guffawed. "He's the one who set it up."

Sister Mary-Frances stopped short. She raised her head and looked behind her, towards the caraganas. Mary-Kate thought her heart would stop. What if her aunt heard them, what if they were caught? She grabbed hold of Paddy's hand; he had gone white. Sister Mary-Frances was like a hound sniffing the air. Mary-Kate began to pray. She went through a full Hail Mary before Father Connelly came toddling out of The Donnybrook and yoo-hooed to the nun. "Sister Mary-Frances," he called. "Yoo-hoo, Sister Mary-Frances."

The nun's head moved slightly, but her gaze stayed fixed on the bushes.

"Donavan says his wife's goiter is acting up. Would like us to check in on her."

Sister Mary-Frances pushed in the last grave marker and wiped her brow on her sleeve. "Her goiter is always bothering her."

"'Tis true, but this time she's thinking it might be travelling to the other side of her neck. That's her good side," he said. "Are you up for a visit?"

"I'm up to it if you are," she snapped, forgetting all about the shrubbery and her suspicion. Mary-Kate let out her breath.

"It's just that you don't seem to be your old self of late," Father Connelly said as he looked down at the stopwatch he had palmed in his hand. "You might want to get rested up for next month." He gently guided her in the direction of the church.

"What's happening next month?" asked Sister Mary-Frances.

"The bishop is coming."

"What? No one informed me."

"Me either. I can just feel it in me bones."

Mary-Kate watched as Father Connelly drew her aunt away. After they had gained some distance, the priest turned, looked in their direction and scowled. A solitary finger touched his lips.

Mary-Kate's face went slack. "Do you think it's a sin?"

"What do ya mean?"

"Being in the bushes with someone I barely know." Her voice tightened. "Deceiving a nun."

"Depends on what you be doing in the bushes with a lad you barely know." Paddy leaned over and lowered his voice. "Sometimes it's the sin that makes life grand."

"Mr. Fitzpatrick!"

"Miss O'Brien." A smile crossed his lips. Mary-Kate ached to kiss them.

22

MR. O'BRIEN

M r. O'Brien examined his wife who sat across from him fussing with a needle and thread. How handiwork could occupy so much of her time was beyond him. The simple drudgery of her repetitive motions sent him scurrying to The Donnybrook every afternoon, to get away from the monotony. This afternoon was different; he had to make up for the previous evening's misstep of coming home at an undesirable hour and interrupting her well-deserved rest. She had been put out by him. He closed his eyes and readied his explanation.

It was all Father Connelly's fault. Despite Mr. O'Brien's domestic strife, of late he made more time for the priest. The two of them had taken to closing down The Donnybrook, drinking the others under the table. He'd tell his wife it was out of kindness. She couldn't get cross at him for that. Perhaps he'd even shed a tear or two. He might say that the little man's countenance had changed. He was no longer light and ready for adventure, and when Mr. O'Brien laid his beefy hand on the priest's shoulder, Father Connelly's skin vibrated, the way a horse's does when it's shooing a fly. It was true, after all, and it was just one more thing that made Mr. O'Brien furious. And all because an English dupe was set upon invading the sanctity of their inner fiefdom. It had shaken Father Connelly in ways that no man should be shaken. To even contemplate such a thing was treasonous.

As Mrs. O'Brien already knew, the pair of them on occasion had caroused until the wee hours. On this occasion though, Mr. O'Brien was obliged to carry the distraught priest home. Unfortunately, it was Sister Mary-Frances who met them at the door and roughly took Father Connelly from his arms.

"He looks like a sweet wee angel," Mr. O'Brien said, tenderly patting the priest's cheek. He cooed over him as a new parent. His plan was to lull his sister into letting down her guard. In that state, she might agree to anything.

"I know, I know," the nun said sarcastically. "I've heard it all before. The next thing you'll say is that 'the breath is only just in and out of him, and the grass doesn't know of him walking over it.'" She looked Mr. O'Brien up and down. "It's an old saying, brother, and believe me, it's grown rather tiresome."

Mr. O'Brien sniffed. She wasn't being lulled. Time for a new tactic — sarcasm. "I'll take your word for it." He leaned against the doorframe and pushed his bowler up with the tip of a finger. "After all, you are the expert on old and tiresome."

Dropping her bundle, Sister Mary-Frances placed her hands on her hips and leaned into her brother. "I'll show you old and tiresome, heathen."

"You have a mirror handy, do you?" Mr. O'Brien leaned over the crumpled heap, so he was nose to nose with his sister.

The nun shrieked and stomped her foot. "First you marry that little strumpet and throw me out of my own house, when it had always been our intention for me to run the family household and you the family business. And then you try to deny me the one thing that would ease my suffering: Mary-Kate!"

"Jasus, Mary and Joseph! That was never my intention. We never discussed you running me household, never agreed to it, so don't be laying claim to it now."

"It was implied."

"By who?"

"Does it matter now?"

"Of course it does. You can't plan me life and not tell me about it."

"Someone had to. Look what happens when you are left to your own devices!"

Mr. O'Brien curled his fists, an act hearkening back to his childhood when pummelling his sibling was a daily occurrence. Pummelling a nun was a different kettle of fish. Even so, arguing with his sister was worse than arguing with his wife, and that was saying something. He let out a breath and tried to keep the temper out of his voice. "Tell me dear sister, what would ease your suffering?"

"Mary-Kate." Sister Mary-Frances's eyes flashed, and there was no kindness in them.

"Never! I've heard about that blasted promise. It was badly done, and you should never have tried to redeem it, not with all those graves in the family plot. I promise you right here and now that won't be happening. I'll never give me dear sweet girl to you! It's a husband and family she'll be wanting. Not to wed herself to Christ as you did."

"She told you that herself, did she?" Sister Mary-Frances examined his eyes and had her answer.

All the way home, Mr. O'Brien fumed. Mary-Kate a peace offering for a malcontent? The thought was ridiculous. If his sister demanded recompense for her imagined slight, let it be someone a little further from the heart. Better yet, someone who was a thorn in his side. He scratched his head. Herself, as he had discussed with his wife earlier, would do nicely. She was a sacrifice he was willing to make.

"Woman," Mr. O'Brien bellowed as soon as he was past his front threshold. "You're needed."

The sound of banging accompanied by the switching on of lights preceded Mrs. O'Brien in her nightclothes coming down the stairs. "Keep your voice down. You'll wake up the household."

"The household be damned. I'm in need of you."

"Well?"

"Well what?"

Mrs. O'Brien thumped him in the chest. "What are you in need of?"

His mind when blank. With all the night's libations, such a thing was expected. "Don't pressure me, woman, I just got through the door." He grabbed his wife's hand and squeezed it.

She gasped before pulling away. "You're the one who called me, insisted I tend you."

"You're the one who came, which in me mind makes us equally at fault. Let's off to bed and catch some winks before the rooster crows."

———

Now, in the light of a new day, he realized he might have been a bit demanding. Calling his wife to him in the dead of night wasn't his best idea. But then again, a woman interrupting her man's thoughts when he's just stepped through the door, regardless how late he's arrived, can't expect him to be coherent, let alone accountable. If she was cross, she was as much at fault as he, and there was enough blame to go around. But how to make his wife willingly pick up her fair share? It was a puzzle that had foiled many a man. He'd have to ask the lads at the pub.

Mrs. O'Brien licked the thread once more before she gave up on putting it through the eye of the needle. Her hands were limp in her lap when she looked up at him. It was the first time she'd looked at him since he'd risen. "How can you just sit there?"

Mr. O'Brien shifted in his seat, not sure how he should respond.

"Are you not worried?"

"Of course I'm worried! The little imp feels expendable, being replaced without a sideways glance. It makes me heart ache. Why do you think I was out until the wee hours last night? Calling you for comfort?" Relief was filling Mr. O'Brien with every breath. The Mrs. must be excusing his previous evening's escapades, as any good wife should. He reached into his jacket pocket and retrieved his pipe.

Rolling the needle between her fingers Mrs. O'Brien's gaze deepened. "Our Mary-Kate being replaced? By who? What do you mean?"

A dry lump rose in his throat. "How am I supposed to know? This is the first I heard of it."

"What do you think we've been talking about?"

Mr. O'Brien shrugged. He didn't want to weigh in. He'd inevitably be wrong. His wife didn't seem to care if Father Connelly was at the end of his rope, barely holding on with his baby priest hands.

Mrs. O'Brien jabbed the needle in his direction. "Mary-Kate left the house God knows when this morning, to go God knows where, and no one has heard from her since." Her voice was vibrating. "But is it any wonder, when her own father hasn't even noticed?"

23

MARY-KATE

Mary-Kate took a deep breath and gathered herself. Trepidation had swallowed her, but she had to face her parents eventually, to seek food and shelter. They had probably foregone afternoon tea, which was a ritual her mother forsook only under the direst of circumstances. She could only imagine how worried they'd been, her father cursing and pacing, and her mother wringing her hands. How could she return and face their demands when she didn't even know her own mind?

Baiting her father at confession held no value now, not after discovering her mother had promised her future to Aunt Mary-Frances. She had wondered why he'd joined her at confession recently, and thought it must have been out of boredom, due to having turned most of his business affairs over to his solicitor. Now that she knew her father hoped she'd commit a limited indiscretion to avoid fulfilling her mother's promise, there was no joy in confessing about buttons to confound him. Was that why she'd done something so completely out of character? Was that why she'd followed the young man who had rescued her a few evenings prior into the caraganas in search of adventure?

With dark clouds mustering and the wind whipping about, shelter was in order. As for nourishment, she felt like she hadn't eaten in days, yet didn't know if she could. Closing her eyes, she placed her hand on the doorknob and repeated her new mantra: Open the door and cross the threshold, open the door and cross the threshold. She had to be as bold as brass about it.

The creak of the heavy front door announced her arrival. Before she even wiped her feet, her mother flew out of the sitting room.

"Where have you been?" Mrs. O'Brien pulled a twig out of Mary-Kate's hair and checked her for wounds. "You look like something the cat dragged in."

Mary-Kate said nothing. How could she tell her parents that she had spent the afternoon in the bushes with a young man? A young man who switched grave markers and watched her aunt replace them? Her parents would be horrified. At least her mother would be; her father was up to his eyebrows in the dirty business. But the truth about the bushes would send him through the roof. That was why she was planning on deceiving them about becoming a nun — deceiving them for now, at least.

"Never mind that." Mr. O'Brien rubbed his hands together and looked his daughter up and down. "I'm wasting away."

"Is that your only concern?" Mrs. O'Brien turned on him with the precision that only comes with years of practice. "Eating? Your daughter comes back from God knows where doing God knows what and your first thought is of food?"

"Good Gawd, woman. Has the day not been bad enough?"

"Apparently not for you. You want to make it worse by expanding your girth."

Mary-Kate left them arguing at the foot of the stairs while she went to her room to freshen up. She wasn't even sure they noticed. Their nattering filled in the background so she didn't have to think. It did cross Mary-Kate's mind to retire early, but her parents would eventually come looking for her. They'd sit on the edge of her bed and might even refuse to leave. When she descended the stairs, she found them in the dining room debating her father's choice of the mealtime prayer.

"I don't like it, not at all," said Mrs. O'Brien.

"Oh, there's nothing wrong with it, woman. Stop complaining about everything."

Laying her napkin on her lap, Mrs. O'Brien pursed her lips for a moment before mocking her husband. "'Three potatoes for the four of us, thank the Lord there are no more of us.' That's your prayer?"

"Aye, and 'tis as Irish as Irish can be. Being grateful *and* remembering the famine." Mr. O'Brien made the sign of the cross. "And there is no reply you can make to that, is there?"

A heavy grunt escaped Mrs. O'Brien and Mary-Kate heard her father's feet tapping merrily under the table. Herself rocked in her chair, plate in lap. "I told you not to marry the man. No sense of rhythm."

"Why, it's me favourite method." Mr. O'Brien's jig abruptly stopped, and he and her gran began where they'd left off the evening before. Each seemed to have a new sling of stones and they hurled them at one another with the zest of zealots. Mae had laid the serving dishes and left the room before Mary-Kate drew her mother's attention.

"You seem preoccupied. What have you been up to?"

"Nothing," said Mary-Kate, refusing to look up.

"Are you sure?"

"Yes."

"Well, if you're sure, I'll let the matter drop."

"I'm sure." Mary-Kate filled her plate as the heat rose in her cheeks. She reached down and touched her thigh, where Paddy's had pressed against hers. The very thought of it over-whelmed her. Being in the bushes with a young man within the reach of the church was unimaginable, and the most exciting thing that had ever happened to her. Mary-Kate felt wicked, not just for her behaviour but for her lack of remorse. She reasoned it bordered on debauchery. "What must he think of me," she whispered.

"What does who think?"

"No one," said Mary-Kate. She set down her napkin, getting up to excuse herself.

"Not so fast," said her father. "Show me your eyes."

"No."

"Aye, you will. Or I'll pry them open meself."

"Don't be ridiculous," said Mrs. O'Brien. She turned back to her daughter. "Sit down. What does who think?"

Mary-Kate hesitated before she re-took her seat. She steeled herself for the barrage, determined to keep her own counsel.

"Who thinks what?" Mrs. O'Brien repeated.

"Does it really matter?"

"Aye it does." Mr. O'Brien brought a closed fist down hard on the walnut table. "When we start something at the dinner table we finish it at the table."

Mary-Kate knew the rule. It had been drummed into her since she was a child. Her mind ran over what she could say without revealing the truth. "Wha... Wha... What does Father Connelly think of Sister Mary-Frances?"

"Is that all?" Mrs. O'Brien sighed and patted Mary-Kate's arm. "That's a convoluted story."

Mr. O'Brien snapped his head towards his wife. "Convoluted? Pray tell, how is it convoluted? The little man pines for that mass of a woman day and night. Been that way since we were children. It's quite nauseating." He put up his hand. "Don't ask me why, I've been sworn to secrecy. Vowed to take it with me to the grave."

"Not much good at keeping your vows, are you?" Herself

dabbed the corners of her mouth with her napkin. "I think the newspaper printed something about it just the other day."

"What the hell are you talking about?"

"Ask your wife."

Mrs. O'Brien brought her hand to her mouth and went white to the lips. She looked as if she would crumble.

"I will not," Mr. O'Brien roared back. "And I advise you to keep your thoughts to yourself." With a grunt he launched a glob of potatoes at her from the end of his fork. "Not keeping me vows. Promised to feed you, didn't I?"

Mary-Kate pushed her plate away, laid her head on the table, and began to sob.

"Mary-Kate, what has gotten into you?" asked Mr. O'Brien. "I'm only lobbing potatoes, for Christ's sake."

Mary-Kate mumbled something and sobbed harder.

"Sit up." Mr. O'Brien leaned in. "I can't understand a word you're saying! You're fading into the table cloth."

Mary-Kate straightened. She hadn't pushed her plate far enough away, and mashed potatoes were stuck in the edges of her hair. "I have to go to confession now. I think I've sinned."

"Tell the maid to get me walking stick. I'm going to confession," Mr. O'Brien squealed with delight. He slapped his wife on the back. "I've not seen Mary-Kate this distraught before. Maybe she's finally done something worth telling the priest about!"

Mrs. O'Brien looked from her husband to her daughter. "That's enough of this conversation. Mary-Kate, go to your room until you calm down. And as for you, Mr. O'Brien, I suggest you sleep lightly tonight."

———

MARY-KATE WAS STANDING by her bedroom window when her mother came to kiss her goodnight. "'Twas a lovely day." Mrs.

O'Brien slipped her arm around her daughter's waist. "Before the rain, the sun couldn't shine enough."

"Yes, it was," said Mary-Kate, laying her hand on her mother's arm. "There was enough blue in the sky to cut out a pair of pants."

Mrs. O'Brien let out a long sigh. "Tell me it will always be like this, you and I together."

Mary-Kate stiffened, and the moment was lost. Everything known and unknown that had transpired between them came rushing to the fore, and she felt herself pull away. "Whatever God wills," she said, sounding more like Sister Mary-Frances than she thought possible.

Paddy's practice was to go during the witching hour. By then, the black convent crows would have finished their pecking and scratching and exchanged their daily habits for bedclothes. But not tonight. Tonight, he waited for the weather to clear. He needed to see the moon, have its breath awaken the sleepy souls that resisted sunlight — tug on them as ocean waves. The only stipulation — it needed to happen before the clanging bells announced early morning martins. The time when night perches were abandoned, and the warbling began.

With one eye on the convent, Paddy picked his way through the tired crosses until he came to the spot. The place, aside from The Donnybrook, where he could find a lifting of his worries.

Near a tilted cross, set apart from the others, was a sunken, hollow shape, the size of a small coffin. The marker was void of any reference to its owner, as if its engraving had been washed away with the memory. Paddy ran a finger across the crackle of white paint. "I'm here," he said settling in the damp grass. At first, only the moon peered down at him, but when he closed his eyes, he felt the shadow of a small boy cover him. "Needed to talk to ya. Wanted to be with someone who'd listen." The boy crouched beside him, turning over a pebble with a stick. "I couldn't bring me concerns to me ma. And to tell ya the truth, there are some things aren't fit for her ears."

Paddy breathed in the moment, the salt of the night air, the peace of the place. "Ya see, there's something troubling me. Never happened to me before, and I fear it may never happen again. I sat down by a girl in the bushes today, right over there." Paddy's chin jutted towards the caraganas that divided the graveyard from the convent. "Not a surprising thing. Wouldn't have thought twice about it. But then she grabbed me hand. I tell ya, it burned like I don't know what. Hellfire, affection. It's hard to say." Glancing at his palm, Paddy tried to see the evidence that matched the feeling. "There are secrets that lie on her skin. But how much are those secrets worth, I ask you that? Been a strange day for me, boy. A strange day."

The breeze lifted the boy's hair and gently laid it down again.

"What's a lass like her to think? Me being so beneath her. I'll forever be walking in the wind."

————

THE MORNING CAME FASTER than expected. Before Paddy had a chance to slip out of the cemetery, he was wakened with a sound kick in the backside. Paddy opened one eye. "Oh, it's ya."

Sister Mary-Frances pushed up the sleeves on her habit. "Who did you think it would be?"

"Don't know. Someone younger that might join me in me repose."

The remark received the response he expected, another kick from the sister's hard-soled shoe. Paddy was surprised, not by the kick, but by the fact Sister Mary-Frances wasn't hobbled — laid up in bed like a worn-out mule. Only yesterday he'd given her a good run, one of his more challenging graveyard switches.

It had been through the adult section — not the foundlings' or the O'Brien's' babes, the ones dead before their time. They were sacrosanct. She hovered over him like some ancient gargoyle perched atop a cathedral. He rubbed his backside as he rose to his feet. "And I thought your only purpose was to scare small children and keep the priest chaste."

"You think so, do you?" Sister Mary-Frances wound up to have another go at him. "You're not satisfied with disturbing the living, are you? You have to disturb the dead as well."

Paddy took off at a run. "I'm not the one who buries them in a deep dark pit and expects them to be happy."

"Ah," the nun called after him, "don't you know anything? They're not supposed to be happy; most of them are in purgatory."

MR. O'BRIEN

I t wasn't passing The Donnybrook's street-front window that irked Mr. O'Brien. There hadn't been a day in his living memory when he hadn't done so. It was the fact he could hear his countrymen make their wagers through the glass, see them throw down their pocket change on his precious roundtable. Mr. O'Brien grimaced. It was as if the lot thought they were at Curragh. He pulled his bowler tighter around his ears and yelled at the glass, "Can a man not pace in peace?"

Cheers erupted from behind the pane. Father Connelly, losing all composure, climbed on the table top and knocked on the glass. "Once more unto the breach, man. Once more unto the breach." Paddy, for his part an unwitting bridesmaid, lifted the hem of the priest's cassock as if to prevent more coins from being swept to the floor.

The scene was one that, at any other time, would have made Mr. O'Brien howl like a schoolboy. Today, to his dismay, he felt conflicted. The exasperation over the change in his daughter was closely matched by the desire to participate in some kind of contest. What that contest was, he wasn't privy to. Even so, it gave him reason to ponder. Was it the length of his stride? The number of times he passed the window? Or perhaps how often he tipped his bowler? The combinations were endless. He shook his head. He had not been treading the length of The Donnybrook for the better part of an hour as some public-house entertainment. No. He was trying to find a way forward that would keep his family intact. Keep his Mary-Kate at home where she belonged.

His only hope lay beyond the pub door, with the lads who threw around coin like the affections of a liberated French prostitute. Even so, he wasn't entirely certain he wanted to open the door and let Pandora out.

"How's the men?" he called. He didn't wait for a reply or a pint. Mr. O'Brien waded through the faceless patrons, his sights set on Father Connelly who had climbed from his perch and was now straightening his robes while the men pocketed their change before hastily excusing themselves.

"Look at the state of ya," the priest said. "Ya look like death warmed over."

"I feel like death warmed over," said Mr. O'Brien, elbowing Donavan out of the way. "Did I not see Fitzpatrick here?"

"Aye, ya did. He's crawling under the table scooping up the drippings."

"Well get the boy up here where I can see him." Mr. O'Brien took his seat and began drumming his fingers on the tabletop. The more he drummed, the more he was convinced his reasoning was sound.

When the three had taken their chairs and exchanged formalities, Mr. O'Brien leaned over the table. "The thing of it is," he said, like some woebegone spy unsure of his compatriots, "I'm in a bit of a fix."

Father Connelly patted the back of his hand. "Ya might as well order yourself a pint. On a day such as today, it would do ya good."

Mr. O'Brien bristled. "What would ya know about me day?"

"Oh nothing, nothing at all." Father Connelly pointed a stubby finger towards Paddy. "But the lad and I are a bit thirsty, and assumed you were likewise." He waved his hand in the air to get the bartender's attention.

"It's not the hour for drinking. These are serious times."

"That's what we've been betting on." There was a gleam in Paddy's eye. "We have Keen on the lookout for the constabularies."

"Constabularies!" Mr. O'Brien could feel the heat in his cheeks. This time they had gone too far, put their hairy toes over the line, and he was about to tell them so when Father Connelly puffed up and shifted on the apple box atop his chair.

"That was me doing," the priest said. "Ya can never be too careful. But I have to give credit where credit is due. It was Paddy who first noticed ya and had us guessing. Said ya probably done in your mother-in-law, with all your striding and sighing. It's a sign of a guilty man if ever there was one."

Paddy leaned back in his chair. "But we were sure you done her in in a Christian way, mind you. Nothing too barbaric or unseemly."

The priest nodded. "Been planning her funeral for the last fifteen minutes. Daisies or petunias?"

"For what?" Mr. O'Brien pounded the table. "I've not come to talk about ruddy flowers."

"For your mother-in-law's coffin." Father Connelly looked dumbfounded. "Didn't think ya would want to splurge on roses. Might give some the impression ya were fond of the old girl."

"The two of ya should never be left on your own." Mr. O'Brien rubbed his brow. "Ya come up with the most ridiculous things. It's like a madhouse in here." He took a deep breath and steadied himself. "It is me Mary-Kate I've come for."

Father Connelly put up a hand and nodded. "No use beating a dead horse. The girl doesn't want any of your buttons."

"Is that what you think?" Mr. O'Brien brayed. "That I've been pacing like a fool about me buttons?"

"Why wouldn't I? It's all the two of ya have been going on about in confession." Father Connelly leaned forward and lowered his voice. "I haven't had the heart to tell ya that no one cares."

"Not even the pope?" Paddy asked, in a tone that Mr. O'Brien was sure mocked wonder.

"Not even the pope," Father Connelly sighed.

"I need a drink." Mr. O'Brien downed three pints before he spoke again. He was never sure if he should take the priest seriously. An impish grin was always playing at the corner of his mouth, waiting to see if one would believe the absurd. It had been that way since their youth, and he wasn't going to fall for it today. "It's not the buttons that have got me so bothered. It's Mary-Kate. She's done something, I swear. Cried in her mashed potatoes, called herself a sinner. It put a hallelujah on me lips, and I was ready to break out me best Irish whiskey. Ya know, I've encouraged the girl to go astray. I thought it was me duty." He got his laugh but then shook his head, a seriousness overtaking him. "Then last night me wife drove reason home. Called me a truculent fool, and I fear she may be right. Won't be throwing me leg over her any time soon."

"It can't be that bad," Father Connelly said. "Not the leg throwing. I'm a little too old for that kind of nonsense meself." As an afterthought he added, "Being a priest doesn't help either. It's not considered seemly." He waved a finger in the air. "But getting back to your daughter. Perhaps Mary-Kate will be more inclined to stay at home now? Not wander off to join the sisters in black?"

"Oh, but that's only a matter of time. Can feel it in me bones.

Every day that girl steps a little farther from me and her ma, and a little closer to that wretched, dried-up sister of mine." Mr. O'Brien pointed out the window towards the convent. "And then there will be no one to carry on me family line."

"I wouldn't worry about your family line," Paddy winked. "A few brick walls can't stop nature from taking its course. Within those skirts, none would be the wiser."

Mr. O'Brien's eyebrows shot up. "Ya say that as if you are trying to make me feel better."

"Don't look a gift horse in the mouth."

Mr. O'Brien was beginning to doubt Father Connelly or Paddy could help rectify his predicament. He wasn't sure if they'd had too much to drink or not enough. Whichever it was, their taunting was wearing thin. "I've come to ask a favour. Nothing grand or unmanageable. A simple favour. But now I see I've come to the wrong place."

Father Connelly pulled a rosary from his pocket. "No ya haven't, son. How would ya like us to help?"

That simple act, pulling out the rosary, seemed to make the ground shift. Paddy took off his cap and looked solemn. Mr. O'Brien, in turn, took off his bowler, and when he spoke his tone was quieter and more reverent. "I need ya to help me stop her."

"A priest usually isn't in the practice of doing such things." Father Connelly looked towards Paddy. "But this lad is another story. He's led many a lass astray."

Paddy went white to the lips.

"That's true." Mr. O'Brien surveyed Paddy with new enthusiasm. "Oh, don't worry about it me boy." He poured what was left of his pint into Paddy's empty glass. "I don't want ya to marry the girl. I just want you to make sure that my heifer of a sister sees the two of you together. Let her see that some fillies are too wild to be bridled."

What irritated Mary-Kate more than her father following her to confession was her father *not* following her to confession. How long would he leave her waiting? She wasn't standing on the church steps for the good of her health. People would talk. Besides, it wasn't worth going without her father. There was no one to spar with, and Father Connelly was more inclined to nap than engage in any meaningful debate. Where was the fun in that?

She was disappointed in herself. When she considered the letter, her meeting with Sister Mary-Frances, and her parents' failure to divulge the promise, she had reason to be furious, but she wasn't. She was a lot of things, but none of them were furious. She was confused, overwhelmed, and besotted, or at least she hoped she was besotted. It would explain her unusual mixture of feelings since her afternoon in the bushes.

As for her aunt's supposition that only her mother's promise had kept her alive, Mary-Kate knew she should be eternally grateful. The promise could be the only reason for her outliving all her siblings. The very idea accompanied her almost everywhere she went, and the colossal debt brought her low. And now, her father had given up their daily trips to the confessional. What was that man thinking? Didn't he realize that it was the only thing holding them together? Keeping her from running to the open arms of her domineering aunt? He couldn't have deduced her true intentions; she wasn't even sure what they were herself.

Mary-Kate pursed her lips. Perhaps she should go over to The Donnybrook, peek through the window and see who was about. That would get his attention. She was halfway across the strip of a park that separated the church from the public house when Patrick Fitzpatrick, the boy from the bushes, appeared.

"Fancy meeting ya here." He brushed off his sleeve and offered her his arm.

Mary-Kate looked at the offer with a measure of skepticism. The Donnybrook was steps away in one direction, the church and convent a few strides in the other, and this virtual stranger was asking her to make a public declaration of familiarity. She stiffened and dared not turn her head to see who observed her. In the bushes, her feelings had gotten away with her, and she wasn't sure she was up for another excursion. As for the offered arm, if she took it, it would certainly get her father's attention, especially if he were hiding somewhere about. He would emerge from behind whatever rock concealed him and reprimand her. That made up her mind.

"Mr. Fitzpatrick, isn't it?" Her candour and indifference masked the hundreds of times she had spoken his name before drifting off to sleep. "What do you have in mind?"

"Oh, a bit of a stroll, if that should strike your fancy. And we can talk about anything ya like, even those buttons of yours."

Mary-Kate could feel the heat in her cheeks. "What would you know of my buttons?"

"No more than any other man in The Donnybrook." Paddy inclined his head towards the building across the way. "Your da has spent many an hour regaling us with tales of their owners' deaths."

She squinted at the pub's grimy window. She was sure she saw shadowy figures raise a pint in her direction. "And if I don't want to talk about my buttons?"

"Then we have to settle for wagging tongues." Paddy offered his arm again, and this time she took it.

They wandered around The Flats for most of the morning. Mary-Kate could feel herself relax. Her laugh was no longer forced, and her voice softened as the tightness at the back of her throat disappeared.

"You're like your da," Paddy said, enjoying the transformation.

Mary-Kate stopped short. "I'm not!"

"Ah, but ya are. If ya let yourself."

"Being like my father is the last thing in the world I want to be."

"Why is that? Although I'm on the edge of his acquaintance, 'tis his company I seek out the most. The man has a way about him. Men stand up and listen. Not many have that. 'Tis a gift, Mary-Kate."

"What good does a gift like that do a woman?"

"Any good she will make of it."

They continued to walk in silence.

"What do you know about him?" Mary-Kate asked.

"Who?"

"My father."

Paddy smiled. "Enough to want him for me own da."

"That's the most ridiculous thing I've ever heard."

"Ridiculous or not, 'tis true. There is a steadiness about him. A soul that doesn't take himself too seriously. There is a stability about that. Catches one unaware."

"And you're saying I'm like that?"

"Ya could be. ya've got it in you."

Mary-Kate became silent again. She tightened her grip on Paddy's arm.

"He's given ya something special, Mary-Kate. Wanting ya to have your freedom."

"How would you know that?"

"'Tis all he talks about. And to be truthful, it's a bit nauseating. The way he goes on about it, as if it's the only thing of any consequence."

"That's where I get confused. If he wants to give me my freedom, as you say, then why does he protest what I choose to do, even if I were to enter the church?"

"'Tis a good question, it is. Would have asked it meself. But consider the choice, Mary-Kate. It's the place that gives ya the least freedom of all."

———

EVENING CAME upon them so fast, it was as if there hadn't been a day. Paddy took Mary-Kate to one of the darkest places in Tnúth, not far from where she had been accosted. To get there, they cleaved to the side streets and obscure places, not to draw attention to themselves. Outside a hall, Paddy brushed off a large crate and boosted Mary-Kate on top of it. He climbed up and took a seat beside her. There they waited for the music to start. When it did, it felt like a cool breeze. Mary-Kate had never heard anything like it, and when Paddy asked her to dance, she couldn't refuse him. She let her body join in harmony with his as he whirled her around the dark alley. Their vibrant movements filled her with wild delight.

When the song ended Mary-Kate was out of breath, and she began to clap wildly. Quickly Paddy put his hands over hers. "Ya don't want to be found out, do ya?"

"No," said Mary-Kate. "I don't want to be found out." She leaned closer and considered his eyes. They were full of moonlight. It made her sigh, and the question that had been occupying her thoughts escaped her lips. "Do you find me fetching?"

"Fetching?" Paddy stumbled on the word. "I suppose. Why do ya ask?"

"I've heard men refer to women in that way. 'A fetching wench.'"

"Some women are that. As much of a fetching wench as ever ya'd care to see. Although you may be fetching, Mary-Kate O'Brien, ya're not the kind men talk about."

"You find me less attractive then."

"Never said that, did I? Ya shouldn't go putting words in me mouth. Being a wench, like some, is something a man finds inviting. Something he doesn't have to work for. But being like ya, Mary-Kate. That be different. Ya are a woman meant to be watched. A man must wait for ya to decide. He can't do it all on his own."

"Is that good?"

"Depends," said Paddy with a smile. "If ya want a beauty for the taking, it is a grand thing. But yours, that's something else. Yours is for the giving. There's a big difference. Ya're a bobby-dazzler."

Mary-Kate stepped closer. Her leg touched his. She felt the burning all over again, leaving them both breathing a little unevenly.

The walk home struck Mary-Kate. The air seemed different. She hadn't intended to be out this late, but the night had been so grand it swallowed her whole. A few times it crossed her mind that her parents would be outraged, not knowing where she was, but she dismissed it, telling herself she would deal with that when the time came.

When they arrived at her house, all the lights were out, as if she hadn't been missed at all. Her parents must have assumed she was occupied in her room. Obviously, neither had sought her out to bid her goodnight, or sent out a search party when she was not found. Their indifference infuriated her.

"We'll go in the back." Paddy interrupted her thoughts.

"The back?" She turned her anger on him. "Is that how you escort all your young girls home? Through the servant's quarters? Is that how you see me? A trollop? A wayward wench? A scandalous tale?"

Paddy dropped her arm and took a step away from her. "Have I done something to offend you, lass?"

"They didn't even wish me goodnight! They always wish me

goodnight. And now you want to take me through the back door."

"Aye. The front is likely locked."

"Oh." Mary-Kate re-adjusted her wrap. "Why didn't you say so?"

She strode through the front gate and around to the back of the house as if she had done so a thousand times before, tripping twice and banging her shin, taking the Lord's name in vain. Paddy was left to scramble in her wake.

Once on the back step, she turned to Paddy and put out her hand. "I've enjoyed myself immensely," she said, more tersely than she intended.

Paddy didn't seem to mind. He took her hand and gently caressed it with his fingertips. "As have I."

Mary-Kate could feel her body grow warm and her breathing quicken. She pulled her hand away and slipped into the house, leaving Paddy standing on the step.

––––––––

ONCE SAFELY BEHIND her closed bedroom door, Mary-Kate retraced the lines Paddy had made on her palm. She scowled. It wasn't the same. How could it ever be the same? In her nightdress she tried to dance the jig they'd spun outside the hall. The steps refused to come to her. Mary-Kate went to the window and peered around her blind towards the tree. She narrowed her eyes. The night was heavy and the foliage thick. Perhaps he was lingering as some medieval knight, hoping for his lady's favour. Putting a shawl over her dressing gown, Mary-Kate went downstairs and snuck out the front door.

"Paddy," she whispered as she stood under the great limbs. "Are you there?"

There was no answer.

"Paddy, I've something to show you."

The only reply she got was from the neighbour's dog. He barked menacingly from the other side of the fence. "Do you have to wreck everything?" she heard herself ask, sounding very much like her father.

Lights from surrounding houses began to flicker on. Mary-Kate ran back inside. When she'd closed the door safely behind her, her father came galumphing down the stairs.

"Jasus, Mary, and Joseph. What's going on out there?"

"I don't know," said Mary-Kate before noticing her father's gait. "What happened to you?"

Mr. O'Brien grunted. "This." He slapped his leg. "A betrayal. What I really want to know is what's happening out there."

Mary-Kate reopened the door and peeked out. "I don't know. I can't see anything."

"Well, you'll not find out that way." Mr. O'Brien limped past her and picked up his bowler and an umbrella.

"You're going out in your nightshirt!"

"Aye. But I've got me bowler on." Mr. O'Brien plopped it on his head and limped into the night to investigate.

As soon as her father cleared the porch, Mary-Kate closed and locked the door behind him. "Serves you right for not coming to confession."

"Y ou're late," Mrs. O'Brien snapped when Mr. O'Brien joined the breakfast table. "You think that Mae has all day to wait on you for breakfast?"

"I don't see why not," he said, navigating his way to his spot. His hobbled gait made the process awkward. "I pay her wage."

"And that gives you leave to treat her with such indifference?"

Mr. O'Brien shrugged. "She's a turnip."

"That's your answer to everything."

He scowled and muttered as he placed his napkin on his lap. Mrs. O'Brien could hardly glance his way without being furious. First there'd been the night he came home bellowing for her, only to claim later, after much thought, that he had carried Father Connelly home. At the time she'd sniffed him and detected nothing untoward. But that didn't mean anything; he'd grown wise to her ways. There was a certain flush in his cheeks and a rumple in his clothes that gave her pause. And now there was this limp. How could he explain that away? A man his age gallivanting around like some lovesick pup. It almost put her off her breakfast.

Her husband, as usual, was ignorant of her musings. He swore as he surveyed the room. "Where's Our Lady of Blessed Misery?"

"She refused to get up," Mrs. O'Brien said without looking at him directly. "Claims all the pounding and barking kept her up for most of the night. Besides, she has a long day ahead of her, trying on habits and memorizing vows."

Mr. O'Brien snorted. "Was thinking the same thing meself. Must have talked about it in me sleep. It's nice to see you taking me initiative."

"It's not your plan." Mrs. O'Brien slapped her spoon on the table. "You never talked about it in your sleep."

"And how would you know?"

"I just know. I came up with the idea all on me lonesome."

"Think what you like, but I know better. Probably be scheming to slip across the hall in the dead of night to whisper me own idea in me ear."

"'Twill be a cold day in hell before anything like that happens again. And if things don't change around here, it's not only Herself that will be rethinking her living arrangements."

A flash crossed her husband's face and she knew, once again, he was half listening. All he heard was that the two women he despised most would be huddled under the same roof. For him it would be a gift beyond measure. She knew, despite her warning, he wanted to lean back and have a good chuckle — but if he dared even a contented sigh she'd pounce.

"And when are you planning to inform Herself of her newfound religious fervour, I ask you that?"

"The same time you stop sneaking around."

He looked up, startled. "I'm not sneaking."

"What do you call it then?"

"My manly prerogative."

"I'd be careful where you're poking that prerogative of yours. You might find it at the end of a sharp pair of scissors."

"What the hell are you talking about, woman?"

Mary-Kate took her usual place at the table. "Am I interrupting something?"

"Why would you think that? It's as good a morning as ever was one." Mrs. O'Brien fibbed, as she had yet to see anything good about it. "Better fill your plate before things get cold."

"Don't be lying to the girl. In this marriage things have been cold for quite some time."

"And by the way your father is spouting off, it grows colder by the day."

Mary-Kate unfolded a napkin and laid it on her lap. "What's all the fuss about?"

"How can you ask such a thing?" Mr. O'Brien barked. "You locked me out of me own house. Spent half the night banging on the door trying to get back in."

"She did no such thing." Mrs. O'Brien's annoyance was at full boil. "That's something you'd do, not me Mary-Kate."

"'Tis true, I tell you. She locked the door and slept well in spite of it." The lines on his forehead doubled. "You yourself said the old bat was kept up all night by the pounding and barking."

"She's in the Deadman's room. It's full of voices and bumps in the night. How anyone in their right mind could sleep there is beyond me."

He slumped in his seat.

Mrs. O'Brien patted her daughter's arm. "Pay him no mind," she said. "I can almost guarantee he wasn't locked out of the house. He's just too ashamed to admit it. Sneaking into the house in his nightshirt no less, with only his bowler and umbrella to shelter him from the weather. Can you believe that, Mary-Kate?"

"She was there!"

"I'm sure someone was there, but I doubt it was our daughter."

Pausing for a moment, Mr. O'Brien seemed to consider what his wife said. "I don't think so."

"But you're not sure? Who have you been cavorting with? And don't tell me the priest!"

Mr. O'Brien looked from his wife to his daughter and lowered his voice. "I've given up cavorting, you know that."

"All I know is you weren't in your bed, and you weren't in mine."

"I was out freezing me arse off." He jabbed a finger in the air. "And it was all because of her."

"Apologize to your daughter."

"What for?"

"For a happy marriage, that's what for."

"It's quite all right," Mary-Kate interrupted, wrinkling her nose. "I half believe him myself." Her feet tapped merrily under the table, like her father's. Mrs. O'Brien looked at her and raised a questioning eyebrow.

29

PADDY

The trick was to make it look innocent. Paddy's first endeavour to dissuade Sister Mary-Frances from recruiting Mary-Kate was unproductive. The ever-watchful nun wasn't watching closely enough that day. His contrived meeting with Mary-Kate, although enjoyable, fell short of its intended purpose. Paddy leaned against a sugar maple and eyed the great door of St. Augustine's. How to fool that wily old nun without making O'Brien livid in the process? It would take Mary-Kate not giving him away about how they spent an afternoon in the caraganas and how he came across her in one of the worst parts of Tnúth. And then there was the dancing. He rubbed his brow. That one couldn't be explained away.

As for Sister Mary-Frances, she would have to be taken unaware, thrown off balance. Paddy closed his eyes as he touched the timepiece in his vest pocket. Snatched from O'Brien himself, and it served him right for dangling it. A smile settled on Paddy's lips. Considering the obvious drawbacks, O'Brien's scheme was already paying off.

The memory of the three of them colluding over their roundtable, arguing what was permissible and what was akin to blasphemy, came to him suddenly. Paddy naturally leaned towards blasphemy, but Father Connelly was unconvinced and felt that even the least of them should step clear of such things. But all came into focus when O'Brien pulled out the pocket watch. Paddy never paid much mind to it before, O'Brien palming it whenever he checked the time. Now he flaunted it like cheese before a beggar. And for the first time, Paddy realized from whence it had come.

First time he saw it, it was in a painted miniature on his gran's bureau. He and his mother slipped into his grandmother's curtained-off corner, just to peek at it. "That's your great-granddad," his mother whispered. "Your namesake. His ma was a bit of a drunk. Hard to tell if she was stuttering or naming him. The last Fitzpatrick worth his salt — until you." She ruffled his hair.

Paddy stood on tiptoes beside his mother to have a closer look. "He was a rogue like the rest of us," she continued. "But he had standards. An Irish Robin Hood if ever there was one." Her ragged fingernail traced the outline of her forebear's face, lingering on his mustache. "That timepiece, the one he's gazing at with such pride, was his one true prize. Had a special hanky just for the polishing."

Paddy was about to trace the remarkable mustache with his thin finger when his grandmother snatched the portrait from his ma and boxed him in the ear. "Stepping on my side of the divide," the baggy-skinned beast belched. "And touching that which doesn't concern you? I'll skin you alive if it happens again."

It wasn't until later, when the nights had grown cold, that Biddy nicked the miniature and brought it beneath their bedcovers so Paddy could have a thorough examination. She pointed at the pocket watch. The light from the candle stump flickered it into view. "Traded it and his life on a bid to keep his wife from the gallows." Her brow knit together. "Not sure she was worth the bargain."

"Where is it now?"

"The pocket watch? Don't know." Biddy blew out what was left of the candle. "I suppose it has been passed down from jailer to jailer. I tell you me boy, most folks are bound by blood, but ours are wound together by the memory of that pocket watch. As fine a piece 'as ever was made, and if luck should have it, someday it will be ours again."

Paddy shivered under the tattered blanket while he waited for his mother to return the miniature to its place on his gran's bureau. It was hard for him to say what he saw in the watch. He couldn't describe the twists and twines that covered its surface. All he knew was that they were the marks of his clan.

It wasn't until later that his gran made the most of Paddy's education. She dragged him to an expensive dress shop window when he was no more than four. "See that pin?" she said, tapping the glass. "You swipe that for me, and your great-grand-dad's pocket watch is yours."

Paddy was confused. "Me ma said he traded it for his wife. That the jailer got it."

"What does your mother know? She's a foolish girl."

It wasn't the first time Paddy stole. He was good at it, dodging trouble as if it was blind to him. He slipped in and out of the shop unnoticed, and no sooner had he plopped the pin into his gran's hand than she pocketed it. "Oh, you're a good lad," she said. "You'll make a fine crook one day. Mark me words, a fine crook." She leaned into him, noting the eagerness in his eyes. "But don't be too disappointed when I tells you there is no watch to be had. It's long gone. You're not to be believing everything you're told. 'Tis a good lesson for you. Besides," she said, straightening up, "that's what you get for going on a fool's errand. You shouldn't be so trusting, me boy."

Paddy hadn't thought of it much since that afternoon; the timepiece was a forgotten relic until O'Brien dangled it in front of him. He grabbed at the watch, but O'Brien was too quick. "Where'd ya get that?" Paddy demanded.

"From me ma. Her father was a jailer. As you know, our lines stand on opposite sides of a divide; what one gives, the other takes away."

"Is that some kind of riddle?"

"If that's what ya want it to be." Mr. O'Brien swung the chain once more before slipping it back into his breast pocket. "I know it was your great-granddad's and holds some fleeting family connection. The value I have for it is far more dear. It's the greatest pledge a man can make to a woman, giving his life for hers. And if I were in the same position, I hope I'd act likewise. A thing that is easy to say; to do it is an entirely different matter." Mr. O'Brien patted his breast pocket. "It's dearer to me than this ring I wear."

"Dearer than your wedding ring?"

"Maybe." He pulled at his collar. "But don't be talking to the Mrs. about it. All you need to know is that I'd be willing to part with it if our mission is successful."

Paddy was doubtful that he and O'Brien would have the same definition of success. More than once, he'd observed others make bargains with the man and walk away with less than they'd agreed upon. Paddy thrust out his hand. Never before had anyone trusted their daughter to him. "It's unlike any scheme I've had the fortune to participate in. My answer is yes."

Mr. O'Brien took Paddy's hand and shook it with the same vigour with which Paddy had offered it.

"Don't let it go to your head, me boy. Ya're only to be letting me sister glimpse ya. Nothing more than that. And if all goes well," he tapped his pocket, "ya know what's waiting for ya."

"And a fine prize it is." Paddy leaned forward so the distance between them lessened. "But the honour is still mine."

He was out of the pub and down the street before he heard the scream. It was O'Brien. "No use crying over spilled milk," Paddy mused, stepping into the shadows and swinging the pocket watch from its gold chain.

Mary-Kate wasn't sure where to spend her time, besides home. There was the library, the convent, and of course confession. But none of these things intrigued her as much as Patrick Fitzpatrick. After their walk, and stint in the caragana bushes, they seemed to run into one another with relative ease. An ease that brought into question how accidental these meetings were. Mary-Kate tapped a finger on her chin. "I need some air," she said, poking her head into the sitting room.

It was Mrs. O'Brien's bridge day. She sat at the head of a small table, around which three other distinguished women were seated. Mrs. Morten, the mayor's wife, was to her mother's left. She fascinated Mary-Kate. There wasn't a soul around who could talk through their nose the way that woman could. Mary-Kate wasn't sure if it was for comic effect, or to draw one's focus from her dowager hump.

Across from Mrs. O'Brien was Mrs. Donavan. Her goiter was near the size of Mrs. Morten's hump, keeping her off balance but lending a lovely symmetry to the table.

The fourth member of the party intrigued Mary-Kate more

than the other two, and if she wasn't off to try to accidentally run into Patrick Fitzpatrick, she would have stayed just to watch her. Miss Nellie Hodgetts wore a boa wherever she went. On windy days she was known to get the feathers caught between the gap in her front teeth. Even so, the woman with the long elegant fingers and translucent skin was hard not to notice. It was no wonder Mr. O'Brien chimed 'come for the game, stay for the oddities.'

"I need some air," Mary-Kate repeated when her first declaration went unnoticed. The foursome nodded at Mary-Kate before looking back at their cards.

Mr. O'Brien grunted from his relegated corner. "Sounds suspicious to me," he said.

"Come now, Mr. O'Brien," said his wife. "Everything sounds suspicious to you." Mrs. O'Brien looked at the other women seated at the table. "I can't get a moment's rest."

"Well, it does." Mr. O'Brien was more insistent than usual. "I'd follow her meself if it weren't for this blasted ankle. The more I walk, the lamer I get." He pointed to his elevated foot. "Nothing but problems since that Patrick Fitzpatrick purloined my watch. What a horse's arse of a name."

The words fell out of Mr. O'Brien's mouth before he could stop them, and the look on his face showed he regretted it. Mary-Kate stepped into the room. "How well do you know this Patrick Fitzpatrick?"

Mr. O'Brien rubbed his ankle as if he hadn't heard her. Then, leaning back in his chair, he touched his empty breast pocket. "Does anyone have the time?"

"It's time for you to leave us all in peace," Mrs. O'Brien said. "That's what time it is."

Ignoring her mother, Mary-Kate repeated her question, but her father was as deaf as before.

"Patrick Fitzpatrick?" interjected Mrs. Donavan. "I've heard a lot about that one, and none of it good. The lad likes the ladies and cares little for the church. Not the kind of body you should be asking about Mary-Kate O'Brien. Only this morning I was talking to Sister Mary-Frances, and she said she'd never met a soul as lost as that boy's."

"His soul is lost, I can guarantee you that," said Mr. O'Brien. "Wish I'd never laid eyes on him meself. Snatched me watch right from under me nose. Would have snatched it back if I hadn't twisted me ankle in the chase."

"So, you do know him," said Mary-Kate, taking a chair by the sitting room door. "How was it you laid eyes on him?"

"Only in passing. Hardly know the fellow at all."

Mrs. Donavan laid down her hand of cards and gingerly fingered her goiter. "That's not how me husband tells it. He says you drink with that lad near every night."

The air grew hot, and Mary-Kate settled deeper into her chair. Mr. O'Brien's anger would surely overtake him. Anyone in the room who wasn't comatose could feel it coming. Miss Nellie Hodgetts inhaled several boa feathers while Mrs. Morten's nose whistled like an in-coming train. Only her mother, Mrs. O'Brien, maintained her composure.

"Your husband says that, does he?" Mr. O'Brien's voice rose with every word. "Surprised he can get a word in edgewise with you going on about this and going on about that. You're like a cat in heat."

Everything but Mrs. Donavan's goiter turned red, even the backs of her hands. She dug her fingers into her protrusion. Her lips began moving and her eyes rolled back in her head as if calling on other-worldly spirits.

"And who said you were welcome in this house, I ask you that?" Mr. O'Brien continued, unaware of any of Mrs. Donavan's apoplexy. "If you were a better wife and minded what belonged to you, maybe your husband wouldn't have to spend half his day at The Donnybrook, drinking like a sieve. Never seen anything like it."

Mrs. O'Brien got up, rolled up a nearby newspaper, and swatted Mr. O'Brien on his injured ankle.

"Jasus, Mary, and Joseph. What did you do that for?"

"For a happy marriage. Besides, I saw a spider." Mrs. O'Brien offered her hand to help her husband to his feet. When Mr. O'Brien balked, she picked up a poker from the fireplace and waved it menacingly in his direction. "I think you would be much more comfortable in the study."

After reconsidering his situation, Mr. O'Brien agreed and rose to his feet.

"Excuse me, ladies," said Mrs. O'Brien, guiding her husband to the door. Mr. O'Brien grumbled something under his breath. Mrs. O'Brien jabbed him in the ribs.

"Good Gawd, woman," he snapped. "I'll deal with that later in confession."

Mary-Kate watched as the ladies inclined their ears in the direction of the study, but the only sounds were muffled scolding and grunts. They were listening so intently that only Mary-Kate seemed to notice Mrs. Donavan peek at Mrs. O'Brien's cards.

When she reappeared, Mrs. O'Brien offered to warm up everyone's tea before returning to her hand. "Lovely weather we're having."

"Aye, 'tis," returned Mrs. Donavan, who was still a bright shade of pink. "A blessing to all. Even Patrick Fitzpatrick."

"And why is that?" asked Mary-Kate.

Mrs. O'Brien turned her attention to her daughter. "Why are you so interested in this boy?"

"I'm no more interested than Mrs. Donavan."

"And I'm hardly interested at all," said Mrs. Donavan.

The bridge game resumed with no more talk of Patrick.

Losing interest, Mary-Kate rose and stepped into the hall. She picked up a parcel, then paused and looked in the hall mirror, the way her mother did before leaving the house. She adjusted her hat. "Will this feeling ever leave me?" she whispered.

"Mary-Kate?" her mother called from the sitting room. "Are you still there?"

"Yes."

"Why don't you take Breasal with you?"

"I'd rather not," answered Mary-Kate, making her way to the front door.

"Who's Breasal?" asked Mrs. Donavan.

From the study, Mr. O'Brien stomped his good foot on the floor. "Gawd, you're a nosey woman," he yelled. "But if you really must know, why don't you have your husband consult your goiter?"

"Don't mind him," said Mrs. O'Brien. "He's a little embarrassed. Hired himself a driver all the way from Ireland, and he hasn't even got a motorcar."

"I've got a motorcar! Ordered it meself. It's just not here yet."

"Yes, dear."

Paddy was running out of things to do with Mary-Kate. After their approved walkabout, things went underground. Their run-ins were clandestine. A picnic on The Flats, fishing in Lough Bane, and a walk in a rose garden at night. He'd taken her on leprechaun hunts and fairy walks. There was hardly a hole and corner that the two hadn't explored. Still, he'd promised something unexpected. Mary-Kate rolled her eyes. "Trying to catch leprechauns is unusual enough. You don't need to impress me."

"Perhaps. But ya do realize Father Connelly isn't a real leprechaun."

"I am aware. But you almost had him convinced otherwise."

"It wasn't hard. The man was well into his cups." Paddy paused and leaned against the gate marking the entrance of the cemetery. The day was bright and the trees were showing their best Irish green. Flowers spread themselves wide in anticipation. Such glories would make the day pass quickly. "There is one place that I've taken no other. One place I want to share with ya alone." He glanced towards The Donnybrook. It was early in the day, not many would have shuffled in for a morning pint, and those who partook this early wouldn't have the wherewithal to spot more than a blur from this far away. He tugged on her hand. "Follow me."

The gate swung open and Mary-Kate pulled back. "I can't. My legs don't have it in them."

"Ya have a lot more in you than ya think." He squeezed her hand. "I'll blind-fold ya. It'll trick yourself into doing it."

"I don't think that will make any difference."

"How do ya know if ya haven't tried?" Paddy waited for her to soften; for a moment of hesitation. A sigh later, he had it. "Don't step too heavy now," he said, leading her past the post. "Ya don't want to make anyone angry."

"Do you think I can do that? Make the dead mad?" Her arms were straight out in front of her, trying to find their way, Paddy's hand on her elbow.

"Only the ones still alive."

"Still alive?"

"Aye. Some stay alive their whole life. Others die long before they hit the grave. Losing a body can't take the life out of ya."

Scowling, Mary-Kate balked. Her gait stiffened.

"Ya're stepping like a horse not sure of its footing."

"I'm sorry Paddy, but I told you I didn't want to come here."

"That ya did, that ya did." He took a deep breath before he guided her around a rough patch. "A little farther, ya're doing grand."

"I don't feel like I'm doing grand." She pulled against him. "I feel like I'm being led to an open..."

"To what Mary-Kate O'Brien?" he chuckled. "Ya think I'm going to lead ya to an open grave?"

"Well, no."

He pulled her close, so his lips almost touched her earlobe. "I'll not be harming ya," he whispered. "Ya have me word on that."

"I want more than your word," she whispered back.

"That's all I can give ya right now." He pushed her away, almost throwing her to the ground. "Sorry. There was a sunk-in spot. Some of the old graves have been known to give away."

"Thank you," Mary-Kate growled. "So glad I came."

"Come now, it's not that bad. Come into the light." As they stepped from the trees, shadows disappeared from Mary-Kate's face and the sun's rays softened the look of doubt. "We're getting closer to the orphans now." He squeezed her arm and gave her a warning. "Ya best be careful around these wee ones. There's not a soul alive who still loves them."

"Not a soul?"

"Forgotten as soon as the last shovel of dirt was thrown on their wayward ma's grave. Many born in the convent where that aunt of yours lays her head."

Mary-Kate bit her lip as Paddy guided her to the ground.

"Now that wasn't so bad, was it?"

"I suppose not," Mary-Kate said, removing her blindfold. "Why are we here?"

"Ya'll see." He stretched out on the grass and closed his eyes.

Mary-Kate scooted closer to him, balanced on her knees and the tips of her toes. Her lips were tight, and one hand gripped the other so hard they both turned red. She looked towards her family plot partially hidden in the trees. She poked Paddy. "Who are we waiting for?"

"Ya'll see," he said without opening his eyes.

She flicked her fingers.

"He'll not come if ya do that."

"Who'll not come?"

"Me boy."

"You have a son?"

"No," Paddy laughed. "Everyone who might have cared for him is long gone. I'm all he has left."

There was a movement and she started.

"What is it?"

"I think I saw something," she cried, climbing on top of Paddy's chest. "But it's gone now."

Opening one eye, Paddy grunted. "Well get off me then." He couldn't believe the words were coming from his mouth. He'd never asked a girl to get off him before, but she was cutting off his air. As Mary-Kate returned to her place, her gaze darted around the graveyard. "Tell me what ya saw then?"

"I'm not sure. A flit of something in the trees." Mary-Kate craned her neck.

"That's who I brung ya to meet." Paddy smiled and closed his eyes. "Haven't brought anyone by before; ya'll be the first. But ya must admit, he's a little livelier than your buttons."

She looked him square in the eye. "You don't think it's odd, me and my buttons?"

"What kind of man would I be if I did?"

She leaned over and kissed him. His lips smiled beneath hers, and he reached up to touch her red hair.

32

In time, Mr. O'Brien was happy with the changes in his daughter. She wasn't venturing any closer to the convent, and the tension between them had somewhat dissipated. She hadn't thrown anything at him for nearly a week, and the only thing it had cost him was a pocket watch. His plans at The Donnybrook roundtable hadn't caused the harm Father Connelly warned, and he wondered if the little priest was losing his touch. "There is fire in those eyes," Mr. O'Brien told his wife one evening as they took tea in the sitting room. "Fire!"

His wife did not seem quite as excited. Her daughter's sudden whimsy seemed to make her suspicious. She looked at her husband with a narrow expression. "But who ignited it?" she asked.

It was a good question. Mr. O'Brien shrugged. "It doesn't matter, does it? I'm just glad she's at home. Snug as a bug in a rug." He opened his paper.

Traditionally, the paper was kind to the O'Briens'. Three generations of O'Briens' had never given cause for a raised eyebrow in Tnúth — Mr. O'Brien's marriage notwithstanding, but those eyebrows had been bought off. As a whole, they always seemed the proper sort, publicly. And of course, they were the most influential family in town. Now, however, more than eyebrows were being raised.

Miss Tenpenny, never one to mince words, had written a short society article, but the brevity of it made it stand out all the more. It left an ample amount of room for a photo. It showed Mary-Kate and Patrick Fitzpatrick walking arm in arm, Mary-Kate's head tilted back in laughter. To Mr. O'Brien's consternation, his daughter's visage was above the fold.

'IT IS *easy for this reporter to find everything about Patrick Fitz-patrick deplorable. Miss O'Brien's choice in men is questionable, as are Mr. and Mrs. O'Brien's methods of child-rearing.*

As for Mr. Fitzpatrick, I have never met anyone so well versed in the gutter. To my mind, they are a dismal couple, and Miss O'Brien should be sent abroad immediately.'

MR. O'BRIEN CRUMPLED it up and threw it into the fire. This was not an article to be cut and pasted and preserved in a scrapbook.

"What will you do?" demanded Mrs. O'Brien.

"Not sure," he said, stalling for time.

Herself cleared her throat. "Well you'd better think of something soon, or your daughter will bring ruin to the whole family." She'd lugged her rocking chair down the stairs and stationed it on the other side of the sitting room door.

"I' didn't ask you for your opinion," Mr. O'Brien yowled back.

"But aren't you glad I gave it?"

"Not really."

Mrs. O'Brien tossed a ball of yarn from her sewing basket,

startling her husband. "You didn't answer me question. What do you think?"

Mr. O'Brien chewed the stem of his pipe. "I've hardly heard of this Patrick Fitzpatrick," he said, turning a little pink in the cheeks. "You think if I had, I would let our daughter have anything to do with him?"

"For goodness sakes, what do you think she's been doing?" Herself rocked hard in her chair.

"Not that it is any of your business," Mr. O'Brien hollered towards the door. "I thought she was just dilly-dallying on the Burren."

"Dilly-dallying at the park doesn't get you into the paper," yelled Mrs. O'Brien, getting up and handing her husband his coat.

"What's this for?"

"Go see Father Connelly and find out what he's been keeping from you."

Reluctantly, Mr. O'Brien took his coat. Father Connelly had nothing to tell him that he didn't already know. He was sure to catch his death of cold wandering around at night pretending to investigate something that didn't need to be investigated. "I'm only doing this because I love you woman," he said, stomping out of the house and slamming the door.

Everything he'd done lately was because he loved that woman. Making plans 'til all hours of the night because he loved that woman. Taking in his meddling mother-in-law because he loved that woman. Involving Paddy and Father Connelly because he loved that woman. Getting locked outside in the middle of the night because he loved that woman. And what did it get him? All this scheming to keep Mary-Kate out of the clutches of his infernal sister? Adoration? Gratitude? No. All it got him was a grumpy wife.

N ot all the O'Briens found the newspaper article upsetting. Mary-Kate came by a copy quite by accident. She was leaving the library with *The Adventures of the Dying Detective* neatly cradled in the crook of her arm, when giggles and finger pointing caught her attention. Mary-Kate paused and looked around. There was no one close enough to have drawn such attention, so it had to be directed at her. She stepped towards the urchins, but they scampered away when she was within striking distance, leaving a copy of the *Tnúth Independent* on the grass. There, on the top of the page fold, was Miss Tenpenny's article. Mary-Kate quickly scanned it. She'd never been the topic of tea time gossip, and the thought of a scandal was surprisingly invigorating.

Placing her book inside the paper, she tucked both back in the crook of her arm and went on a search for Paddy. She found him in the graveyard switching markers. "Paddy," she called leaning over the fence. "Come here. I've something to show you."

Paddy wiped his brow with the back of his hand. "I don't have a lot of time, Miss Mary-Kate. Father Connelly's keeping the brute occupied, and I'm only halfway through switching the markers. There's a big challenge coming up and the old gal needs all the practice she can get."

She nodded. As she waited for him, her gaze ran over the graves but halted when she came to the O'Brien section. She avoided that spot, more so now that she knew of the promise. She envisioned a gaping hole, snuggled in amongst her siblings' graves, whispering her name. Mary-Kate brought a hand to her throat.

"All right, what do ya want to show me?"

Mary-Kate refocused and flipped open the paper. Paddy made her read it aloud twice, nodding as she read. "It's a fine day when a lad such as meself graces the same page as someone as fine as ya."

Mary-Kate curtsied. "The pleasure was mine," she said. "But I would feel even more pleasure if we moved away from here."

Paddy nodded and jumped the fence. "Should have thought of that meself. Once Father Connelly sets the old gal free, there's no telling what she might do if she finds us lingering about."

He brushed off his sleeve before offering Mary-Kate his arm. "A wee bit of a meander?"

"Where to?" she asked, taking it.

"Glad ya asked, Miss O'Brien. Would have asked the same question meself. To purchase a few papers. If I'm going to be connected to one of the wealthiest families in the city, it would be a shame if anyone missed me debut."

———

THINKING BACK, it was only by happenstance that Miss Tenpenny had come across Mary-Kate and Paddy, and that the pair made their way into the *Independent* at all. "Mary-Kate O'Brien," Miss Tenpenny called. "I'm glad I caught you."

When Mary-Kate turned, her smile disappeared. It was the first time Miss Tenpenny had pronounced her name correctly. Usually it was Mary-Jane, Mary-Kathleen, or some other deviation.

"Out for a stroll are you?" asked Miss Tenpenny.

"Yes."

"And who is your friend? I ask because I was looking out my office window and I saw the two of you. An intriguing couple if ever there was one," she touched Mary-Kate's arm, "if not unevenly matched. When I realized it was you, an O'Brien, I grabbed my hat and wrap and ran into the street to join you."

Mary-Kate stiffened. She could feel the light drain from her face.

Paddy tipped his hat. "Patrick Fitzpatrick, and I'm pleased to make your acquaintance." He bowed, stiff at the waist. Mary-Kate giggled and flicked her fingers.

Miss Tenpenny clicked her nails on her teeth as she sized Paddy up. "I've heard of you," she said. "And none of it I care to repeat."

"Good," said Paddy. "And I'll do the same for ya. Except I've never heard of ya."

The society writer grunted her disapproval. "Oh, surely you jest. Everyone who's anyone has heard of me."

"I only jest with women I find attractive," said Paddy.

Miss Tenpenny wheezed. Stepping back, the heel of her shoe caught on a loose plank and she lost her balance. Paddy reached out to steady her.

"Do you really think that's necessary?" Miss Tenpenny righted herself.

"What?"

"Offering me your hand!"

"Aye, that. Probably not, probably not." Paddy withdrew his offer. "It was an insult then, me offering me hand?"

"Of the most grievous kind. Men like you do not touch women like us," Miss Tenpenny said, more to Mary-Kate than to Paddy.

Paddy turned to leave, but then he hesitated. "While it's on me mind, I've got a message for ya. Something from Mr. O'Brien."

Miss Tenpenny looked at Paddy intently. Paddy shuffled his feet and lowered his voice. "It's kind of hard to say."

Miss Tenpenny leaned in closer. "Go ahead," she said.

"I'm not sure ya can be trusted. Maybe I should speak to your superior."

"You can trust me," Miss Tenpenny snapped.

"Are ya sure?"

"I'm sure!"

"Have it your way," said Paddy. He grabbed her, pulled her close and kissed her full on the mouth. "I think ya should've taken me hand."

Miss Tenpenny's article was kinder than it might have been. She kept Paddy's forward advance to herself.

————

WITH A NEWSPAPER FOLDED NEATLY under his arm, Paddy tipped his cap to all he met, while Mary-Kate curtsied. "Has there ever been a finer day?" he asked.

Mary-Kate giggled. "Not that I can recall."

He said it came to him in the night, the solution to all their ills. Finishing school! Upon first hearing it, Mrs. O'Brien couldn't help but oppose the notion. As of late she'd barred him from any nocturnal encounters, but her husband was determined she hear him out. "'Twould be good for her," he said. "She's been cooped up too long. She needs to find her wings."

"And where will she fly?" demanded his wife. "Farther away from us?"

"No, no, no. Sister Mary-Frances. She will fly away from that soul-sucking nun."

Mrs. O'Brien leaned back on her pillow and sucked on her teeth. She hated being fearful of that nun. In fact, she did secret penance for it. But now she worried her child would be cut in two, and she would get the smaller half. As it was, she and her daughter were hardly on speaking terms, and when they did speak, the tension was palpable. At the breakfast table when she asked Mary-Kate what her plans were for the day, Mary-Kate threw down her napkin. "Don't you trust me?"

"It's not about trust, dear, it's about judgement."

"And my judgement is inferior to yours?"

"You said it, I didn't."

Mary-Kate stood abruptly and stomped out of the room.

Mrs. O'Brien tried again. Passing Mary-Kate on the stairs, she touched her arm. "Do you want to spend some time with me pasting?"

"What are we going to paste?"

"Execution stories. Ne'er-do-wells and ruffians. I think some may be related to that Paddy from the newspaper. He seems to be walking the same path."

Mary-Kate yanked her arm away, continued to her room and slammed the door.

"There's no talking to you," Mrs. O'Brien called after her. "It's enough to make a preacher swear."

As far as she was concerned, it wasn't just Sister Mary-Frances's influence that had grown far too strong and needed tempering, but that Fitzpatrick character's too. Maybe finishing school was the answer. "How can you be sure you'll get Mary Frances away from Mary-Kate?" she asked her husband.

"Because we'll be sending her to New York. The Lady Jane Grey School in Binghamton. Mr. Bailey, a gentleman I met on business, sent his daughter there. Said it did her wonders."

"But that's so far away! And the school, it doesn't sound Catholic."

"Aye, it's not," grinned Mr. O'Brien. "That's why 'twill be so grand. If the Protestants can't get her to stray *and* keep her away from the church and that Fitzpatrick character, I don't know who can."

Mrs. O'Brien grunted. "I'll have to think on this awhile." She didn't want to admit that her husband's plan would kill two birds with one stone.

By morning, after being disturbed another half dozen times

so her husband could expound on the brilliance of his plan, Mrs. O'Brien was convinced it was the best thing for Mary-Kate too.

When breakfast was finished, Mr. O'Brien approached his daughter with a gleam in his eye. He seemed so overjoyed that he babbled. Mrs. O'Brien interpreted.

"You will love it," she said. "So many girls to meet and things to learn. We won't know you when you come home."

"Oh," said Mary-Kate. "You think not knowing me is best?"

"That's not what I mean, dear. It's just that you'll have grown. You'll be a much rounder person."

Mary-Kate patted her slim waist. "But it's not Catholic."

"No, dear. It's Protestant."

"I don't think I know anyone who's Protestant."

"I'm sure you'll manage," said Mrs. O'Brien. "No doubt there's a church nearby."

"Besides," smirked Mr. O'Brien. "You can pretend you're Joan of Arc, sent to be tortured by the ruddy English."

Mary-Kate burst into tears. "I already pretend that."

"Really?"

"Every day."

Mr. O'Brien stopped smirking.

After her parents used all their best arguments, she still resisted. Mary-Kate turned white and started biting her nails. Mrs. O'Brien sat by her daughter's side and stroked her hair. "You are strong and you will find that time passes faster than you can possibly imagine."

Mary-Kate crumpled into her mother's arms. "I can't imagine not being here," she said. "Not being with you."

"Come now, me dear; it won't be that bad. You'll see."

"Have the rumours been too much for you?" Mary-Kate whimpered.

"What rumours?" Mr. O'Brien bellowed, turning red. "No

one told me about any rumours. And if there were I haven't believed a word of them. Born of jealousy they are, a playground for a fool's tongue."

Mrs. O'Brien rolled her eyes before putting her face closer to her daughter's, so that her breath fell upon Mary-Kate's cheek. She started to recite a poem that had been passed down for generations, mother to daughter, daughter to son. "Me great-great-gran wrote it when she came over from Ireland. Her heart was as lonely as yours."

Oh, that I could get back again to home and friends so dear,
with husband and one brother
And little children twain
Myself that forms our family
In our coastal home.

Dear mother, brother, sister
Though away in this Northwest
I never can forget past years
That with you I have spent.

Oh how I miss your presence
While away in the Northwest
And through the long dreary winter
Lonesome hours I have spent.

But winter now is past and gone
And summer drawing nigh
And it with all its luxury

Time will pass swiftly by.

AND OFTEN IN *my slumbers*
    I think that you are near
    But oh what disappointment
    When I find you are not here.

IT MAKES *me long for home again*
    But I must long in vain
    But months and years will pass away
    Before I get back again.

BUT IF MY *life to me is spared*
    And yours to you the same
    I hope to see you all again
    I may not wait in vain.

BUT IF GOD *wills that we on Earth*
    May never meet again
    I hope we meet beyond the skies
    Never to part again.

MARY-KATE DIDN'T STIR. She lay on Mrs. O'Brien's lap, sleeping as sweetly as a babe.

Mr. O'Brien knelt in front of her, took a strand of her hair and twisted it around his finger. His big hands trembled and there were tears in his eyes. "Me sweet little lamb," he whispered. "Me dear sweet little lamb, I will never let your mother send you away."

Mrs. O'Brien flinched at the words and thumped her husband in the chest. "I should have known," she snapped. "The worm hasn't just turned, it has rotted to the core."

MARY-KATE

I t had to be a sign. There was no way that her parents would send her to a Protestant finishing school if they were in their right minds. It was an act of desperation, one that defied all reason. The mere mention of sending her abroad to live with heretics had to be Divine Providence to nudge Mary-Kate in the most virtuous direction — a Catholic destiny. Her parents were unwitting pawns in fate's elaborate game. Though the thought made her gag, Sister Mary-Frances had been right all along.

She rolled over on her bed and reached for her jar of buttons. The very act could irritate her father, yet today she found no joy in it. Mary-Kate loosened the lid and poured the buttons through her splayed fingers. They tumbled over one another in a cascading pile, and their weight made a hollow in the quilt beside her. She closed her eyes and let her fingers drift through the mound. It was like greeting old friends.

The green button with worn edges belonged to her grandfather. In her mind, she could see his heavy white mustache, grown to hide a scar. The button had come off an overcoat he wore the day he learned Sir John A. MacDonald was elected prime minister. Her grandfather drank a pint to the victor but, being a fair man, he also drank a pint to the loser, George Brown. Another button, in the shape of a red squirrel, was from a sweater her mother knit her first-born son, the one who never opened his eyes to the sun or cried for sustenance. Mary-Kate longed to know him.

Catching herself, she stifled a sob. She never knew who was lurking in the hall, and she wouldn't let anyone hear her cry. The posy sisters had a habit lately of dusting her bedroom door frame when she was inside. More than once Mary-Kate had gotten a face full of feathers when she opened her door unexpectedly. She was fairly sure her mother had put them up to it, a way of letting Mary-Kate know she was watching.

Mary-Kate placed the buttons back in their container. "Something has changed," she whispered, by way of an apology. "Where I'm going, I won't be taking you. It's not a place for daydreams and fairy stories." She looked towards the door. "You'll have to stay here with my parents. As for me, there'll be no new memories. None worth putting in a jar." She opened the drawer of the bedside table and deposited the jar gently inside. "Sleep well." It felt overdramatic, something her gran would do, but for Mary-Kate the thought of not being able to while her days away smothered her. Made her feel that the best part of her life was already behind her.

Mary-Kate flopped back on the bed. For the first time since her mother's secret had been revealed she let it run unimpeded through her thoughts. No distractions, no frolicking with Paddy or trying to understand her father's behaviour. Now that she was convinced her aunt's claims were true, that her life was dependent on a promise made before her birth, Mary-Kate had no future of her own. It was the most terrible feeling.

At least if she joined the convent, she could stay where life was familiar. See her beloved Tnúth from a cold and cloistered window. The Lady of Shalott, watching Paddy go on without her. She brushed away a tear and shook her head. Most of her friends were already married, some even had little ones. She had resigned herself not to do the same. Men seemed much more attentive when they were in pursuit than when they'd achieved their goal, as if bedding a new bride was the epitome of marital bliss. Her indifference had caused a division between her and her old chums.

And if she considered her mother, nine children had taken their toll. The woman looked older than she ought. That was the reason for some of Mary-Kate's reluctance. On one hand a life of solitude with Mary-Frances, on the other, marriage, which — as of late according to her mother —meant a life of unending suffering, one that festered with unspoken grievances.

She looked towards her closet and all the outfits she had worn to frustrate her father. They all seemed quite fanciful now, considering what her future held. All the arguing and teasing between her father and herself seemed futile. Its only purpose, a distraction to blind her from the inevitable. And if it hadn't been for the mention of Lady Jane and her Protestant education, she would have never capitulated, never given in. She would have gritted her teeth and held out until the end. But once said, there was no taking it back. A Catholic God would have never wanted that. Her aunt was right. Whether she desired it or not, it was Divine Providence for Mary-Kate to become a nun.

"Ya've been summoned," said Father Connelly, patting Paddy on the back of his arm. "And if ya're not coming of your own free will, ya will be fetched."

"Dockworkers?" Paddy asked, knowing the answer.

The priest nodded.

It was always dockworkers. Men who could sling a chap over a shoulder, without a thought to his size, and Paddy didn't want to be carted down the street for all to view like someone's chattel.

"I'll accompany ya," he said, "but only because ya are the least of two evils."

The priest puffed out his chest. "Well if ya are going to be the least of something, it might as well be of evil."

Paddy trudged towards The Donnybrook behind the priest. To be summoned wasn't a good thing. It rarely went well. In his mind, Paddy went over what he could say to appease O'Brien. The man would be sitting in the great chair, the one dragged out for such occasions. Its square, high back decorated with notches for those who were no longer welcome, their names not worth remembering. Each reduced to a nick on the gnarled wood.

When they entered, The Donnybrook went silent, and the men took off their hats as if Paddy were leading a funeral procession — his own. A man going to his doom. When Paddy was close enough, O'Brien reached over and put his massive hand on Paddy's shoulder. The weight of it caused Paddy's legs to buckle, forcing him on to a small stool, placed in the large chair's shadow.

"Seeing ya makes me feel that me troubles are all but over," O'Brien said, and he lifted his glass in a toast. "Here's to Paddy," he called. "The lad who'll make things right." The words should have had a merry ring to them, but the tone in which they were said had no warmth.

Paddy lifted a glass that had been slipped into his hand, but he didn't know how he could make things right. Or for that matter, even have an opportunity.

O'Brien grabbed Paddy's collar and pulled him close. "Ya see lad, it's like this, our plan didn't have the effect I desired. And I put the blame directly on your shoulders." He squinted his eyes. "Miss Tenpenny's little article didn't help, I'll give ya that. But that's all I'll give ya." O'Brien leaned back into the great chair and touched the notches that ran down the length of its arm. "The whole debacle forced me sister's hand. She's doubled her efforts. Sent for Mary-Kate this very morning." O'Brien finished the remainder of his pint and wiped his mouth on his sleeve. "I'll even be charitable and overlook the incident with me time-piece. In return, ya'll do anything I ask, when I ask it."

Paddy wanted to say he was grateful but wasn't sure he should interrupt the man.

"And to tell ya the truth, Mary-Kate didn't respond well to her mother's idea of finishing school. She is bound and determined to enter the convent now, and I am bound and determined to stop her. At any cost. That's where ya'll come in handy."

A confused look crossed Paddy's face. If Mr. O'Brien was asking what he thought he was asking, it was the first time a father requested such a thing. "Ya want me to put her in a position where that's impossible?"

"In a manner of speaking," said Mr. O'Brien. "But if ya can do it without catching too much of her attention 'twould be best. The last time ya opened your mouth things went awry."

"That might be difficult. It's me words, me charm that persuades the girls. I'd be hard-pressed to do it without them."

"Jasus, Mary, and Joseph. What in the hell are ya talking about? I don't want ya to put Mary-Kate in any position. Ya're to deal with Sister Mary-Frances!"

"A nun? Jasus, sir. Spare a thought for me soul."

Father Connelly placed his hands firmly on the table and interrupted. "This is getting us nowhere," he said. "The two of ya will go 'round this tree 'til doomsday. Paddy, O'Brien here, would like ya to enter the convent and keep Sister Mary-Frances occupied so that she hasn't the time to hector Mary-Kate to take vows."

"How am I supposed to do that?"

"As the caretaker."

Paddy stifled a laugh. "Take a job as a caretaker? There's no one alive would believe that foolish notion. I can guarantee it."

"Aye, that's exactly what I told him," said Father Connelly. "But do ya think he'll listen to me? No! The man is thick in the head and won't listen to reason. I've told him deceiving a nun is a short step from blasphemy."

Mr. O'Brien put his hand over Father Connelly's mouth. "Blasphemy doesn't bother Paddy. Does it, me boy? That is, if you're up for the challenge?" Mr. O'Brien took his hand from the priest's mouth and retrieved a pipe from his coat pocket. He tapped it on the heel of his boot and filled it. "There are those I'll not name who think ya're past your prime, Paddy.

That what ya did as a child ya can't do as a man. Some even think it was all your ma's doing and that ya had no talent at all."

Paddy's eyes widened. "I'll box any man who says such a thing."

"Actually," said Mr. O'Brien lighting the pipe, "it was Father Connelly."

The priest jumped to his feet. "I've said no such thing! And I'll not keep company with anyone who claims I have." He looked Paddy square in the eye. "I give ya me word, son. Only had the best thoughts about ya. Held ya in the highest regard a scoundrel can be held."

"And to prove it, ya promise not to interfere?" asked Mr. O'Brien.

"I do," said the indignant priest, but then added, "unless we cross paths. But if he can stay out of me sight, I'll stand clear."

"Good," said Mr. O'Brien. "Then 'tis settled."

In Paddy's mind, nothing was settled. Working at a convent hadn't occurred to him, not even on the coldest of nights. The only deceptions he'd been contemplating of late didn't concern the church, even though since his falling out with his mother he had been sleeping on one of its pews.

Mr. O'Brien's new plan was simple enough. Get hired as a caretaker, by claiming a changing of his ways. As luck would have it, the hiring of the caretaker fell under Father Connelly's jurisdiction. According to Mr. O'Brien, Sister Mary-Frances might turn a blind eye to Paddy's shortcomings if it were to save her from opening the convent's coffers. Even Father Connelly agreed. "'Tis true lad. That woman watches her coin more closely than most maidens watch..." He hesitated, then dropped the subject.

"Ya'll make a fine handyman, Paddy. Ya were made for it," said Mr. O'Brien.

Paddy frowned and looked at his hands. "Handyman," he repeated. "The word feels heavy on me tongue."

"I agree with ya, Paddy," said Father Connelly. "Any ruse to hoodwink nuns is one ya should be leery of."

"Holy Mother of God. That's where ya're both wrong. 'Twill be the finest scam ever fashioned, I promise ya that." Mr. O'Brien looked around the room. "I'll even have the lads lay a wager or two — Paddy keeping his ten percent, of course."

"Sounds tempting," said Paddy, "but I'm still of the mind to say no. With the weather improving as it is, I think I'll take me chances on the street."

"Do what ya like." Mr. O'Brien leaned over and patted Paddy's vest pocket. "I won't be wasting any more of your time. But mind when ya're about. Your next encounter might be with the local constabulary, who'd like to see ya swing with your ancestors."

Paddy frowned and nodded, not so much in agreement but in recognition of his likely fate.

"But wait," Mr. O'Brien said. "I've not even told Paddy the best part."

"What best part?" Father Connelly asked. "Ya've not told me either."

"I know," Mr. O'Brien gleamed. "Was saving it for confession."

The priest made the sign of the cross, and Mr. O'Brien reminded him he had given his word not to interfere. "While Paddy is distracting my swine of a sister, Mary-Kate will be tending her gran, my wife's ma." Mr. O'Brien grinned. "The old woman is under the weather."

"No one told me," Father Connelly widened his eyes. "I haven't even offered up a prayer."

"Well, that's because I haven't informed her of her condition yet. When me wife approached Herself about taking Mary-

Kate's place at the convent, the foul creature refused. Said she'd rather die first. It's only logical that getting ill is the first step toward that. I have no doubt the old bat will play her part."

"Pretend to be ill? Temp fate? And that pleases you?" The priest was dismayed.

"Not in a good way, I give you me word on that. Only in a way that's convenient."

"What if fate takes her up on the offer, and sends your saintly mother-in-law to an early end?"

"She won't be dying," scoffed Mr. O'Brien. "She can't make me life as miserable from that side of the grave as she can from this one."

"And what is Paddy supposed to be doing with the nuns?"

"Anything he wants." Mr. O'Brien winked and let the words sink in. "Let's tip a glass to the lad's success." Downing his drink he looked from the priest to Paddy. "I've got to go home and help with me mother-in-law's arrangements."

"But ya said she wasn't sick, let alone dead." Father Connelly rubbed the back of his neck with a checkered hanky.

"But that doesn't mean I shouldn't stop encouraging her."

"I know you have your heart set on the convent," Mr. O'Brien picked his teeth with the tip of his tongue. "And I'd be the last man on earth to get between you and the church."

Mary-Kate frowned. Her father was going out of his way to sound like he was not trying to dissuade her. Yet when she looked at it more closely, that was precisely what he was doing.

"But just look at her," he said, pointing at Herself who sat across the table. "Have you seen anything sadder in your life?"

She examined her gran. She looked as she always did. An old woman ready to pounce.

Herself wiped her mouth with the corner of her napkin. "You talk as if I don't have ears in me head. I've been sitting here this whole time."

"We know that, woman," snapped Mr. O'Brien. "That's what I've been talking to me Mary-Kate about." He turned once more to his daughter. "It wouldn't be kind of you to leave the care of her in your mother's hands. Wouldn't be charitable. And after all, isn't that what taking those vows are all about? Charity?"

Mary-Kate wasn't of the mind to agree with her father on any front, but he did have a point.

"Listen to the way she breathes," he paused. "Did you hear it, the way it catches? There is no denying it, the end is near."

Herself put a hand on her chest as if measuring her own breath. "It doesn't catch," she said after a time. "I've been breathing this way for years." A look of doubt darkened her features.

"Aye. And it's wearing on you. Can you not hear it, Mary-Kate?"

Mary-Kate shook her head. They'd had some version of the same conversation every morning at the breakfast table since she had announced her decision to enter the convent. A departure that was to take place in a matter of days was now turning into weeks. Each morning her father had some new complication that kept her where she was. His twisted ankle. The pending arrival of distant relations that never showed up. Now it was her grandmother's health, something that until this morning had never concerned her father. In fact, at an earlier time, he would have celebrated her ague as if it were the second coming of Christ.

"Of course, she can't hear it," Herself snapped. "There is nothing to hear."

Mr. O'Brien squared off. "So, you're telling me that you're fit as a fiddle and there is no need for your granddaughter to put off her leaving for the convent to tend to your needs?"

Herself's brow furrowed. "Oh, so that's the way it is? You're going to place this burden on me?"

"When have I asked anything of you before?"

"You haven't asked. You've taken!" Her eyes narrowed.

Even Mary-Kate knew a line had been crossed — something that made her settle down in her seat and wait to be educated.

"And what harm did it do her? I doubt there has been a day she has regretted it."

"Oh, I think there have been many. Each time she donned the black and trudged her way to the graveyard, for starters."

The veins in Mr. O'Brien's neck pulsed, and Mary-Kate wondered if her gran would make it out of the morning room in the same manner in which she'd arrived.

"You can tell me anything you like, but I don't remember you standing by her side, holding her up when her legs gave way." Mr. O'Brien's eyes were dark and his voice low.

Herself sucked at her teeth, and when she spoke again it was less vigour and more trembling. "Let's leave the past in the past. It serves no purpose now." She turned her attention to Mary-Kate. She blinked as if trying to avoid the light. "Your father's right. I'm not as strong as I once was. Twenty years ago, I could match the strength of a woman half me age. Now I'm not so sure that would be the case."

"There you have it." Mr. O'Brien slammed his hand on top of the table. "The woman is growing weaker by the day."

Herself coughed into her napkin, checking the linen for blood. "Consumption. Been trying to keep it to meself."

Mr. O'Brien leaned back, and the anger that once overwhelmed him seemed to dissipate. "It'll be a quick death," he reassured Mary-Kate.

Mary-Kate looked from her father to her gran. It was no use. She put her hands up in the air in an act of capitulation, secretly relieved her father had come up with something new to keep her from the cold stone walls of Sister Mary-Frances's embrace.

Sister Mary-Frances was putting straight the grave markers when she caught sight of Mary-Kate leaving the church in a drab and shapeless dress. She wrinkled her brow. "She's wearing that? In public? This will not do. She looks like the kitchen help." A certain amount of decorum was expected from an O'Brien, even the ones answering a higher calling. "First the picture in the paper, and then this."

In fewer strides than usual, Sister Mary-Frances crossed the graveyard and met her niece at the base of the church steps. Mary-Kate seemed oblivious to her approach, her mind elsewhere.

"Mary-Kate." Sister Mary-Frances cleared her throat. "Another uneventful confession?"

Mary-Kate looked up as if seeing her aunt for the first time. "Uneventful indeed. My father didn't even show up."

The nun stifled a grunt and ran a finger along the wooden cross she still held in her hand. "You know Mary-Kate, time is running out."

"Running out?"

The nun tightened her grip on the cross. "Yes, running out.

Don't you remember our conversation? The one we had when you came to see me at the convent?"

Mary-Kate nodded.

"That week we agreed upon has come and gone. I've written you three more times regarding the matter, and I know you've received the correspondence as you told me so yourself. Still, you dither when it comes to setting a new date."

Mary-Kate nodded again, but Sister Mary-Frances wasn't convinced anything of substance was sinking in. The nun squared herself. "I don't know what's occupying your time of late, but whatever it is, it needs to be set aside for what is important."

Mary-Kate nodded, the vacant look undisturbed.

"You're not a lamb being sent to the slaughter, for God's sake." The nun's temper rose with every word. "You'll be a postulant. Do you know what that means? A postulant?"

Mary-Kate looked passed her aunt as if she weren't even there. Her gaze locked on something beyond her.

The nun bristled. "Are you not listening to anything I've said? A postulant doesn't have to make her vows for a year or two. It will give you time to make sure it's what you want to do with your life. We will ease you in."

The part that indicated Mary-Kate had a choice slipped from her lips, and as soon as Sister Mary-Frances realized it, she started backpedalling. "That is, if you were a regular postulant, not one promised to the church since birth."

Her niece nodded again, but her gaze stayed fixed. Sister Mary-Frances bit the inside of her cheek as she turned and followed it — to The Donnybrook.

There, through the mullioned window, her brother sat, head down, both fists pounding the top of his table. That wasn't the unusual part; it was the person dancing on the table that drew her attention. It couldn't be Father Connelly. He was taking confession. Besides, the tabletop dancer was too tall. His head and shoulders disappeared above the frame. But the robes were undeniably those of a priest. Sister Mary-Frances narrowed her eyes. "Who is that?"

Mary-Kate shrugged and watched as the tabletop dancer bent over, relieved Mr. O'Brien of his bowler, and kissed him squarely on his pate.

Sister Mary-Frances gasped. "Father Browne! I didn't know he was due for a visit." She swung the cross in the air. "What's he doing here?"

Mary-Kate gave no response. Not that the nun expected one.

"And what on earth does he have in his hand?"

Mary-Kate squinted. "I think it's a stopwatch."

"Suffer the little children," intoned Father Connelly. His voice rose until it echoed within the chapel's walls.

Sister Mary-Frances thumped Paddy in the chest with two fingers. "This one is no child."

"Aye. 'Tis true. Any fool with eyes in his head can see that." The priest tapped his temple. "In body at least."

Sister Mary-Frances huffed and circled the applicant again. He stood cap in hand, head bowed. Altogether too passive, as if life somehow had defeated him. "His reputation precedes him."

"As it does all of us."

"Really? I've chased him out of the graveyard on more than one occasion, and that's not to mention the sanctuary." Her brow furrowed. "I've seen him in the paper."

"With your eyesight you're bound to have seen almost anything." Father Connelly rocked back on his heels. "But being our new caretaker is this lad's road to Damascus. And we can't be denying him that."

The nun snorted. She doubted Patrick Fitzpatrick had a road to Damascus or ever would.

"And," Father Connelly said, as if noticing her hesitation,

"he'll do it for nothing, out of the goodness of his heart." He slapped Paddy on the back of the head. "Won't you, lad?"

Paddy's head snapped to attention, and the grip on his cap tightened, so much so that Sister Mary-Frances noticed his knuckles whiten. She couldn't help but smile. "For nothing?"

"Well, his room and board, just enough to keep the chill out of his bones and hunger at bay."

"And why? Why now? Isn't it up to the prisons to rehabilitate?"

Father Connelly looked from Paddy to the nun. "I've heard the same thing meself. And that may work for some, but sadly for most that is not the case. Besides, who's to say when a calling should strike? Draw a man to his knees?"

"And who's to say there was a calling at all?" Sister Mary-Frances considered Paddy's eyes. "He might just as likely be claiming sanctuary. My brother isn't fond of having his name, or daughter's for that matter, dragged through the mud."

"Oh my God, woman! Can you let it go? Your brother can take care of himself. I've come to you out of the goodness of your heart. Don't disappoint me now."

"Don't you tell me to let it go. I've been dealing with riffraff for more years than I care to count. And as for the goodness of my heart, I'm standing here aren't I? Listening to your drivel."

"It's not drivel; it's me Irish brogue."

The nun reddened. "Can the boy speak for himself? I've seen him often enough charming the young ones on the street."

Father Connelly stepped between Sister Mary-Frances and Paddy. "Rather not. Begged me to do it on his behalf. Your reputation precedes you as well, sends most quaking in their boots." The priest's hands were steepled together, the tips of his fingers tapping. "Besides, I wouldn't worry about it too much. Not with Father Albright on his way, probably as we speak, to lurk around. Or should I use his Irish name?" His voice hardened.

"Father Not-Bright. If the two of you can't keep the lad on the straight and narrow, then there is no use getting up in the morning."

"What are you talking about? You're the only priest in this parish, now that Father Browne has finished his tabletop dancing and returned home. The two of you, a pair of French strumpets, kicking up your heels. Where's the Inquisition when it's needed?"

"Don't look at me. I've never run with that sort." Father Connelly reddened. "Too busy putting communion wine on me oatmeal. Not into wearing pointy caps and swinging incense."

Sister Mary-Frances took a deep breath. He was trying to distract her. Lead her down some God-forsaken path until she lost all sight of where she was going. There had to be a reason, something she had yet to ferret out.

Father Connelly sat down on the nearest pew. "As I was saying, it was you yourself who thanked me for taking this one duty off your hands, and now that I've done so you can't claim ignorance. Besides, if the church can't find it in her heart to be charitable now, when will it?"

Sister Mary-Frances looked towards Paddy who was turning over pew cushions looking for loose change. "I suppose it might be charitable after a couple more imps have been burnt at the stake."

After his morning constitutional, Paddy thought it might be time to inform his mother of his plans. He slid off the roof with more than his usual thump. "Good morning to ya, miss," he said, sussing out her better side.

Biddy stopped sweeping the front step and rested on her broom. "And what's so good about it?"

"A good morning is to be discovered, not told about." He leaned into her. "Where would be the fun in that?"

Biddy grunted. "Haven't seen you for a month and you think we're playing a game of hide and seek. Spit it out, there's things I need to be doing."

"And what do ya need to be doing?"

"Never mind you that, I'm not the one who's dropped off the roof to interrupt the day."

"I just dropped by to tell you where to forward me mail. I've had a change in vocation. I'll be doing God's work." Paddy slipped a thumb through a vest buttonhole. "The kind of things a cutpurse would never understand."

"And what kind of things are those?"

At first there was no response. Paddy 'hadn't been expecting to be held to account. "Mending whatever needs to be mended, raking and planting." He could feel the colour drain from his face as the list expanded. "Sweeping, washing and polishing. Fetching, carrying and ..." His voice trailed off.

His mother's expression hardened as he unfurled his new opportunity. "I understand those things well enough. I'm not daft." She cuffed him on the side of the head. "Why would you go blistering your palms, when me made it me life's work to keep them pristine? All I can do is shake me head. But you've made your choice, decided on a job. Generations will be turning in their graves." As she looked him over, a greater measure of disappointment entered her expression.

"A little exercise won't hurt them. They'll be more spry come Judgment Day."

"You think it's a joke?"

"Just lightening the mood. Didn't know making something of meself would stir your ire."

"Oh, you've stirred me ire all right. Been gone for a month of Sundays, and not so much as a how are you, or did you miss me?"

"Aye."

"Can you see yourself picking up after the pious and holier-than-thou? You think it's something a Fitzpatrick would willingly lay his name to?"

Paddy nodded, not quite sure what his mother was getting at. "Well, not exactly."

"Then what exactly are you to be doing? I ask you that."

"Keeping O'Brien's daughter from taking her vows."

"O'Brien is leading you up a garden path, and you don't even know it." Biddy pursed her lips and raised an eyebrow. "Keeping the O'Brien girl from taking her vows? I can think of only one way you can make that happen, and it won't if you spend all your time raking leaves and pulling weeds."

Paddy didn't care for her skepticism. "If ya were at The Donnybrook it would have made sense."

"Over a few pints, everything sounds reasonable." Biddy resumed sweeping. "If O'Brien wants his daughter to stay out of the convent, he should marry her off." She lowered her voice. "Not that anyone in their right mind would want to be caught up with that family."

Paddy could feel his frustration overtake him. He had come to see his mother out of kindness, to let her know he'd not held her previous outburst against her, and this was how she received him? "Father Connelly was right; women are fickle. First ya say ya want me to get a job, and then get mad when I do. Can a man not have a moment's peace?"

"An afternoon at a public house and you call yourself a man?"

"I do. Been fending for meself a long time."

Biddy arched an eyebrow but let it pass. "And as for you getting a job, I know that's what I said." She looked at him as if any fool could have seen through her guise. "But it's not what I meant, and O'Brien knows it." She swept harder, so much so the straw broom was leaving more bristles in its wake than it was picking up. "Flouncing around with those men in skirts. I can think of a thousand things I'd rather do."

Paddy fingered the timepiece in his vest pocket, remembering O'Brien's threat. "I have me reasons."

"And most of those reasons don't lie between your ears, I tell you that much."

S ister Mary-Frances ignored the knock at her door. The day had been full enough of oddities, and she was just comfortably settled. First, there was the hiring of the new caretaker. That was an unmitigated failure, and the boy had yet to pick up a broom. Then there was Father Browne's unexpected visit. His unusual behaviour troubled her. That priest hadn't set foot in her parish for — she paused to count — at least four years. The last time he came, he and Father Connelly had a bitter argument about a competition. Father Browne claimed it was staged, whatever *it* was. Father Connelly, for his part, had grabbed her habit and lifted it well above her knees. "Look at those gams! You can't cast your eyes on those monstrosities and claim fraud." She cuffed her little nemesis soundly for his familiarity. The thought almost brought a smile to her face, but then she remembered that after the priest was hospitalized, the bishop had written of his disapproval.

She grunted. The banging persisted. She knew her young protégé would knock herself raw, so she barked, "Yes?"

Sister Bernadette opened the door just enough to let her

voice be heard. Sister Mary-Frances smiled. The young thing was learning. You can't hit a target if it won't reveal itself.

"The new priest is here."

"What new priest?" Sister Mary-Frances tried not to, but, from somewhere deep inside, hope entered her voice.

"I don't know. The one standing on the front step demanding entry."

"Well, let him in, let him in." Standing with haste, she knocked over her chair. News this good had to be met head-on. Sister Mary-Frances rushed out of the office with such speed she didn't notice she'd bowled Sister Bernadette to the ground. The girl lay prostrate. "No need for formalities," the older said to the younger as she stepped over her. "Save your prayers for vespers."

By the time she reached the main entrance, she had to pause to catch her breath. She couldn't be huffing and puffing over the new priest like some lovestruck school girl. It might give him the wrong impression. After waiting what she thought was the appropriate amount of time, she opened the door. "Yes?"

A thin, young man stood on the step, looking a little dismayed. He shivered, even though the weather was mild. "I've been sent from the diocese." He handed her a letter. "There was no one at the church, so I came here."

A chill filled the nun. "You're English."

"That I am. Is that a problem?"

"Could be." Sister Mary-Frances opened the message and began to read, while the Englishman shifted from one foot to the other.

"Didn't Father Connelly inform you? The diocese sent him a letter."

"He may have," she said, remembering an earlier conversation. She could feel herself redden. She had been demanding a replacement for years, and now they'd sent one but informed Father Connelly instead of her. It was an intentional slight, and one she felt bitterly. But she wouldn't let this one see it. "We have been so busy of late, it might have slipped my mind. And you are?"

"Father Albright." The young priest drew himself up to his full height. "Might I come in?"

"If you like." The nun stepped aside. "But you will have to share a room with the Damascus boy. I haven't made any other arrangements."

Father Albright coughed discreetly. "The Damascus boy?"

"Yes, The Donnybrook kind."

I t may have started out as wishful thinking on Mr. O'Brien's part, his mother-in-law contracting some communal disease, but not long after Herself feigned ill at the breakfast table, she took a tumble while hauling her rocker down the stairs. A broken hip was the result. "Oh just leave me," Herself wailed as she lay in a heap beneath the rocker. "Easier for the undertaker to fetch me here."

"Don't be ridiculous," Mrs. O'Brien snapped. "The posy sisters will never get their work done if they have to step over you."

It took almost the entire household to get Herself settled back in the Deadman's room. Mary-Kate fanned her gran and Mrs. O'Brien directed traffic from the rear, while the posy sisters took the head and Mr. O'Brien the foot of a makeshift stretcher. "Watch her head," Mrs. O'Brien instructed. "We can't afford any more injuries before the doctor arrives. He'll think we're trying to do her in."

"You are," Herself moaned from her prone position. "Making me fetch and haul me own rocker and sleep in that goddamned room."

Mr. O'Brien stopped short, turning first to Herself, and then to his wife. "It's a roof over your head when no one else would have you, so count yourself lucky. And as for doing her in, would that be so bad?"

The posies twittered and Mary-Kate narrowed her eyes. Her parents could bicker about how her gran should be transported until the cows came home and still never arrive at a consensus. "I think she's passing out," Mary-Kate said, tapping her gran on the cheek.

"Glory be to God," Mr. O'Brien said, increasing his speed. He was soon barrelling down the hall towards the Deadman's room, causing the rest of them to trot or be run over. "Maybe we'll make our destination before she comes to. I can only deal with one caterwauler at a time."

After the mishap on the stairs, things went from bad to worse, as they often do. Herself began to complain of bed sores, and a cough that settled in her chest soon turned into pneumonia. The only bright side to Herself's decline was that Sister Mary-Frances stopped her badgering, leaving Mary-Kate to avoid her calling for the foreseeable future.

"She needs you dear," Mrs. O'Brien said one day when they were changing the bedclothes. "The convent isn't going anywhere. I'm afraid it isn't so for your gran."

Peering down at the frail woman, Mary-Kate sighed. Although it was heart-wrenching to see Herself waste away, it wasn't as depressing as it could have been. True, they were relegated to the Deadman's room, but the place was bright and airy, and the soon-to-be-departed had a pleasant look about her. Her face was smooth and tame, not tight with knots as it usually was. Mary-Kate tucked in the spread around her.

"Mary-Kate is that you?" Herself asked.

"Yes, Gran."

"Well don't just stand there, kiss me on the cheek and get me the book."

"Oh, you don't need that," Mary-Kate said as she leaned over and kissed her gran.

"Don't tell me what I'll be needing. I'll not be hearing that from you. Me time is short, and I want to find out why."

"Why is obvious, considering the tumble you've taken."

"Nonsense. That has nothing to do with it."

Mary-Kate crossed the room and picked up a book from the dresser before taking the chair next to the bed. Both her mother and grandmother relied on Lady Wilde's book, *Irish Cures, Mystic Charms, & Superstitions.* Each woman examined it closely whenever something disagreeable happened. "Where were we?" Mary-Kate flipped through the pages. "Ah, here it is. Whit-suntide."

"Aye, that's when I fell." Herself took a deep breath. "I lit a candle without making the sign of the cross, and on Whitsun-tide of all days. Beginning of June. Doomed meself. Now what does Lady Wilde have to say about it?"

"She says there is a great possibility of death. That and evil spirits may try to carry you off. You're not to be left alone or in the dark."

"I knew it. Me own foolishness for being so careless. At me age I should have known better."

Mary-Kate ran her hand across her gran's cheek. "You're making something out of nothing."

"Making something out of nothing? Your ma marrying your da, that's making something out of nothing." She poked Mary-Kate in the chin with a bony finger. "Don't tell me I'm making something out of nothing. You forget who you be talking to. I know the signs. How about the magpie? Have you thought of that? Came to me window and stared right at me. Death might as well have been sitting in me lap! There is no stronger omen that that."

"That's an old wives' tale. Look at my red hair. Has that brought you bad luck?"

"Your hair's not red, it's auburn."

"Oh. I beg to differ with you. What does the superstition say?"

With the back of her hand, Herself wiped the spittle from the corners of her mouth. "It says a redheaded woman is unlucky to the bone."

"So is a whistling mother-in-law but that's never stopped you."

"Aye. But I did it to bring your da bad luck."

"Did it work?"

"He had a redheaded daughter didn't he?"

Mary-Kate got up and put the book back on the dresser. She paused and looked at her reflection in the mirror. "To be born with red hair is an unlucky curse," she muttered. "Even more than the habit to cover it up." She turned back to her gran, took a seat and waited for the old woman to fall into another fitful sleep.

The care of Mary-Kate's gran was shared equally. There wasn't a time Herself was alone, whether asleep or awake. As the days passed she became more restless, and even Mrs. O'Brien voiced doubts of her recovery. "I've thrown more salt over me shoulder in the past weeks...I've tried everything, and nothing seems to help," Mrs. O'Brien said when she came to spell Mary-Kate off. "There's little more to be done but wait. You'd best go have something to eat."

Mr. O'Brien was sitting at the dinner table reading the paper and humming when Mary-Kate entered the room. He didn't acknowledge her. She had almost cleaned her plate when he finally spoke. "Saw your paperboy this afternoon."

"Where?"

"At the convent with Sister Mary-Frances. Those two are thick as thieves."

"That's a lie."

"Ask anyone you like. 'Tis no lie. Father Connelly will tell you the same. He was there with me he was, sitting at our table."

"I don't believe you."

The room grew quiet, and when Mae came in to clear the table, Mary-Kate told her not to bother bringing her any dessert.

"The more for me." Mr. O'Brien flipped down the corner of the paper and grinned at Mary-Kate, who was dabbing her mouth with a napkin. "Don't you want to know what they were up to?"

"Not really."

"Stay seated and let me tell you. They were conspiring."

Mary-Kate opened her mouth to speak but closed it again.

"It infuriates you, doesn't it? You think I'm trying to bait you."

She grunted.

"Well I am." Mr. O'Brien flipped up the corner of his newspaper and resumed humming. His feet tapped under the table.

"You're unbearable."

"In me humble way, I suppose I am."

"What's that supposed to mean? That you're humbled by your own grandeur?"

Mr. O'Brien laid the paper in his lap and lowered his head. "Is that what you'd like it to mean?"

"I give up." Mary-Kate handed Mae her napkin. "If you're trying to upset me, you're not going to succeed. My aunt has obviously seen the good in my paperboy. Good that you seem to be blind to, otherwise you'd have not threatened to send me away after that harmless article."

"Harmless! It was anything but harmless. Your mother locked me out of her room."

Mary-Kate narrowed her eyes. "And why would she do that? You've already told me that you don't know Patrick Fitzpatrick. Or is there more to the story than what's printed in the paper?"

Mr. O'Brien scoffed. "What gave you that impression?"

"She's locked you out of her room."

"Can you blame her?"

Mary-Kate felt like pulling out her hair. "This is going nowhere."

"You're just like your mother, complaining about everything." Mr. O'Brien scratched his chin. "But getting back to that paperboy of yours. From where I was sitting they were up to something, Mary-Frances and Paddy. Or maybe the two have been scheming all along, wanting to guilt you into the church. Can't trust anyone who'd be doing that. "

Mae set what she was carrying on the sideboard and wiped her hands on her apron. "Well, all I can say is she wasn't teaching him the stations of the cross, now was she?"

Mr. O'Brien slapped his knee. "Amen to that, sister. Amen to that."

His first few days as caretaker went smoothly enough. Paddy spent much of his time lounging about as he thought of ways to get under Sister Mary-Frances' skin and entertain the lads in the pub simultaneously. When Sister Mary-Frances wasn't about, his target was Father Albright.

He caught the priest as he covered the ground between St. Augustine and the convent. "Tell me, good Father," he said, offering the priest his hoe, "does a Catholic work a garden any different than a Protestant?"

Father Albright scowled but didn't extend his hand. "Oh, Damascus boy. You are an absurd young man."

"Absurd I may be, but at night ya regale me with tales of English superiority. I've almost come to believe it. Ya see, out of me Irish ignorance, I'm blind to such things." Paddy looked at the hoe he held. "Would that superiority not apply to all things?"

"It may."

"Including hoeing?"

"I suppose."

Paddy walked to the nearest flowerbed, the one Sister Mary-

Frances insisted he attend to that morning. "So, tell me, Father, how would a Protestant work the soil differently from that of a Catholic?"

Father Albright, in a contemplative stance, gazed from Paddy to the garden.

"Oh, never mind," Paddy said, seeing the other's resistance. "An Irishman is as capable of discovering such things as an Englishman."

The priest's contemplative look dissolved, and in its stead, a look of disdain appeared. "Let this be a lesson to you." Taking the hoe, Father Albright raised it above his head. "Notice the gentle fervour with which the blade strikes the ground, dividing weed from flower."

Squatting, Paddy examined both the swing and the result. "Aye, I see it. It is slight but there."

"It's not slight," Father Albright struck the ground again, with more vehemence than before. "It's dramatically different to a discerning eye."

Paddy shrugged. "Perhaps, but would an English Catholic work the plot better than an Irish Catholic? Of that, I'm not so convinced."

Father Albright threw himself into the task, not acknowledging Paddy's presence until the chore was complete. With a hand on a hip, Father Albright surveyed his accomplishment. Paddy nodded. "I see," he said, taking back the hoe before making his way towards the workshop.

"See what?" Father Albright shouted to his back. "English or Irish superiority?"

Paddy shrugged and continued walking. He envisioned Sister Mary-Frances surveying the turned bed, evidence of the headway she was making. And if Paddy should be so lucky as to have Father Albright keep the matter to himself, all the better. Sister Mary-Frances could boast of her influence unfettered, and who was the reedy priest to disagree? It was only recently he had seemed to gain the old nun's favour, and Paddy doubted he'd risk losing it by correcting her.

He smiled to himself. The benefit of residing with a pious padre was that Paddy learned much from him without raising his head off the pillow. The good father prayed until all hours, and Latin was his language of choice. Paddy stayed on his cot and gave a rough translation of the priest's supplications.

"Praying for Sister Mary-Frances's piles, are we?"

"I should think not!" Father Albright reddened.

"Then it's your own." Paddy fluffed his pillow. "I sometimes confuse me Latin he's, she's, and me's."

Father Albright stood and stalked over to where Paddy stretched upon his cot, his rodent features twitching to life. "I'll have you know the prayer was regarding Sister Bernadette."

"Uh, 'tis clear to me now. Wondered why she lumbers about the way she does."

"Sister Bernadette doesn't have piles!"

"Well, ya don't have to announce it to all and sundry. Nun or no, there's not a woman alive would appreciate such a thing."

Lying in the shadow of the twitching priest brought back the tales his mother, Biddy, used to coo Paddy to sleep, like the drooling overlord haranguing guiltless Irish lambs. Paddy blinked demurely, only to bring on greater spasms from the other.

The arrangement worked well. Rooming with an insufferable priest, on the outside, looked inconvenient and untenable, but Paddy soon found it advantageous. A churchman full of his own pre-eminence was only too pleased to correct his inferior, and Paddy was confident that Father Albright found no one quite as inferior as the Damascus boy. That was, until he came into Sister Mary-Frances's sightline.

"What do you think you're doing?"

"Oh, Sister Mary-Frances." Paddy raised a hand in salute. "I was wondering where ya got off to."

"But it didn't occur to you to get up off your fanny and look for me?"

"Why would I?" Paddy squinted up at her through the dappled light that filtered through the spring leaves. He'd been reclining ever since Father Albright finished the gardening duties. "Ya found me well enough on your own. Ya didn't need me looking. And if I hadn't found ya I'm sure Father Albright would. He seems skittish when he's not standing in your shadow."

"What would you know of Father Albright?"

"We bunk together, remember. He twitters at the mention of your name — a little English song sparrow."

The nun's lip twitched as she stepped closer to Paddy. "He is your bunk mate to be a godly example, not to be ridiculed by a heathen such as yourself."

"If ya mean by godly example a man who for penance licks his lips repeatedly to chap them, he certainly is."

The twitch from the nun's lips metastasized to encompass the whole of her face. Her proximity to Paddy was such that it eclipsed any view that the lads in the pub may have had, and Paddy was tempted to get up and reposition her but thought better of it. She might pummel him.

"Are you finished?"

"I haven't even started," he said, inching his way around her to change the perspective.

She rapped her knuckles on his head. "Where are you off to?"

"Nowhere." Paddy rubbed the spot before raising his gaze to meet hers.

"Well, where's the gate? The one you were to mend when the hoeing was completed."

"I fixed it."

"If you fixed it, it would still be here, wouldn't it? Where is it?"

Paddy pointed to some nearby bushes where the gate was nestled. "Doesn't squeak now, does it?"

"I could have done that myself."

"Aye. You could have. Save me some time."

Sister Mary-Frances raised her hand, but Paddy darted out of the way. "You're trying my patience."

"Ya sound like me own ma." Paddy put his cap over his heart. "Brings tears to me eyes."

"I'll bring more than tears to your eyes!" The nun stepped forward and grabbed Paddy by the scruff of the neck. "Scoundrel or no, you will mind me." She dragged him to the bushes, picked up the gate and thrust the two together. "Do you have any questions?"

Paddy stared blankly.

"I thought not. Be done in an hour. I'll be back to check."

M ary-Kate practiced her Holmes as she made her way to the Deadman's room. It was time to spell her mother off, and she thought she'd find a bit of a mystery to solve before settling in to the monotony. She paused outside the door. Her mother and gran were in the middle of a hushed conversation. She was sure to find something to deduce, so she inclined an ear.

"Cough it out."

"I can't. It hurts. And after five births a little coughing has its costs."

"But there are six of us."

"I may have had six, but on most days I only care to acknowledge five."

"Please tell me I'm the sixth."

"I'll do no such thing."

More coughing.

"That's better. You don't want to be here 'til doomsday."

"Oh doomsday has come and gone — and it didn't claim me then, so it won't come back and claim me now."

Mary-Kate edged closer to the door of the Deadman's room,

hoping to catch a glimpse of the two bantering matriarchs without getting caught. They seemed to be getting along, and she wondered how long the peace could hold. She didn't have long to wonder, for the playful ribbing turned when Herself brought up a newspaper article.

"Have you had a chance to read that piece I pointed out? The one with the woman outside The Donnybrook, calling that man to account?"

"Why would I do that?"

"I saw you slip it under your bottom. Must have been for a reason."

"Used it to stoke me bedroom fireplace."

"None as blind as those who will not see."

"That was a long time ago. He's changed."

"A leopard never loses his spots. He may hide them away, but don't be fooled. He keeps them in a pocket to pull out whenever he chooses."

Her mother's sobs were an end to the conversation.

When Mary-Kate formulated the bits and drabs, she felt light-headed. The only man the two could be possibly talking about was her father. She stepped away from her post, chiding herself for ever occupying it in the first place. Skulking around corners only brought misery — that was now perfectly clear. If her mother couldn't trust her father, where did that leave her? She'd always thought of her father as steady, reliable, minding his own sheets. The thought of him being any different wasn't a thought worth merit. Not then, not now.

Mary-Kate found it hard to breathe.

45

The days at Herself's bedside were short-lived. The old woman's health declined as expected with someone in her condition. "There is nothing more to be done," the doctor said solemnly, heading to the door. "I'll check on her in the morning."

Mrs. O'Brien sniffed and walked downstairs with him.

"Prepare for the inevitable," the doctor said before disappearing into the night.

During the last hours of her life, Herself called for her family. One by one they passed before her. Mary-Kate was the first to pay her respects.

"I've come to sit with you, Gran," she said, scooting her chair as close to the bed as she could.

Herself opened her eyes and examined her. "You're not the biggest disappointment in me life," she said. "I just want you to know that."

Mary-Kate bristled. She had come to bring her gran comfort in her last hours, not to be insulted. "I should hope not."

"Don't get your nose out of joint," she wheezed. "I'm telling all me loved ones the same thing, makes them a little more competitive, a little less proud. Closer to the heavens that way."

"What a gift."

"It's all I have." She motioned to the corner. "That and me cursed rocker. Should have known it would be me demise. The thing has always been a point of pride. And what does the bible say about pride?"

"That it comes before a fall."

Herself touched the side of her nose. "Exactly."

Mary-Kate could have told her that wasn't the spirit of the verse, but why tax a dying woman? This once she could go unquestioned.

"I've always wanted to tell you something, me girl."

Mary-Kate leaned closer.

"You're the one thing that made me daughter becoming an O'Brien worthwhile."

————

Seeing his mother-in-law off was a sombre event that didn't appeal to Mr. O'Brien. "I didn't care what she had to say when she was living, why do you think I'd care what she has to say when she be dying?"

His wife placed her hands hard on his cheeks. "For a happy marriage."

"All marriages be happy. 'Tis spending time together that causes all the troubles."

Mrs. O'Brien grunted and pushed him toward the door. "Get on with you," she said.

"Well, I won't believe a word she has to say. She's not cared for me, and I won't pretend any different now."

"Do as you like, but for now I suggest you get in there. She's waiting."

Fumbling with his bowler, Mr. O'Brien made his way towards the deathbed. The room was bright, and the curtains were open, but with a closed window and the old woman's hacking coughs, it felt stifling and stale. "What took you so long?" Herself croaked. "Thought I'd die if you lingered about?"

Mr. O'Brien turned to leave.

"We're not through. That's not all I have to say." She cleared her throat. "You're not the biggest disappointment in me life. I just want you to know that."

A look of relief crossed Mr. O'Brien's face. "'Tis the most pleasant thing you ever said to me. I'll leave now and savour the memory. Besides, I don't want to wear you out. 'Twould be selfish of me."

"Too late. Time has beat you to it. Take a seat, I won't take long."

It took a while for Mr. O'Brien to bend his legs. The smell of death seemed stronger the lower he went.

"I have nothing to say about you. Hope you're not disappointed. Just can't imagine you will get any better with time. It's Mary-Kate that troubles me. She's not meant to be a nun. I feel it in me bones. She hasn't even found her feet yet. Nothing but misery can come of it. You need to put an end to it."

"What do you think I've been doing?"

"Nothing. 'Tis me who took the tumble, broke me body and shortened me breath to keep her here. Why, I've prolonged me own death to keep her here. I can't prolong it any longer."

Mr. O'Brien nodded.

"I've not seen hide nor hair of you."

"Been deliberating at The Donnybrook. Didn't think you'd be needing me help."

The old woman rose a little higher in her bed. "I do now." She laid her hand over her son-in-law's. "We may have come from different sides of the track, but we both know what's best for this family."

He nodded again.

"It's for Mary-Kate to wed and have a wee one. A babe named after me."

"Herself?"

"No, Edna."

————

WHEN MR. O'BRIEN emerged from the Deadman's room, he looked a little grey in the face. His wife reached out and took his hand. "That wasn't so bad was it?"

"No," he said. "It wasn't. She feels as strongly about Mary-Kate as we do. Wish I'd talked to her earlier. Might have ended up liking the woman." He slid a finger along the rim of his bowler. "'Twill be roses for that one, not petunias or daisies like Father Connelly suggested."

"Roses?" Mrs. O'Brien questioned.

"Aye. A rose for every day she drew a breath. And a shamrock for the days we have to live without her. We'll need a greater measure of luck when she's gone."

————

IT WAS curiosity that drew Mrs. O'Brien back to her mother's side. She knew she should want to be there, gather whatever grains of wisdom the withered hag might have to offer before her last gasp. But want had little to do with it. It was curiosity that won the day. The fact that there hadn't been a brawl when her husband made his visitation was a miracle unto itself. And right now, there were precious few of those going around.

"Is that you?" Herself croaked.

"It is." Mrs. O'Brien pulled a chair to the bedside.

"You're not the biggest disappointment in me life," Herself said. "I just want you to know that."

"That's nice."

"Just because I'm dying doesn't mean I'm beyond kindness." Herself let out a death rattle. "But to tell you the truth, you're not the you I was hoping for."

"Who were you hoping for?"

"Any of your sisters would do, crawling on their bellies, begging for me mercy. It'd be music to me ears." She coughed. "Send in one of the posies. They can feather dust me nostrils and chase away the staleness of this place."

Mrs. O'Brien rolled her eyes. "What am I to do with you?"

"Besides locking me away and waiting for me breath to desert me?"

"Yes. Besides that."

Herself didn't respond. Her gazed fixed somewhere beyond the room in which they sat. Her lips parted and closed again, indecision rising. "I've been meaning to tell you," she reached over and pinched Mrs. O'Brien a little too hard on the cheek, "I want to give you something to remember me by. Wash away any sadness between us." She folded her hands across her chest and closed her eyes as if readying herself for the coffin. "That great oaf of yours isn't so bad. I've been watching him, thinking he was the fool that Tenpenny woman wrote about in the paper, off chasing some skirt. As much as it pains me to say it, I was mistaken. Couldn't believe I'd not seen it with me own eyes, but the lout doesn't walk with the same spry step he did when he was pleasing the masses."

Mrs. O'Brien brought a hand to her mouth. "Sweet Jesus. How many women did he please?"

"Just one that I be aware of, but she wasn't tiny." Herself

raised a tired eyebrow. "That being said, it was years ago, and who be counting?"

It wasn't a conversation that would cause most to weep for joy, yet that was exactly what Mrs. O'Brien wanted to do. Hours of imaginings had occupied her days — of young women with slim waists and long lashes giving him sons and wearing ropes of pearls without feeling ridiculous. She hated the very thought of them, envisioned sneaking into their bedchambers at night and branding them with scarlet letters. Mrs. O'Brien gave her mother a half smile and let out a breath. It was a breath she'd been holding since the day she'd buried her first little one, hoping he'd be warm enough in his white box. "I've been so worried, ma. I thought I was to lose the both of them."

Herself sniffed. "I'd been relieved, meself. The lout bothering someone else with his late-night urgings."

Mrs. O'Brien sank deeper into the chair as her mother rambled on. In all the years she'd been saddled with Herself as a mother, the woman had not shown such grace. Why so charitable now, when the end was near? It had to be a ruse, an assurance so she'd let down her guard. It niggled at Mrs. O'Brien. How could she trust this woman? As long as she could remember, the old bat never went out of her way to be kind. In fact, quite the opposite was true.

It was as if Herself read her thoughts. "Let me give you this one thing. Let me die a kindly ma. One whose grave is covered with costly flowers, and paid mourners come weekly to weep over me demise."

"Is that why you're telling me this, for paid mourners and flowers?"

"I'd be lying if I said it wasn't, and only a fool would lie this close to the grave. But it's not me only reason."

"And your other?"

"That would be wee Edna. The two of you will have to pull

together for her sake. And you only can do that if the truth be known."

Mrs. O'Brien hesitated. She wanted to believe. She had to. If she did, for once she could rest in her mother's shadow. She'd waited a lifetime for that. Closing her eyes, she took a breath. The old bat had to be more than a maven of misery. "All right," she said. "I'll try. But who's wee Edna?"

"Never mind that now. What's important is what is, and what will be. Deep down, you know it to be so."

Mary-Kate dressed and packed in silence. There wasn't much to take — a hair brush, her gran's old broach and some photographs. Everything else was filler. Her mother was busy down the hall arguing with the posy sisters who were balking at cleaning the Deadman's room. They claimed her gran's essence was still there, as someone had neglected to cover the mirrors. Mrs. O'Brien seemed to be of the same mind, as she refused to cross the threshold as well, which made it difficult to collect the body and plan the wake.

Looking around one last time, Mary-Kate picked up her carpet bag, stuck out her chin and stepped into the hallway. She looked towards the Deadman's room, where her gran lay cold and stiff and her mother pushed a posy sister across the threshold. Mary-Kate gave a half smile, turned the other way and descended the stairs.

She didn't pause long enough for goodbyes. She wouldn't know what to say and didn't think she could stomach it if she did. Her gran's passing had set her on her heels. She 'hadn't been expecting the emptiness, and wasn't quite sure how to embrace it. The only thing that brought her comfort was a verse

Paddy had whispered to his graveyard-boy. '*Tis a fearful thing to love what death can touch. A fearful thing to love, to hope, to dream, to be — to be, and oh to lose.* She'd asked him where he heard it. He wrinkled his brow and said he wasn't sure. Such a thing of beauty from a baggy-pants boy. Mary-Kate repeated the verse. If anyone could bring aching joy, it was her gran. And now it was all Mary-Kate could do to get away from it.

The route to the convent was unmemorable. If there were birds songs, she couldn't recall. If a gent had tipped his cap, she didn't acknowledge him. Her life, as far as she was concerned, was over. Now it was just a matter of living out her days.

At the door of the convent, Sister Mary-Frances met her. They greeted one another with a nod, and Mary-Kate dutifully followed the other to the cell that had been prepared. She paused on the threshold and caught her breath. This would be her new sanctuary, unwelcoming as it was. Stepping into the room, Mary-Kate shut the door, sank into her cot and wept.

M ary-Kate didn't just make an impression on Paddy. The lads in the pub nearly climbed on top of each other to get a better look. It wasn't often they were on hand for a virgin sacrifice. They were in a heap by the window when Mr. O'Brien entered.

"Did you see that?" asked Keen.

"Aye. I did," returned his brother. "But I wouldn't mind seeing it again."

Mr. O'Brien pushed the boys away from the window. "She's behind locked doors now. It won't do ya any good sniffin' around. Besides, we only have room for one womanizing-care-taker in The Donnybrook. I suggest the lot of ya put your tongues back into your mouths and go back to your seats."

With a little grumbling, the boys cleared the window. They removed their caps, and one by one the line of men bowed their heads. "Sorry for your loss," each said in turn. "The Mrs. must be beside herself."

Mr. O'Brien nodded back, not allowing any show of emotion to betray him. "She's at a loss all right," he said. "Have to build an ark with all her blubbering. We're bound to float away. Burnt toast at breakfast, tears. Pillows left unfluffed, tears. Pigeons pooping on the windowsill, tears. I tell ya, a woman's heart is the strangest thing. 'Twould baffle ," Mr. O'Brien paused. He couldn't think of who it would baffle, but the men here wouldn't question him. "Ya fill in that last bit yourselves, gents," he said. "I can't do all the philosophizing."

The group consulted one another, and after a little back and forth Keen stepped forward. "'Twould baffle a man such as yourself."

"Good enough," Mr. O'Brien said, ordering a pint and taking his seat.

Father Connelly was already seated at their round table. "Glad ya joined us."

"Didn't have a choice. If it hadn't been for Breasal, wouldn't have known me Mary-Kate had left. She was at the convent before I could catch her and drag her back home. Would have locked her in the Deadman's room if I had me way."

"I'm sure she'd have liked that."

"It's better than where she's gone, and I have to say I'm a little uneasy about the whole thing, I am. Not just me daughter entering the church — that's bad enough — but involving the lad wasn't me best idea."

Father Connelly patted the back of the other's hand. "He wasn't even your second best idea, and that's saying something."

"That very well might be." Mr. O'Brien shook his head. "For the life of me, I don't know why she's gone. We've been getting along better. Since her gran's death, there's been no strife. Haven't even spoke. It's like she got up one morning, packed a bag and walked out the door."

"When did this happen?"

"Why, this morning, o' course." He looked towards the convent. "Did ya not see her?"

"I did." The priest scratched his chin. "I wasn't sure it wasn't a ruse. Laid a bet on it."

Mr. O'Brien ignored his friend. "Me wife is at home waiting for me now. Laying out her ma, and heartbroken that none of me ploys worked. How can I look her in the eye when I know I've let a fox into the henhouse?"

"Oh, I wouldn't worry about that. Ya've carried out many a deception that hasn't come to light."

"Name one."

"Your wedding. She hasn't found out about that little fiasco, has she now?"

"I'd forgotten about that." Mr. O'Brien sank deeper into his chair. "After all these years it hardly crossed me mind. But now ya've reminded me, I'll have to fret about that too." The colour faded from his face. His marriage proposal to Mrs. O'Brien may have been hasty, and he may even have insisted on eloping, but he'd had his reasons. There was no doubt about his fondness for the woman, but if she discovered the truth, fondness would do little to appease her. The hurt she would feel fell heavy upon him. Had she guessed the elopement was to win a bet with a mate to be the first to wed, she would never have done it. Mr. O'Brien knew it for a fact. They wouldn't have shown up the first day of their honeymoon at the same mate's wedding, standing arm in arm as man and wife.

"Paddy will give Sister Mary-Frances a run for her money. Take me word for it." Father Connelly made the sign of the cross.

The little priest's words didn't bring Mr. O'Brien any peace. Sweat speckled the lines of his forehead. "What if me wife finds out? Even worse, Mary-Kate?"

"No use wringing your hands about it now, is there? Let the pendulum swing. I'm most certain ya'll keep your head."

"Aye. But after it's swung, there may be no reason to have what little is left of me head."

The men sipped their pints and watched Paddy out the pub window. From what they could tell, the lad seemed to be enjoying himself, despite having to lay his hand to menial tasks. He waved to them every so often, and when Sister Mary-Frances was around, Paddy situated himself in such a way that they had a clear view.

"He's making her too angry," said Mr. O'Brien. "She'll regret she listened to ya and hired him at all. And if I know me sister, she'll find some reason to toss him."

"Oh, she regrets her decision all right, I can guarantee ya that. But she'll not throw him out."

"I wouldn't be so sure." Mr. O'Brien finished his pint and turned back to the window. "The woman's got a heart of stone."

"That she may," Father Connelly grinned, "but God forgive me, I've intervened a little more than was intended."

"Intervened? What are ya talking about?"

"Are ya losing your mind? I've already told ya, remember? I asked your sister about the new caretaker. Said I'd be disappointed if she didn't treat him as Christ did Mary Magdalene. Not that I think he should wash her feet with fine perfume and dry it with his hair, mind ya. That wouldn't be fitting, though I've thought about doing it meself on many a cold night. But when it came to Paddy, she got her back up, just like I knew she would. Insisted she'd only had the boy's best interests in mind. Ya watch. She'll go out of her way to prove me wrong."

Slamming his hands on the table, Mr. O'Brien shouted, "Ya told me no such thing. I'd remember something like that. Besides, ya promised not to get involved. If I can't take ya at your word Father, what good are ya?"

Father Connelly crossed his arms and stared hard at his

companion. "Do ya remember when you came to your last confession?"

"Aye."

"And do ya recall what was said?"

Mr. O'Brien thought for a moment, scratched his head, and looked sheepish. "Ya told me ya had intervened."

Since the evening Mr. O'Brien had first approached Paddy about entering the convent, he'd reversed positions with Father Connelly. The priest was now fully in favour of the deception, while Mr. O'Brien feared it might be the end of him. The turnaround for Father Connelly came when he saw the advantage of having Paddy roam the church grounds, stirring up difficulties for the English invader.

"Anyone with eyes in his head and a soul in his body can see me troubles weigh as heavy on me as yours on ya. An English priest can hardly mouth the words, and it burns me bum just saying it."

"There's no comparison," Mr. O'Brien brayed. "And I'll not sit here and listen to ya spout such nonsense."

"I'll spout whatever nonsense I like. But ya think my heart isn't breaking as yours? To have your sister, and her immeasurable girth, seek out an Englishman, when I've waited a lifetime for her to cast her eye in me direction, and tremble beneath me — why, the very thought brings me to me knees. The woman may not walk in beauty like the night, but she walks. And to me that's all that matters."

Although it was against his former judgement, the argument somewhat appeased Mr. O'Brien. Lacing his fingers together he leaned back. "I'm listening."

"'Tis like sending us a plague," Father Connelly began. "I wrote back telling the diocese so, but they won't hear of it. Think I don't know me own flock. I'll show them."

"Ya do that, Father."

"Aye. I will. And I'll be damned if I don't run him off. There's no place in this parish for an invader of Ireland." Father Connelly paused to collect himself. "And worse than that, I can't open me heart to him. The braggart thinks Sister Mary-Frances is his gift from heaven. Can ya imagine that? His gift. And the two have plans to close down The Donnybrook."

Unlacing his fingers, Mr. O'Brien pulled in his legs and sat up. "This is worse than I thought. Not as weighted as mine, mind ya, but worse than I thought. Trying to shut down our wee little establishment. The lads won't like it, they'll be fit to be tied."

"That's what I thought. I'll leave the intruder to run the convent, I will. He'll have his hands full. Instructed Paddy to be himself, as much of a scoundrel as he can be. If the place is going to fall apart, it might as well be under the direction of an English imbecile."

"It's a sound plan, if I say so meself," Mr. O'Brien mused, but after some thought his brow furrowed. "What about me Mary-Kate?"

"Don't worry, It's all part of me plan. She won't last long."

P addy shut the workshop door and set down the hoe. It had been a good day, for he was able to irritate Sister Mary-Frances and Father Albright in one fell swoop. Couldn't have done better if he planned it. Flying by the seat of his pants was always something Paddy excelled at. Being a Fitzpatrick had its benefits, even at a convent.

A succession of sneezes interrupted Paddy's musings, bringing him back to his present surroundings. They weren't his. He looked around the empty workshop, and his fingers twitched as he searched. The closet was the only place large enough to hide an intruder. He tapped on the door before opening it, but no sound betrayed whatever trespasser lurked inside. Taking a step back, Paddy considered the situation. If he opened the door it might bring trouble. If he didn't, he'd deny his curiosity, something he hated doing. "Trouble it is," he said, turning the handle and yanking open the door. Mary-Kate almost fell out of the crowded closet, blinking like a blind mole. With an unlit cigarette dangling between her lips, she gave him a stiff smile. "What can I do for you, my son?"

Paddy leaned closer, examining Mary-Kate more thoroughly. "What would ya like to be doing for me, Mary-Kate?"

She thumped him in the chest. "What kind of girl do you take me for?"

"The kind that hides in closets and smokes cigarettes."

Bringing one shoulder to her ear, Mary-Kate blushed. "It's not lit."

"But ya were thinking about lighting it."

"Well, I have to if I'm going to discourage my aunt. If the church rejects me..."

Paddy's finger brushed the tip of his nose. "Ya won't be breaking your mother's promise."

"Exactly."

The two considered each other. For a moment, Paddy thought about getting into the closet with her and closing the door. It was an out-of-the-way place to get lost in, as was the workshop itself. The building was so full of things to be fixed, along with the tools to fix them, that it took a good search to find anything. It was hidden from the street, so Paddy utilized it often. Mostly to roll around on the floor to cover himself with sawdust and shavings. A man worked all day to look like that; it took him minutes.

Mary-Kate mimed a drag. "I was wondering if you'd show up. And I have to admit I'm kind of relieved. Can't imagine being found out by anyone else."

"The pleasure has been mine."

"So, what brings a nice boy like you, to a place like this?"

"I work here."

"You?"

"To win a wager," he shrugged, "and avoid the constabulary."

"The two finest reasons I've heard of." She lifted a shoulder and rolled her eyes. "I'm here," she stifled a sob, "because my gran died."

"I didn't know."

"If she'd lived I'd still be sitting at her deathbed whiling away my days. Changing her bedpan, mopping her brow. I know it doesn't sound like much, but after a few hours within these walls, it is ever so appealing. My gran would have known what to do. Probably have smoked this cigarette and flicked the ash devil-may-care. Can't you see it? Now I'm on my own."

"What about your parents?"

"My parents? You mean the ones who gave me away? I don't want to talk about them!" She gave a half smile. "Not very good company, am I?"

"Since I've come here I've spent me days with nuns and priests. Considering that, ya're a sight for sore eyes."

"Thanks."

"Don't thank me lass. 'Tis the truth."

"It's times like this," Mary-Kate looked him over and stepped closer, "that I realize how much I have to lose."

"Aye, and I how much I could gain," Paddy returned.

Mary-Kate passed Paddy her unlit cigarette. "And what would you like to gain, Mr. Fitzpatrick?"

"What would ya be willing to lose?"

Mary-Kate raised an eyebrow. "You are a dark horse."

"Aye," said Paddy, bending over and brushing the sawdust from her skirt. "Maybe we can pull in the same direction."

"And what direction is that?"

Paddy placed the unlit cigarette back between Mary-Kate's lips and brought his body closer to hers. He felt her breath fall on him. Before he could go any further, Sister Mary-Frances bellowed Mary-Kate's name from outside.

"She calls," he said. The nun yowled again. "And she be getting closer."

"I'd better hearken." Mary-Kate took the cigarette from between her dry lips, slipped it into her skirt pocket and headed in the direction of the voice. "But I think I'll show my true colours another day, when I know what they are." As she disappeared, Paddy watched her shaking herself, trying to get rid of any evidence of sawdust.

Nothing could bring Mrs. O'Brien's blood to the boil like family, and the family that were stoking the fire at the moment were her sisters. "They're not coming!" Mrs. O'Brien fumed upon opening the telegram. "Claims that the weather's not conducive for travel."

Mr. O'Brien snatched the dispatch from her hand. "Not conducive? We haven't had a drop of rain in over a week."

"That's the problem. They say it's overdue and they don't have proper footwear."

"The lot live across town. At a brisk pace they could be here in less than an hour."

"You're preaching to the choir, Mr. O'Brien."

All the hours she had spent fussing over the dead woman seemed for naught. Herself hadn't looked that good in years. And in spite of the unseemliness of it all, Mrs. O'Brien wanted to show off her handiwork.

Her husband looked to the street. "Doesn't look like anyone is coming. Good thing I popped down this morning and paid Donavan a visit. Told him his Mrs. was welcome to come by and ply her trade — two bits for a goiter prediction. They'll be lining up around the block. If we place her by the coffin, she should be able to suss out who will survive the year." He stuck a thumb in a vest buttonhole, proud of himself.

The first response that came to mind was to call him a great oaf, but Mrs. O'Brien squelched it. There might be some value in his approach. What would look worse in the societal pages, an unattended wake, or free-spirited parlour games? She wasn't sure. "Do you think that was wise?"

"The old bat would have liked it."

There was more truth in the statement than Mrs. O'Brien cared to admit. The most pressing concern now was whether Mary-Kate would attend. It wasn't something they had discussed before she snuck off to the convent. But she couldn't think about that now, or she'd burst into tears and give her husband one more reason to hound her about her weepy state of late. "I'm going to check on the preparations in the kitchen," she said, handing him her empty cup and saucer.

"What will I be needing these for?"

"A happy marriage."

The kitchen was a bustle of activity, Mae a sergeant major at its helm. Mrs. O'Brien couldn't help but examine the counter-tops and be pleased. Crustless sandwiches, bread and butter pickles, and dainties of more varieties than she cared to count. It was enough to choke a horse, but since no horses were at hand, Miss Tenpenny would have to do.

A commotion brought Mrs. O'Brien back to the sitting room. The front door had barely closed on their first guests when the knocking began again. She called the posy sisters who, in a matter of minutes, disappeared under piles of wraps and coats. Mrs. O'Brien could feel the twins' disapproval. They were sputtering under their loads, and she wasn't of the mind to offer them relief.

"Put them in me study," Mr. O'Brien instructed the girls.

"Why would they do that?" Mrs. O'Brien intervened. "More handy here, for those who want to come and go."

"Look at the pair of them," Mr. O'Brien spread his arms, "they're bending under the weight."

"Good." Mrs. O'Brien's voice hardened. "They've been spiteful ever since Herself came to stay and have only grown worse with her end. Thinks the likes of her wasn't good enough to be sleeping between clean sheets or laid out in refinement." She looked the girls up and down. "And to top it all off, they think I was too daft to notice. The burden will do them good. Put a civil tongue in their heads."

"I'm all for civil tongues." Mr. O'Brien turned and waded into the swelling crowd.

The sounds of an Irish wake, of laughter and merriment, reminded Mrs. O'Brien of her old life — the one before the fancy drapes and hand-crafted furnishings. To be truthful, part of her missed it. She stood in the middle of the milieu, feeling torn. To join in, or skirt around the edges? If she participated, she might never regain her hard-fought parity, and if she didn't, something deep in her would shrivel. She was in the middle of her indecision when a stranger, a little out of breath, entered the family residence without knocking.

"Biddy Fitzpatrick," she said, introducing herself to the posy sisters.

Mrs. O'Brien tugged on the stranger's arm. "Never mind those two. They're of no importance. Can I be of service? You look lost."

"I've never been lost a day in me life." Biddy rose on her toes. "Where's the man of the house? I've come to collect me son."

"And who is your son?"

"Patrick Fitzpatrick. O'Brien will know him."

"The boy from the paper?"

"Oh, you know him as well?"

"Not formally," Mrs. O'Brien frowned.

"As I said before, your man will. He's quite a cad. Mr. O'Brien, that is. Though I haven't seen him since that night in the rain. We did have a laugh."

Mrs. O'Brien could feel her hackles rise at this intruder, not just for referring to her husband with such familiarity, but for believing her mother when she'd said Mr. O'Brien wasn't stepping out on her. It had been against her better judgement, yet she'd done it. Let her hope overtake her. She would never do that again. "You're the woman from the paper?" she asked, her hands balling into fists.

"Guilty as charged."

Her nostrils flared. "You're not that attractive."

"And you're not that thin," Biddy fired back.

Mrs. O'Brien gasped. All her planning and fussing to give her mother a proper send off was now for naught. She wanted to call for Herself, so that the two of them could make short work of this strumpet. Drive her from Tnúth as the snakes from Ireland. The only thing stopping her, besides a dead mother, was Miss Tenpenny lurking about. The less fodder she could give that woman the better.

"Biddy, may I call you Biddy?" Mrs. O'Brien asked without waiting for a response. "If you haven't come here to show your respects or get a goiter prediction, you'll have to leave. Come back when the man of the house, *my* man, has time to dismiss you properly."

Biddy didn't seem to hear a word she said. "Thanks, but I'll keep me coat. Don't want anyone to go through me pockets. Can never be too careful in places like this." She pushed past Mrs. O'Brien. "Oh, looky there — didn't know you'd be handing out fancy pastries."

Mrs. O'Brien trailed the younger woman, determined to

have her tossed, but the stranger flitted about like a pickpocket, impossible to pin down.

"Where is she?" A new voice thundered above the mix.

Mrs. O'Brien turned to see a brute with a face so covered with coarse hair it was hard to make out his features. Her own Mr. O'Brien would have cowered in his presence. Gathering herself, she stalked back to the door. "Who are you referring to?" She covered her nose with her hand to lessen his stench. "This is a respectable gathering, with respectable people."

A large hairy hand pointed to the other side of the room, to where Herself's coffin rested between two large chairs. Staring into the casket was Biddy Fitzpatrick. Mrs. O'Brien was sure she saw the vixen pocket her mother's brooch.

"I've not sent her here," the large man roared. "What kind of cat house is this? Poaching another man's property!"

"This is not a cat house," Mrs. O'Brien yelled. "And I'll not have anyone say otherwise."

"Pardon me French. Using fancy words are you?" He cleared his throat. "Who's the proprietor of this brothel?"

"No one!"

"Let me offer me services then." He bowed slightly at the waist. "Black-Hearted John is the name."

Mrs. O'Brien's humiliation was complete. She looked from the black-hearted brute to the posy sisters, knowing they'd heard every word and were drafting up a whole new list of judgments.

"Mary-Kate!" Mr. O'Brien's voice boomed, bringing Mrs. O'Brien out of her mortification. She turned towards the commotion. Mr. O'Brien had swept their daughter up in his arms and was swinging her through the air as he had when she was a small child, knocking over two guests waiting for their fortunes. "You've come back, lass. I knew we couldn't be parted."

By the time Mrs. O'Brien reached the pair, Mary-Kate had

pulled free from her father and was explaining that she'd come to the wake and couldn't stay long — Sister Mary-Frances was in hot pursuit.

"Let her try. That woman will have to pry you from me cold, dead hands."

"That can be arranged."

Mrs. O'Brien stiffened. It was the same voice she had heard in the kitchen weeks ago, the same one that had opened this Pandora's Box. Sister Mary-Frances. Losing all composure, Mrs. O'Brien turned and flew at the nun. "Tenpenny be damned," she screamed, grabbing hold of the other's habit, ripping it from her head. The act exposed a crop of ragged hair, as if it had been cut in the dark — a mark of self-loathing. "You'll not be threatening anyone under this roof. Not again."

The nun's striking resemblance to her brother elicited gasps.

Mrs. O'Brien took a step back and dropped the black wimple to the floor, a little shocked by her own behaviour, as well as the results.

Snatching up the wimple, Sister Mary-Frances fixed it back to its former position, though slightly askew. "I'm not getting into this with you today," she said, shoving Mrs. O'Brien roughly to the floor. "I've come for my postulant."

Mr. O'Brien stepped in front of his daughter and his sprawling wife. "Well, get it and leave this house now."

"I will. Mary-Kate is my postulant, you idiot."

———

WHEN THE DISHES were cleared and crumbs swept away, Mrs. O'Brien considered the disaster that was her mother's wake. The posy sisters had caved under their burdens — first one, then the other — toppling over as felled trees. Black-Hearted John had chased Biddy Fitzpatrick throughout the house, until threats of being carted off by the constabulary sent the pair of them careening down the street. In the midst of it all, Mary-Kate left with that horrible nun, despite her protests and that of her husband. The girl was as small as Mrs. O'Brien had ever seen her. A wee, broken lamb.

S ister Mary-Frances cracked her knuckles as she readied for morning prayers. She couldn't remember the last time she felt this much fervour. She even had to steady her hands when she put on her headpiece, like some skittish bride. It made her wrinkle her brow in disgust. What was to become of her if something as simple, as commonplace, as innocuous, as a new priest got her ruffled? He pulled her thoughts into a thousand pieces until she lost her place altogether. Still, she couldn't recall when eagerness so thoroughly filled her. Perhaps in her younger days, when God could be compelled and persuaded. It had been years since such amity overwhelmed her, but it was a welcome intrusion.

Upon leaving her cell, Sister Mary-Frances checked herself. There was no need to thunder down the halls. Her steps needed to be measured, giving others the illusion that today was no different than any other day. But when passing Sister Bernadette in the hall, she clapped her so soundly on the back the young nun toppled to the floor. Stepping over the pile of jumbled robes, Sister Mary-Frances continued towards the chapel. "Keep up," she called over her shoulder. "There will be time enough to contemplate the goodness of God."

"Yes, Sister," came the muffled whimper.

As she entered the chapel, she spied Father Albright. He was an early riser, another check mark in his column. Not many reached the altar before her. Despite his nationality, the priest was beginning to appeal to her. He had more resolve than Father Connelly and wasn't inclined to roam with the locals. If it hadn't been for his slicked-back hair and bird-like features, she might have called him handsome, but then she had been in the convent for so many years she wondered if she'd lost perspective. As it was, with hair like that, she imagined he slid off his pillow in the morning and counted himself lucky to have stayed between the sheets at all.

"Father."

"Sister," Father Albright tilted back his head.

The nun scowled. There it was, the thing that burrowed under her skin, the way he addressed others, looking down his snout like a swaggering popinjay. If it irked her, she could only imagine the response at The Donnybrook — sweaty, tweed-clad yokels, half drunk, tilting back their heads and plugging their noses. And the one who would mock Father Albright most was her very own brother. She was tempted to correct the young priest, ask him to temper his tone, but she knew it was futile. Years of practice must have been employed to produce a sound that pungent. Her sole choice was to disregard his antics for the moment and shift her thoughts to the morning's activities. "Joining us for early morning Matins?"

The priest nodded. "Of course. Shall we wait for Father Connelly?"

"Oh, I suppose we could if you are willing to wait until doomsday. Was probably up half the night at The Donnybrook."

Father Albright pulled a pad of paper and pencil from his pocket and licked the lead. "Does he do that often?"

"Do what? Miss morning prayers or slip off to the pub?"

"Both."

"Yes."

"I can see why we need to burn that place down."

The nun smiled. "You're a man after my own heart. We're going to make a strong team." She rubbed her palms together. "I've kept track of his lack of devotions on a calendar in my office. How many years do you want to go back?"

As she enlightened Father Albright on Father Connelly's folly, Paddy strolled into the chapel and tipped his cap, as if he were on a Sunday turn. The nun and priest stiffened.

"The boy from Damascus." Father Albright narrowed his eyes. "What possessed him to become a caretaker?"

"Regrettably, another one of Father Connelly's shortcomings. He hired him, and I don't mind saying I think it was a mistake. For starters, there was the episode in the paper."

"What episode was that?" The priest's tongue darted out to lick his pencil lead.

"One that should never be repeated." Sister Mary-Frances shook her head. "There's something not right about that boy. He has no more intentions of finding God than I do of flying to the moon. A dog in the manger, put there to aggravate me."

"Maybe he was, Sister. But better to aggravate you than to lust after the innocent." Father Albright pointed to Mary-Kate who had entered the sanctuary.

Sister Mary-Frances looked from Mary-Kate to Paddy. They were on different sides of the chapel, each bowed in prayer. "True Father, but some days I'm not sure she is as innocent as she appears."

Father Albright shrugged. "Who are we to judge?"

The nun nodded. "Yes," she said. "It's good to have you here to bring back perspective. We must never judge."

No sooner had the words come out of her mouth than Paddy tossed what looked to be a rolled-up sock towards Mary-Kate. The foolish girl giggled.

Turning to the priest, Sister Mary-Frances growled, "Not to judge you say? Whose idea is that?"

"God's."

"Well, God never met Patrick Fitzpatrick!"

Pushing her sleeves past her elbows, she turned back towards Paddy, but he was gone. He had disappeared when she'd turned her back to talk to the priest.

Mrs. O'Brien peeked under the napkin covering the basket. Irish soda bread, oatmeal cookies and coffee cake. If Mae's baking didn't remind Mary-Kate of home, nothing would. Eyeing the cake, she hesitated before replacing the cloth. She should test it for its quality, pinch off a morsel from its underside. Who would be the wiser? She sucked her teeth. That was the first place Mary-Kate would check, for Mr. O'Brien was notorious for pinching bits of cake and hiding the evidence. She must love the girl considering all the sacrifices she made.

Stepping out in public was a prime example, especially after Miss Tenpenny's flogging. The shrew took notes on all the goiter predictions, named the most unseemly guests, and even went so far as to critique Herself's funeral attire. When her rant hit the paper there were snickers in the street. It had been years since she'd heard snickering, and Mrs. O'Brien cringed at the memory of it. The words flashed in front of her eyes.

If I'd known there would be entertainment, it began, *I would have worn my comfortable shoes. Those fit for a more common experience, like a jumble sale or a circus. But what can one expect from the*

O'Briens? Ever since he married that woman, the family's reputation has gone downhill.

Mrs. O'Brien shook herself free of the memory. It had forced her to re-examine everything — all the decisions she'd made, every threshold crossed and barrier climbed. And then there was Mary-Kate. Mrs. O'Brien wondered if her affections were sufficient. The girl must realize how much she loved her, ever since Mary-Kate came to her pink and naked, with lungs far too large for a babe, wailing louder than whelps twice her size. Mrs. O'Brien had loved her then and took her to the breast without hesitation. It was no different now. The girl could rail and rant, and she would still claim her proudly as her own. A statement that no longer applied to her husband.

The closer Mrs. O'Brien got to the convent, the more self-conscious she became of her attire. She felt like her daughter going to blasted confession. Tread-worn boots, a hobgoblin shawl, and a dress barely fit for the ragbag — a disguise in which she could be mistaken for the turnip cook's mother. In her tattered wrap, Mrs. O'Brien faked a limp as she travelled around to the far side of the building, careful not to attract attention. The only thing she was lacking was the tin cup for alms.

The ruse, although out of character, lightened Mrs. O'Brien in ways she hadn't felt for weeks. She slid through the streets of Tnúth with hardly a notice, as invisible as her costume intended, a poor beggar seen but never acknowledged. It was the only way she could get past the bloodhound at the convent door. She knew Sister Mary-Frances would thwart her every effort to converse with Mary-Kate, intercept and forbid her entrance. Even if she fell prostrate at the nun's feet, begging for mercy, there would be little pity. Gooseflesh prickled Mrs. O'Brien's arms as she envisioned the scenario. If there was a place of charity in Tnúth, the convent wasn't it.

Coming to a door partly obscured by vines and leaves, Mrs.

O'Brien hunched her shoulders and redraped her shawl over her head. She sniffed the air. Not a whiff of her nemesis, only the scent of dusty desperation. Rubbing her thumb across the inside of her fingers, she considered how she should proceed. A light rap would serve the purpose, no use letting all hell and yonder aware of her presence. She tapped on the rough wooden door. There was no discernible response. She tapped again. Nothing.

Mrs. O'Brien cursed aloud. Those nuns were deaf to all but the call of the cross. Giving up on tapping, she tried the handle and it gave way with ease. Mrs. O'Brien smiled. She'd barely passed the threshold when the new priest and Father Connelly came thundering towards her in the most unbecoming manner.

"There's one," Father Connelly clamoured, waving a fist full of rosary in her direction. "She comes here like clockwork." His cheeks were flushed with excitement.

Mrs. O'Brien stepped back towards the door, but Father Connelly was too quick for her and prevented her escape. Father Albright closed in on Father Connelly as if they were linked together in a three-legged race. It was not the greeting Mrs. O'Brien had anticipated, and she was further put out when the younger of the two grunted, letting his English gaze cover the length and width of her. Mrs. O'Brien dropped her shoulder and receded farther under her shawl.

"Sister Mary-Frances hasn't mentioned her," Father Albright said primly.

"Why would she? The woman works herself to the bone. Doesn't have time for riffraff." Father Connelly winked at Mrs. O'Brien, though too quickly to recognize who she was. "Come for your weekly blessing, have you?" He spoke to her as if she'd not only lost her hearing but was brain-addled too.

Mrs. O'Brien hunched her back as the older priest

rummaged through her basket. "We call her The Widow of Zarephath. Needs me to bless her meagre portion, so it will last her a week." Father Connelly made the sign of the cross and said something unintelligible.

"It's tiring," the old priest continued, turning back to Father Albright. "Performing all these miracles. Some call me Elijah." He poked the young priest in the chest. "You can write that down."

Father Albright kept his notebook securely in his pocket. He breathed deeply through the end of his pinched nose, as his hand reached out to take hold of Mrs. O'Brien's upper arm. "For a pauper, she seems rather plump."

Mrs. O'Brien stiffened. It was bad enough for an Irish soul to insult her, but for an English imposter, it was intolerable. She considered the weight of the basket on her arm. If she were to swing it sufficiently and with enough speed, she could thump the invader on his pate without spilling a crumb. "Plump my arse," she mumbled, sliding the basket from the crook of her arm to the palm of her hand. She was about to start her windup when Father Connelly intervened.

"'Tis me particular specialty, plump paupers." Father Connelly steadied the basket before turning back to Father Albright. "We'll check in on the lepers later this afternoon, shall we?"

"There are lepers in New Brunswick?"

"Well, not real lepers, mind you. Just parishioners with warts. But you must give them full marks for trying."

Mrs. O'Brien was still fuming when the two Fathers disappeared down the hall out of earshot. If she weren't preoccupied with Mary-Kate, she'd drive the English snake out of the church herself. The nerve of the man. If Herself was still about and not laying stiff next to her father in Tnúth's graveyard, as she'd done

all their married life, she'd ask her for an old Celtic curse — one
the church wouldn't recognize. See how the simpering dolt dealt
with the Old Ways, the ones outside his pious purview. Mrs.
O'Brien savoured the thought. It had been hardly any time at all,
and already she was missing Our Lady of Blessed Misery. But
who'd believe her? Not her husband surely, who deserved an old
Celtic curse of his own. She and Herself had always been at
odds. "See what you've done to me, you old bat?" she whispered.
"Not going to visit your grave 'til you loosen your grip. Don't say
I didn't warn you."

She scratched her backside. The rough-hewn cloth wasn't
conducive to her upper-class sensitivities. Perhaps she could call
on Mary-Kate's buttons. There might be some use for them yet.

With a sniff, Mrs. O'Brien shifted the basket back up her
arm. She was here for Mary-Kate, she reminded herself. But
where to start the search? Squinting her eyes, she examined her
surroundings. There were dozens of rooms, evident by the
number of doors that marked the corridor. And that wasn't
considering the out of the way places, the ones only known to
the residents. The task was more than she'd bargained for. She
sucked her teeth.

"Me girl, where are you hiding yourself?" Her voice was
barely above a whisper. Her shawl slipped back, and she
straightened her spine. There was no use hiding now. If there
was any residue of affection left, surely Mary-Kate could feel her
presence as likely as hear her call. "Mary-Kate?"

She strode down the hall, opening doors and calling into the
empty rooms. The hollowness of the place was all that received
her. No nuns or postulants scurried from the great unknown to
shout rebukes. It seemed there wasn't a living thing within the
convent walls. A thought Mrs. O'Brien hadn't allowed wiggled
its way into her consciousness. She brought a hand to her

mouth. What if Mary-Kate had been sent away, out of her reach? To some moth-eaten place, not to be heard from again? Mrs. O'Brien braced herself against the wall and let her basket drop to the floor. If that were the case, she didn't know how she could survive it.

Mary-Kate consulted the list nailed to her cell door. Her aunt had given it to her, revising it each time Mary-Kate met with her disapproval. Mary-Kate had more meetings with disapproval than anyone who passed through the convent's door. Her list had been revised at least a dozen times, leaving it marred, scratched, and requiring divine revelation just to decipher it. Running her finger across the page, Mary-Kate narrowed her eyes. Confession. She frowned. Scheduling confession was inconvenient. In her mind, if one didn't schedule a time to sin, it was ludicrous to think one should pencil in time to confess. At her first opportunity, she would tell Father Connelly so. Perhaps they could play a rousing game of *I Spy* on her trips to the confessional.

It would be better than repeating fictional transgressions, like feeling envious of the length of Sister Bernadette's fingers and how elegant they looked when the nun turned the pages of the hymnal. Or how grieved she was at her lack of empathy for the children of Persia. Not that Mary-Kate knew anything about Persia, let alone its children, but she liked the way the word lifted off her tongue, as if she were a foreign operative on some clandestine mission. Still, that was another thing to repent — her indifference. For now, her only objective was to see how many offences she could contrive before Father Connelly fell asleep. Once the old man had drifted off, she confessed her feelings for Paddy. The things they did, the things she thought about doing. It worked better for both of them that way. She had a clean conscience and the father didn't have a stroke.

Father Albright would be an entirely different matter. Confessing to him was like dealing with a shiftless rodent, one who dodged both trap and poison. Mary-Kate sidestepped him whenever possible. But if by chance he should take residence on the other side of the partition, she would consult him on the mating practices of carrier pigeons and whether it was wicked to discuss such things.

"Forgive me, Father, I have sinned." She lowered her head and made the sign of the cross, one ear cocked towards the screen, hoping the smaller of the two priests resided beyond the divide.

"What can I do for ya, me daughter?"

Mary-Kate squinted and brought her face closer to the partition. "Paddy?"

"Aye."

"What are you doing? Aren't you supposed to be fixing something?"

"I'm giving Albright a little time to himself. Here to grant some wishes."

"Priests don't grant wishes."

"Are ya sure?"

"Yes."

Paddy scratched his chin. "Ya should've told me that before. I've granted six this very morning."

"Paddy!"

"What?"

"You should get out of there before you get caught. Father Albright isn't an even-tempered man."

"He'll thank me someday."

"No, he won't."

"He should. The last time I was here..."

"The last time you were here?"

"Aye. There was an old lady convinced she was a sinner, she was. The poor dear wept and crossed herself like mad." Paddy lowered his voice and leaned into the confessional wall. "There's not enough Hail Mary's to cover that kind of guilt."

"What did she do?"

"Swore at her dog. She asked me to forgive her. Can ya imagine such a thing?"

"What did you do?"

"Told her I couldn't forgive her in a month of Sundays. 'Twas her dog she should be asking. She said she wasn't going to ask any animal for forgiveness. So, I told her to buy it a pearl neck-lace, and she did. Pearls before swine, pearls before canines, what's the difference?" Paddy puffed up with pride. "Any fool could do this job."

Mary-Kate smiled. "Well, not any fool."

Paddy chuckled and leaned back. "Mary-Kate?"

"Yes."

"Come over here and sit on me knee. I'll give ya something to confess."

"Patrick!"

"Ya don't have to worry. Albright is out in the graveyard changing the wooden grave markers. He'll be there for a while."

"You didn't."

"Aye, I did. Did it for the boys in the pub. And Albright's time is almost respectable. Mind ya, he's yet to catch Sister Mary-Frances."

Mary-Kate winced. "You'll never make it into the church."

"I don't care." Paddy sighed as he got up to leave. "This place is a bit musty for me."

Paddy was almost at the door when Father Albright came in wiping his hands on his robes. "You again!" he screeched. "I thought we'd talked about this! You're not to be in the sanctuary without supervision."

Paddy smirked and raced past him. "Aye. I see your memory's not failing ya. Just wanted to check to see if anything had changed." He pointed to the confessional. "Was keeping the seat warm for ya. Don't thank me now. Give yourself time to let the gratitude build."

Paddy looked up at the stained-glass window he was supposed to be cleaning. "How many Stations of the Cross could there be?" He shook his head. "One window I can see, but fourteen? That's just bragging." Paddy tucked the rag into his back pocket. Polishing them would only be encouraging frivolous bravado. How could he be part of that? Stepping back, Paddy stopped to admire the work he hadn't done and wondered if his lack of effort would go unnoticed.

"It is a thing of beauty."

"I suppose," Paddy said, a little startled. He turned to see Father Albright hovering behind him. "How long have ya been standing there? Slithering in like a snake, ya gave me a fright."

"I have been here long enough to see you hesitate to touch the divine. Don't blame you. It's too much for the common sort."

"Aye," Paddy said, handing Father Albright the dust rag. "And ya can't be any more common than me."

The priest took the cloth in hand. The look on Father Albright's face reminded Paddy of the first time he saw Peggy Murphy without her bottoms on. The awe was near identical. Paddy wanted to drape an arm across the other's shoulder and tell him he was a lost lamb, that he had missed a part of his youth that could not be replaced. That he had it ass backward, so to speak.

"What are you two up to?"

Paddy turned. "Oh, Sister Mary Francis, there ya are. The good Father here is showing me how to polish a virgin. Give her a good rub."

"I don't think you need instructions in that department." The nun grabbed the rag from the priest's hand and flung it at Paddy. "By the way you look at my niece you've had plenty of practice."

Paddy inclined his head towards the priest. "Good Sister, Father Albright's no different. I've seen him sneak a peek or two meself. That girl brings some life to those dark robes she does." He elbowed Sister Mary-Frances. "Now there's a nun. Just looking at that one gives a boy at least half a dozen reasons to repent. She swings her rosary as if it were a cheap string of pearls. Makes me think about becoming a priest meself. Can't look at a lass more purely than that."

Father Albright reddened and licked his lips.

"As ya can see," Paddy winked, "takes more than a few Hail Mary's to assuage that kind of guilt."

Sister Mary-Frances placed a hand on her ample hip. "Mary-Kate's not a nun. She is a postulant. Do you hear me? A postulant. I suggest you let her be one in peace."

"I will when Father Albright does, as ya already told me he's to be me godly example. Why, he's the one who told me Jesus was Irish. An Irish Jew, now that's a heavy cross to bear."

The priest shook himself from his stupor. "I did no such thing."

"No use being modest now, ya being me inspiration. Have me looking on our blessed saviour in a whole new light." Paddy waggled his eyebrows and began whistling *The Rising of the Moon*.

"Do you never stop?" Sister Mary-Frances threw her hands in the air. "I can hardly turn around without finding you up to your eyeballs in some kind of debauchery." She looked from Paddy to the priest. "I've been forbidden by the diocese, but Father Albright hasn't. Get him," she instructed her slippery side-kick.

Father Albright flung himself at Paddy. "Beelzebub!" he roared.

"I think he may be me cousin, but I will have to ask me gran. Hard to get to her in prison, and she's tight-lipped about that side of the family," Paddy said, sidestepping the mass of black robes as a matador would a bull. "If he is me kin, I swear I haven't seen him in years, but it's kind of ya to think of him. As I told Sister Mary-Frances this very morning, ya're a precious man if ever there was one."

"I am not precious," Father Albright said as he made another run at Paddy.

"Aye. That's because ya're not an Irish Jew, such as meself."

Paddy would have taken up caretaking earlier if he had known how invigorating it could be. "If you lift your skirts higher," Paddy advised, running backwards down the nave, "ya might be able to keep up."

Father Albright charged once more, running Paddy out of the church and onto its step. He seemed surprised at his victory and quickly slammed the large oak door and bolted it behind him.

"And how are ya going to explain," Paddy called through the barrier, "why the windows aren't clean? I ask ya that."

When the priest gave no response, Paddy headed for the graveyard. He couldn't have planned it better. Now he had time for his ritualistic switching of the wooden crosses, something he was sure Father Albright would grow to appreciate. When he finished, he made his way over to the section in which the orphans were buried.

"Been feeling a bit guilty," he said, by way of an apology. "Not that I've forgotten ya. I give ya me word, that will never happen. It's just that I've been a little preoccupied, chasing Irish skirts and having the English ones chase me back." Paddy took his place against a red maple, leaning on its rough trunk and stretching his legs out in front of him. "But enough about me. What shall we be talking about today?"

The little grave was silent.

Paddy cleared his throat. "Has that annoying Father Albright been bothering ya lately? I suppose not. Not way over here. If he does, let me know. I'll switch some more markers for him. He likes that. Keeps him limber." Paddy smiled and closed his eyes.

He imagined a small blond boy climbing out of the grave and onto his lap. The boy's blue eyes lit up in the sun. Paddy was glad for the company and loved whiling away the afternoon with him.

"Ya should have lived," he said. "The two of us would've had a time."

The little boy's eyes danced as Paddy spoke.

"A grand time."

Paddy's graveside visit lightened his mood. He took the steps to the convent two at a time, and when he slipped back among the nuns, it was as if he hadn't been missed. "Evening ladies," he said between verses of a saucy tune he'd picked up from his mother. He left out the risqué parts — those he whistled. Most of the Sisters found the song charming and didn't discourage him. In time, he even caught them humming the catchy ditty. "It's such a pretty song," they said. "Too bad you don't know all the words."

"**D**eo meo Jesu Christi, adoramus te, et dixi tibi gratias ago pro omnibus data est gratia estis hodie mihi. Offero tibi momenta somno nocte peto ut non peccetis. Latus meum ponam in medio sub pallio beatae." The nasally voice of Father Albright enunciated each syllable, drawing some out, dropping others short. Paddy restrained himself on his cot, holding back his Irish translations, and his mocking retorts. The priest cleared his throat and started again.

"Oh, for the love of God," Paddy rose on an elbow. "Get on with it man."

"Without all your interruptions," Father Albright explained, "I lost my place."

"Ya were well into your penance."

"I don't think so." The priest put a hand to his mouth. "My lips are quite dry."

With a groan, Paddy placed his pillow over his head. If it were possible he would suffocate himself — anything to get away from the monotonous drone. Every other evening he reveled in harassing the priest, it had become as much of his nightly ritual as the prayers were Father Albright's. But not this evening. This evening Paddy had other things to attend to.

"Mihi sta super me et custodiant vestra sanctis angelis in pace. Et benedictio tua sit super me. Amen." Paddy said, throwing his pillow as he finished the prayer.

Father Albright stiffened. "You know it?"

"I've been enduring it for weeks. Now lick your lips and call it a night."

By the time Father Albright finished and dissolved into his own version of sweet oblivion, Paddy was coming out of his skin. With his luck he'd missed his opportunity. Mary-Kate could have already drifted off, and the way that girl slept it would take a lot more than a little tapping on a window to wake her. He swore as he slipped out of bed and out of the rectory.

————

MARY-KATE SAT on the edge of her bed and surveyed her surroundings. Her gran was right, this was no place for her. But where was her place? Not at home, not with her parents. And certainly not at some finishing school. If she could she would ask her gran, or look at some obscure line from Lady Wilde's book on superstition. She 'hadn't thought she'd ever want to do that. Now she longed to.

As it was, where her aunt had dumped her there wasn't much to survey. Each evening she went through the same routine, and each evening she was disappointed by the result — hoping her initial appraisal had been misinformed, and rediscovering it had not. The room was small, with barely enough space for a bed, dresser, chair and night table. On the floor lay a rug so well-worn it was hard to make out it was braided. Mary-Kate hated the thought of putting her feet on it, not knowing what vermin's waste had been trodden into its fibers. If this was a measure of living an austere life, she wanted no part of it. Marginal refinements, as her father would say, were intolerable.

Flopping back on the bed, she examined the ceiling. Even the flop was disappointing — hard and lumpy. A spider had taken up residence in the corner. Even he seemed resigned to his predicament, spinning endlessly, until Mary-Kate was sure he was mad. In her other life, Mary-Kate would have insisted he be removed. Here, she was thankful for the company.

As for counting to pass the time, that was getting her nowhere. She had stopped counting days ago. Now she talked to the walls. "You may have my body, but you will never have my soul. And I don't care how long you tap on the glass." Mary-Kate lifted her head and looked towards the window. There was Paddy holding precariously to the vine-wrapped lattice.

She smiled. "What a fine kettle of fish you've gotten yourself in. You'd think you'd have learned."

Paddy tapped again.

"And you want me to open the window and let you in? For, what is it now," she counted on her fingers, "the third time?"

Paddy grimaced.

"If you insist." Getting up, she undid the latch and slid up the window. "But, as I told you before, I don't think men are allowed in the sleeping quarters. Not even the caretakers."

Paddy swung his leg over the ledge. "Aye. But I am no regular caretaker."

"What kind are you?"

"The kind that is willing to risk life and limb climbing up to your second story window."

Mary-Kate curtsied and faked a swoon. "Well I'll give you marks for that, my brave knight." With a sly grin she took a chair from the corner and wedged it under the doorknob. "Now we can talk."

Paddy swung his other leg over the sill.

"I don't know what I'd have done if you hadn't come by tonight."

"Oh, postulant, my postulant. Ye of little faith. Didn't ya read the note I wrote ya?"

"What note?"

"The one in the sock." Paddy looked at her as if she were daft.

"I don't read crusty sock messages."

"Ya should, they're the best kind. But it doesn't matter. I'm here now."

"I suppose it doesn't." Mary-Kate patted a spot on the bed beside her. "I've prayed for a miracle. A sign. And here you are. You are the answer to my prayers."

The bed creaked as Paddy took his place. "Usually I hear that climbing out of a window, not coming in." He brushed the dirt off his shoulder. "Not that it's ever happened before."

At times Paddy's comments delighted Mary-Kate, but then there were others, when they revealed the chasm that lay between them. She may have allowed a common man into her sleeping quarters, but that didn't make her common. She narrowed her eyes. "I think you're taking liberties, Patrick Fitz-patrick. And if you're questioning my virtue, there's the window. You can go out as fast as you came in."

Paddy took off his cap. "I wasn't questioning anything." He hesitated as his fingers rubbed the rough tweed. "I'm not playing with your honour, Mary-Kate. I would never do that."

"But you are." Mary-Kate could feel the blush rise in her cheeks. "If we were caught, even suspected, my reputation would be in tatters. The same way my father's was after that newspaper article."

"What are ya talking about?"

Mary-Kate made a face. "The woman who accosted him in front of The Donnybrook. Claimed he'd," she couldn't finish.

"Oh that," Paddy chuckled. "That was me ma."

"Your mother!" Mary-Kate was regretting opening her window. What kind of people did Paddy come from? "Why didn't you tell me?"

"Why would I? It's common enough for her to pull that scam. She's been doing it since I was in short pants. All of Tnúth knows of it. She claims to be in a bad way and the gents empty their pockets to shut her up."

"If everyone knows it, why would she try it on my father?"

"Don't know. I suppose she wanted to get his attention, have him pass me a message."

"And what was that?"

"He never said."

Mary-Kate wasn't convinced. Threatening men in the street over unseemly behaviour — what kind of woman would do that? She bit her lip and considered Paddy.

"Ya see," he interrupted her thoughts, "'tis a point of pride where I come from, fleecing our betters. Ya da has done that a thousand times. How do ya think he's built his fortune?"

"I don't know. He doesn't concern me with his financial dealings."

"And as for me reputation," Paddy said, lowering his voice. "I wouldn't have risked everything to climb up here to see ya. I'd have walked straight through your cell door, and let folks think what they like."

Mary-Kate rolled her eyes. "You say you've risked everything. What have you risked?"

"Almost all that is dear to me. If your da finds out, I'll be tossed from The Donnybrook. Not a soul will risk knowing me. I never gambled so much for anyone before, not even me own ma."

"Well," Mary-Kate said, her tone softer than before. "My father's driven others away for less."

"Aye. I remember a time when he banished Aibeart the Scott." Paddy paused and eyed Mary-Kate. "I hate to say it in front of a lady such as yourself, but I've begun the tale, and I'll bring it to its end. He banished him for flatulating in O'Brien's pint. Aibeart was well into his cups and mistook ya da's mug for mine. Even when the confusion was explained, the man and his kin never graced the door of the pub again."

She stifled a grin. Her father was a man of extremes, and to be honest, since coming to this stone monstrosity, she missed his strange ways. "Sometimes I close my eyes and imagine the sound of my parents bickering in the hall." She sighed. "It's like Christmas. How could I have not seen it?"

Paddy shrugged.

Mary-Kate flopped back down on the bed. "I was tired of this place before I heard all the prayers and hushed voices. My knees hadn't even hit the floor." She looked up at Paddy. "I just have to make sure it's my aunt who dismisses me. Then if God was of the mind to smite someone, he could smite her."

"Uh, the old 'let this cup pass from me to her' trick."

"Exactly."

"Not very Jesus of ya."

"I'm sure after a few Hail Mary's she'll get over it."

Paddy flopped back on the bed beside her. "You sound like me ma. Always playing the long game."

Putting a finger to her lips, Mary-Kate inclined her head towards the door and listened for a while. "She's always sniffing around. Trying to put me in some box."

There was a shuffling in the hallway and an attempt at turning the knob. Mary-Kate froze.

"I hear voices. Is someone with you Mary-Kate?"

Mary-Kate rolled her eyes. "I was talking to myself."

The handle jiggled again. "The door is stuck."

"Yes, it is."

"That's the third time this week," Sister Mary-Frances yelled, clamouring to get in.

"Yes," answered Mary-Kate. "Isn't that odd?"

55

PADDY

It was black as pitch when Paddy crawled out of Mary-Kate's cell. He waited on the ledge, hoping she'd linger with him, pull him back to her. But she said she was cold and almost shut the window on his fingers. He smiled. That one had spunk, a no-nonsense kind of lass that would keep a lad guessing. And if Paddy liked anything, it was guessing. He touched the pane once more and waited, but Mary-Kate had drawn the blind. "I'll be back," he whispered.

His eyes might as well have been closed as he started his descent. The moon, if there was one, wasn't inclined to show its face. Even so, he was confident that he could navigate his way down using the vines and trellis, as it wasn't the first time he'd made the trip. "Oh, sweet Mary-Kate," he whispered to the closed window as he climbed down. "My sweet, sweet, Mary-Kate. Ya are a goddess to me."

Inch by inch, he made his way through the dark, humming and whistling to himself. He was halfway down his traverse when, reaching for a foothold, there was none to be found. In his mind he retraced his descent — he was directly under Mary-

Kate's window, same as before, and the trellis that should be there was gone.

"Drop."

Paddy's throat tightened.

"Drop. It won't kill you. You might break a limb, but limbs mend." There was a pause. "Eventually."

By the tenor of the voice, he knew his foe — Sister Mary-Frances. Paddy froze. She was the last person he wanted to come across in the dark.

"I've taken it upon myself to relieve the stonework of its lattice. And to break your fall, I've laid about some rakes and shovels."

For an instant, Paddy considered climbing back up to Mary-Kate's room and crawling through the window. He might be able to make it out of the convent if he hoofed it. But, as much of a scoundrel as he was, he would not take a chance of exposing Mary-Kate like that. He looked towards the ground. Black as pitch. If he couldn't see her, then it was only reasonable to assume she couldn't see him. He'd be safe enough, if he could hold on. It was a matter of making a plan before sunrise. Then he heard a pistol cock.

"Drop," came the nun's voice again. "I can't see you, but my hearing and sense of smell work perfectly well. I've won prizes for hitting my target blindfolded, and I'm certainly up for the task tonight."

Paddy found her glee unseemly and was about to tell her so when the lattice supporting him creaked under his weight. In the dark, he could envision the old woman aiming her weapon in the direction of the sound. "Sister Mary-Frances," he said, a lilt in his voice. "Ya wouldn't want to be doing that. I have just climbed up here to check the pipes. The ones I might remind you have been giving you trouble."

"And it's best to check them in the middle of the night?"

"Aye. Less distraction."

"I'm sure. So much so that the pipes I was talking about are on the other side of the building?"

"And this is a fine time to be telling me. When I've risked life and limb just to please ya. That's the church for ya, never satisfied 'til there's blood."

If there were any colour left in his face, Paddy felt the rest of it drain at the sound of the nun repositioning herself. He could envision her bracing, unfurling fangs and claws — which left him somewhat perplexed. Was it better to die clinging to the side of the building, like a petrified squirrel, or drop to where she lay in wait?

"I know you're a stubborn lad, but if you hang there 'til the break of day, it will be Mary-Kate's reputation that suffers. You clinging outside her window, like the thief you are, will do nothing to improve her situation."

"Not conceding to your assumptions, finding me dead beneath it, I would argue, would have the same effect. Didn't even know her room was in this wing."

The two were at an impasse, each not wanting to give in to the other. A cricket disturbed the silence.

"You have a point," she said finally. "Drop, and I'll count to five before I shoot. It's the best offer you'll get this evening."

Sister Mary-Frances found Father Albright skulking on one side of the sanctuary while eyeing the confessionals on the other. It was one way of keeping Father Connelly in check, if not a little on the nose.

"He did it again," Father Albright shouted. "Did you see it? He did it again."

Sister Mary-Frances put a finger to her lips to shush Father Albright as she made her way to his side. "Did what?"

The wide-eyed priest pointed to the confessional, "Whenever someone finishes their supplication that imp opens the curtain and waves at me."

"By imp, I assume you mean Father Connelly?"

"There, did you see that?"

Sister Mary-Frances looked to the confessional. And there was Father Connelly, waving and winking as if he were in a parade, his short legs swinging in the air.

"Oh, take no notice of him. He's trying to get your goat."

"He got my goat long ago." Father Albright waved a fist in the air. "At this point, he's after the farm."

"We are participating in surveillance," said Sister Mary-

Frances through gritted teeth, as she caught hold of the back of Father Albright's robe, keeping him from breaking away. "Not dredging up the dark past. Or need I remind you that fisticuffs in the sanctuary are strictly forbidden?"

Shaking free from her hold, Father Albright regained his composure and interlaced his fingers. "As they should be," he said with great piety.

"How demure of you."

Under their casual surveillance, Mary-Kate came gliding into the church as if the previous night's incident hadn't occurred. For the briefest of moments, Sister Mary-Frances wavered. Was she wrong? Did the urchin's drain pipe blatherings hold water? No. It had been the drivel of the unprepared. She shook off her misgivings. The girl was up to something.

"Where's her shame?" Sister Mary-Frances flinched with regret. Sometimes her tongue went off all on its own, not giving her thoughts time to muster a measured observation.

"At the foot of the cross," Father Albright said in his pinched way.

Sister Mary-Frances closed her eyes and gritted her teeth. If the mealy-mouthed man weren't her cohort, she'd pummel him into the ground.

But there would be no pummelling today, at least not before afternoon tea. By that time she'd have sussed out the truth of the matter. She looked her niece up and down. For a young thing, the girl had a stride. Not even a hint of regret. "'Twould be a blessing to live in such an empty abyss, oblivious to decency and godly living."

Father Albright's face slackened. "Of whom do you speak?"

Sister Mary-Frances waved a hand at him, giving no credence to his question. "Mary-Kate," she called. "Do you have a minute?"

"Father Connelly's waiting for me," Mary-Kate returned over her shoulder, as she quickened her pace.

"That Father can wait. Come here, Father Albright and I have something to discuss with you."

"We do?" Father Albright reddened and tugged on Sister Mary-Frances's arm. "I try not to speak to them face to face or outside of the sacrament."

"Speak to who?"

Father Albright rolled his eyes like it was obvious. "The female persuasion."

"If you haven't noticed," the nun boomed, "I'm one of them."

"I suppose, but I never think of you that way." The priest licked his lips. "Penance," he said by way of explanation.

She looked the priest over. Why did she always end up with the defective lackey? The thought of involving him in family matters wasn't something she relished. "Go feed the pigeons in the park."

"Are there pigeons?"

"There might be if someone had the foresight to feed them."

Father Albright hunched down as if he were in a starting gate, and when some imaginary bell that only he was aware of sounded he was off. He cleared the distance to the door in less time than Sister Mary-Frances thought possible. It was only a guess that the little man had an unnatural penchant for aviary. They may be allies, but she was tempted to throw him off the roof to see if his bones were hollow.

Sister Mary-Frances shifted in her habit as she turned from the priest to her niece. "Mary-Kate," she said through tight lips, "did you sleep well?"

Mary-Kate yawned and stretched, a little too leisurely in Sister Mary-Frances's estimation. "I did, and you?"

"My sleeping habits are no concern of yours." Sister Mary-

Frances stepped closer to her niece. "What should be your concern is who was tapping on your cell window last evening."

"That black crow? You've seen him? He hardly gives me a moment's rest." A look of relief covered her face. "I thought I heard a shot, was that you? You must be a good aim, killing crows in the dark."

"It wasn't a crow I was after." The nun took hold of the cross that hung around her neck. "My aim was after a featherless intruder. The kind that can heal a girl of," she paused and thought carefully of what to say next, "chlorosis. You know it?"

Mary-Kate shook her head.

"Well, by the looks of you, if you had it before, you most certainly don't now."

F ollowing his freefall, it was only by luck Paddy outran
the nun. He zigged while she zagged, each hearing
rather than seeing the other, and when a shot sailed
past him, he thought he was done for. "We will no longer need
your services, Patrick Fitzpatrick. God be with you. If I have it
my way, no one else will."

"Succubus," he cursed over his shoulder.

The words didn't mean much to him then — just the sound
of an old woman rambling — but now in the shadow of The
Donnybrook, he wasn't so sure. They might mean the end of
him. His knees quaked when he stepped through the pub's
doors. Paddy paused and breathed deeply. The smell of stale
beer and pipe smoke rivalled no other. He tipped his cap at a
gent or two, who in turn raised their glasses in salute.

"'Tis good to be back in me own place," Paddy said with a
little bow. "Would kiss each and every one of you, if you were
anything to look at." The men laughed, and Paddy felt a tingle in
his spine. He was home.

Perusing the room Paddy saw that Mr. O'Brien wasn't there,
but Father Connelly was. The priest was sitting at their usual

table. And when Paddy sat down, there was hardly a grunt from the other.

"'Tis good to see you, Father."

"Can't say the same for you."

"And why not? It's been near a month since we've had a chance to sit at our table and have a pint."

"Aye, 'tis true. Just yesterday I saw you out there switching grave markers, more than usual." He lowered his head and raised his brow. "Have you seen the state of Sister Mary-Frances? She looks like death warmed over. Can't be racing her around like an old plow horse."

Paddy lowered his voice. "Not for her this time, Father." He placed his hand over the priest's. "This time I did it to Father Albright."

The priest lightened a little and looked out the window. "Albright," he said.

"Aye. And he is only half the man she is. I tell you that."

"Aren't we all?"

Paddy had to concede the priest was right. That nun could undo all she met, and by the new priest's times, she could outrun them as well. He leaned back in his seat. "Keen's been keeping the times when you're not here to hold the watch." He waved in Keen's direction, and Keen ambled over with a tattered black book, his full pint slopping over to spray its hard cover. In it were rows of times and wagers. "Here," said Paddy. "Here are her times."

The priest slowly flipped through the book, examining the pages. "And Albright?"

Paddy took the book and flipped to the back. "Here," he said.

The priest frowned. "Not too promising for a man his age."

"Nay, they're not."

"Hasn't even come close to her slowest time." Father Connelly closed the book and ordered another round. He was more pleased with himself than Paddy had seen for quite some time, as if the nun's accomplishments were his own.

"I'd like to place a wager then," said Father Connelly, sliding a coin across the table.

———

FATHER CONNELLY and Paddy were still at The Donnybrook when Mr. O'Brien came barrelling in. He didn't give his usual greeting. Heaviness clung to him like a dead man's cloak. His gaze caught Paddy's. "Why aren't you at the convent?"

"Been tossed."

"Jasus, Mary, and Joseph! Is me Mary-Kate still there?"

Paddy slipped down in his seat. "Aye."

Mr. O'Brien sat down with a thump, more bewildered than when he'd come in.

"Can't her gran get sick again?" asked Father Connelly.

Mr. O'Brien threw his hands in the air. "You buried her man, do you not remember? Not even a woman as crotchety as Herself could bring — Herself — back from such a circumstance."

"Some never cease to disappoint." Father Connelly stirred the foam in his pint with a finger, before narrowing his eyes. "That's not good."

"'Course it's not good," bellowed Mr. O'Brien. "Even a fool can see that. Mary-Kate's probably making her vows as we speak."

"Doesn't happen quite that fast," said Father Connelly, with a reassuring pat on Mr. O'Brien's arm. "Will be at least a year."

"That's not very comforting." Mr. O'Brien ground his fist into his thigh. He looked out the window towards the convent. "To lose her to that place...I don't think I can do it, I tell you that."

"You won't have to," Father Connelly said. "Just this morning

I heard Sister Mary-Frances conspiring in the conclave with Father Notbright. Said something about a broken lattice and that it might not have been her best idea to have her niece join her. Says the girl is too much like her da. Went so far as calling her 'a dog in a manger.'"

Paddy's lips twitched. "A broken lattice?"

Mr. O'Brien laid a hand on Paddy's. "No use worrying about your caretaking duties now, lad. My sister has seen the light. She's thinking about sending me Mary-Kate packing."

The place looked better than Paddy had ever seen it. He rubbed the palms of his hands together. The guilt that had niggled at him in the early morning hours had been for naught. The boarded-up kitchen window was fixed — a new pane of glass, and curtains to boot. Paddy didn't remember it looking so sharp. It made him want to buy a walking stick. There was a potted plant by the front door, the only one on the block.

"She certainly has moved up in the world," Paddy said to no one in particular. "Don't know if I can live in a place that's so fancy." He leaned over and plucked a flower from the pot. That mother of his, he couldn't imagine what she would do next.

For the first time that Paddy could remember, he wiped his feet on the mat before opening the front door. But when he went to turn the knob, he found it locked, not willing to budge, no matter how hard he cajoled it.

"You'll not get in that way."

Paddy turned. On the step across from him stood Maggie. She looked particularly pleased with herself.

"Still using your new clothesline, I see."

Maggie stuck out her chin as she hung a shirt. "Well, we do what we can. And our side of the road seems to do better than most."

The tone had a hitch in it. Something that caught, as if a warning. He stepped forward and ran his tongue under his lip. "Is there something ya want to be telling me Maggie?"

"Not something I would seek you out to say." she bent over and pulled a wet tablecloth from her basket. "But now that you ask, I suppose it would be the Christian thing to do."

Paddy could feel her prolonging their interaction, as a cat does before devouring a mouse.

"The shoe is on the other foot now, isn't it?" She snapped the tablecloth. "The way the two of you taunted me. I couldn't do anything about it. But now I can. I can stand here and toy with you."

"No, ya can't." Paddy, red-faced, tipped his cap and turned to leave.

"She's gone," Maggie called after him. "Was dragged off in the middle of the night." She lowered her voice. "By her hair."

Paddy froze.

"Didn't leave quietly though. Was kicking, screaming, calling for you."

He felt like a tinker, wandering from neighbourhood to neighbourhood trying to peddle an outdated service. But it didn't matter how many doors Paddy pounded upon, there wasn't a soul that would tell him what happened to his mother. "Are ya telling me she's fallen off the face of the earth?" he asked, infuriated that everyone's seemed to know his mother's plight except him.

"I'm not telling you anything of the sort." One-Eyed-Bob pushed past him. "Minding me own business."

Paddy quickened his pace to keep up with the hollowed-eyed man as he made his way to the back of the warehouse. "It's like pulling hen's teeth to get an answer from any of ya."

"And for good reason." Bob half closed his good eye before heaving a feed sack over his shoulder. "It would be better for you to do the same."

"What did she do?"

"Nothing. Your ma did nothing." One-Eyed-Bob leaned over, so his lips brushed Paddy's ear. "It was your gran."

"Me gran? That hag?" Paddy was dumbfounded. "That doesn't make any sense." In his bewilderment he stood stock still as men shuffled through the dust around him, sending up specks, breathing in their own drudgery. He scratched his head. His gran hadn't been heard from since she'd become a guest at one of Her Majesty's best penitentiaries. As far as Paddy was concerned, Her Majesty could keep her.

Paddy didn't remember slipping out of the warehouse. He only became aware of his surroundings when he was more than a mile away. He left One-Eyed-Bob with not so much as a fare-thee-well, and he owed him more than that. The man had risked something in the telling, though Paddy was unsure of what that something was.

The crux of the situation became clear the following evening. Paddy was meandering through old haunts, seeking out any who could clear up the confusion, when there, under a bent street lamp, stood a stranger. On the first pass, Paddy didn't make much of her. She seemed a fine gentlewoman, if not a bit out of place. Her hat and veil concealed her features. The longer he watched, the more appeal she had — the odd way she fussed and twisted under her dress, as if it somehow pinched.

The most striking thing to Paddy though, was when a sort outside her station approached her she didn't show reproach as he expected. She tilted her head and drew a finger along the length of his chin — a dead eyed playfulness, encouragement. He fished out a handful of change from his pocket, and the two of them disappeared into an alley.

When the stranger returned, her ungentlemanly friend was nowhere about. Paddy tipped his cap as he started in her direction. "Sorry to be bothering ya, Miss, but I think ya've lost your way."

The woman snorted but kept her back to him.

"Did ya hear me, lass?" he asked, pulling on her arm.

"I heard you," she said. "But I am long past caring." Biddy

Fitzpatrick turned to face him. Her face was swollen and discoloured.

Paddy's fingers twitched. He wanted to reach out and touch her but thought better of it. Her tone warned off all affection. "What's got into ya? Ya took to street fighting? There's got to be better ways of filling your stomach."

"Street fighting, my arse!" She grabbed him by the front of his shirt. "Where were you when I needed you? Went to the O'Briens to fetch you, but was run off with only this brooch to show for it."

Paddy pried himself free, peeling back her fingers one at a time, as he examined the filigree cameo nestled at the base of her collar, "'Tis a fine piece. Didn't know the lot of ya were exchanging gifts."

"We're not. I came for you."

"While ya were pilfering, I was in the church." He cleared his throat. "Tipping the holy chalice with the best of them. Don't ya remember? Ya're the one who pushed me to get a job."

"Oh, don't you be throwing that in me face. I told O'Brien to send you home, that it wasn't the same without you. But of you I saw neither hide nor hair."

"Well, O'Brien never told me. But me being away hasn't hurt ya any. Think ya're so fine, in your store-bought dresses and fancy hats. When did ya start dressing like the queen of Sheba?"

"When did you start dressing like the queen of Sheba?" Biddy mimicked. "Since when did you start caring? Would think you were too busy running after some spoiled girl to be thinking of me. A girl who wouldn't lay claim to you in public."

"Think ya have any right to talk about what me girl would do in public? I saw ya slip into the alley. Ya weren't playing tiddlywinks."

Biddy's face changed, hardened at the edges. "It may not have been tiddlywinks, but it's not something I'm going to talk to you about." She turned back to the street. "You should go. He'll be here soon."

"Who'll be here?"

"Him." Biddy pointed down the dark street, to the lump that was lumbering towards them.

Paddy narrowed his eyes and looked in the direction his mother was pointing. It was hard to make the figure out, a moving shadow, too distant to be sure. "How can ya make rhyme or reason of that?"

His mother frowned. "Comes like clockwork. There's no mistake about it."

"Who?" Paddy blinked, but the shape wasn't any clearer than before. "Who's that?"

"Someone who'd put his foot through you as soon as look at you."

"How'd she get out?"

"She?"

"Gran."

"Gran? She's not out."

"Then who would put their foot through me?"

Biddy's voice was placid. "Black-Hearted John."

"That lout! What's he got to do with ya?"

"Everything."

The closer Black-Hearted John came, the faster Biddy spoke. "He's been asking about you Paddy. Wants to know who your mates are, where you like to spend your time."

"And what have ya told him?"

"As little as I can. He wants to have a chat with you, make sure you're not going to cause trouble." Biddy pulled Paddy close, her nails digging into the back of his arms, and put her cheek against his. "You weren't there to say the words for me," she said. "And now it can never be the way it was, the two of us picking pockets and scamming strangers."

Paddy's mouth went dry. "Why? What's he got to do with ya? Us?"

"She sold me to him, your gran. First day she had a chance, dangled me before him like a prized jewel. She got a better life inside those walls, and I got a worse one outside them."

Biddy's gaze didn't leave the distant figure. "He was fixed to have me." She shivered. "Now he does."

The distant mass began to take shape, bringing back with it the worst parts of Paddy's young memories. He could feel his bowels turn to water. It had been years since the sensation had visited him, the one where Paddy was left shivering on the step waiting for his gran to grant him entry. The one where he lay and watched his mother's body shudder as she tried to stifle her tears. He was back on a slow-turning spit, and he had to admit he was at a loss as to what to do about it. "I'll come for ya," Paddy said, pulling away from her. "I promise ya that."

Biddy nodded. "Run boy. Better to be a coward for a minute than be dead for the rest of your life."

Mary-Kate sucked in her nostrils and pinned back her shoulders. A piece of paper wasn't going to do her in, but a doorknob might. She stood before the front door, hesitation consuming her. It hadn't been long since she'd left home, it shouldn't be hard going back. Surely her parents would embrace her.

The posy sisters must have sensed her, as Rose, feather duster in hand, flung open the front door while Daisy twittered in the background. "What are you doing here, Miss?" Rose looked her over from head to toe. "Avoiding rumours?"

Without waiting for a response, the sisters twittered once more before turning on their heels and heading down the hall towards the kitchen. As they went, Mary-Kate was sure she could hear them chime, "*Ashes to ashes, dust to dust, if it weren't for Paddy, Miss Mary-Kate's lips would rust.*"

Mary-Kate narrowed her eyes. How could she have let herself be out-Sherlocked by empty-headed foliage? It had to be the blasted letter that threw her off her game. And why did she care so much? She didn't want to be a nun in the first place.

"Oh," Mrs. O'Brien said, as she strolled out of the sitting

room with a teacup and saucer in hand. "I wasn't expecting company."

Mary-Kate's hopes were dashed, and she muffled a sob. "I never thought I'd be considered company here."

Her mother's face blanched. "It's not that, I promise you." She reached back to set her cup and saucer on a hall table, but missed the mark and the pair went clattering to the floor. Mrs. O'Brien seemed oblivious and stepped towards her. "I don't know what to say. You caught me unprepared. You're a soul saved from the clutches of — well, God knows what." She reached out and lightly touched her daughter's hair. "And not a mark on you."

Mary-Kate bit her lip. "If you read this," she handed her mother the letter, "you might change your mind."

The sheet fell to the floor. "Never me, dear girl." She took Mary-Kate's face between her hands. "Never. There is not a thing you can do that would drive me away. Not a place you can go that I wouldn't follow. I'd give you me first and me last breath. Do you hear me? Me first and me last breath."

Mary-Kate nodded.

"I could swallow you whole."

The O'Briens didn't knock or pause at the door to the office of Sister Mary-Frances. In fact, Mrs. O'Brien felt emboldened, striding shoulder to shoulder with her husband. It was the first time in weeks they were truly united.

"Mary-Frances." Mrs. O'Brien vibrated as she waved a letter in the air. "What do you have to say about this?"

The nun shrugged and shifted a stack of papers on her desk. "A missive," she said. "Something not worthy of my attention."

"Not worthy of your attention? You wrote the damned thing."

"I may have written it," Sister Mary-Frances pushed back from her desk, "but it was inspired by your husband."

"My husband?" Mrs. O'Brien stepped forward and placed both hands squarely on the nun's desk. "Don't be blaming him. He hasn't inspired anything in his life."

"'Tis true." Mr. O'Brien pushed passed his wife. "I've prided meself on that very fact. Just this morning I mentioned it at the breakfast table. Didn't I?"

"He did." Mrs. O'Brien lifted her chin as if it were a point of pride. "'Tis why I married him."

"Well, I can't argue with you there." The nun smiled in a way that made Mrs. O'Brien realize they were making her case for her. "The two of you are the definition of buffoonery."

Mrs. O'Brien slapped the top of the desk. "How we suit one another is none of your concern. This," she waved the letter once more, "is our only concern."

The two women eyed each other for some time before Mrs. O'Brien noticed her husband inching towards the door. "Where do you think you're going?" she said, without dropping her gaze.

"Nowhere in particular." Mr. O'Brien took another step backwards. "It's just that the two of you seem to have things in hand. Thought I'd pop out and check on Father Connelly."

"You'll do no such thing, Mr. O'Brien. No one is leaving this room until we get to the bottom of things."

"I think that would be lovely." Sister Mary-Frances raised her eyebrows at her brother.

"And let's be sure not to skip any details, shall we?"

The three eyed each other warily.

"Well," Sister Mary-Frances said after a time. "Let's get this over with." She looked Mrs. O'Brien up and down. "Since you were the one who barged in here, invading my sanctuary, you can be the first to stand there and give account." She paused and rapped impatient fingers. "Speak up now, don't stand there like a scared rabbit."

"She'll stand any way she likes," Mr. O'Brien interjected.

"Do you think defending your wife," she jabbed a thick finger in Mrs. O'Brien's direction, "will get you out of the line of fire? It is a foolish notion."

Mrs. O'Brien turned on her husband. "What is the penguin talking about?"

"She's flapping her jaw, that's all." Mr. O'Brien cracked his knuckles. "That's all she's ever been good for."

"That's not what I asked. Anyone can see she's flapping her jaw. It's what she's implying that I need to know."

Sister Mary-Frances snickered. "Tell her. Tell her everything. Tell her how you were the one who insisted Father Connelly hire the scoundrel. The very cad who became your daughter's downfall. That you were the one who egged him on and turned a blind eye to his dubious past. The two of them, your Mary-Kate and that boy, got along like a house on fire."

Mrs. O'Brien's lip quivered as she tried to hold herself with dignity. "What scoundrel? What are you talking about?"

"Patrick Fitzpatrick." Sister Mary-Frances spat before Mr. O'Brien could respond. "They have been compatriots for years, viewing the world through their small grimy window at The Donnybrook."

"Let me get this straight." Mrs. O'Brien's hands tightened into fists. "You're saying my husband, the man I've shared my bed with, was part of this?"

"He wasn't just part of it. He was, as I've stated before, the orchestrator."

Mrs. O'Brien didn't remember sitting down. "And what about her?" She looked up at her husband. "What did she have to do with it?"

"Me sister?" Mr. O'Brien puffed up. "Her fingers dipped far deeper than mine."

"Not that 'her.' The 'her' that has been keeping you out late at night. The one who has been drawing you away from me."

"Father Connelly? That her? He may wear skirts, but he's no woman."

Mrs. O'Brien furrowed her brow and examined her husband's face. "You mean, there's no one else?"

"Good Gawd woman, you bring this up now?" He leaned closer and his voice dropped to a whisper. "I skirted around on you once, and I promised you then it would never happen again, and on me word, it hasn't."

Reaching up, Mrs. O'Brien hesitated before she stroked her husband's cheek. "You daft fool. Why didn't you tell me?"

"I tried! Stood outside your bedroom door, shivering in the dark. But after all these years, if you didn't know me heart, why would you have believed me words?"

Mrs. O'Brien had no answer for him. He was right. The great oaf was right. And her mother saw it first. Not her, her mother. How could she have been so blind? The exhaustion of recent events overtook her, and she put her face in her hands, trying to hold in the deluge. For his part, her husband, her dear sweet husband, squatted, put his forehead next to hers, and began to rub her back. The touch stilled her, and she realized how she'd missed it, needed it, longed for it.

"I forgive you," he purred, a hint of self-satisfaction in his tone.

Mrs. O'Brien stiffened. The softness of the moment passed. "You forgive me?" Her voice grew louder with every word. "You forgive me?"

"Aye. I do."

She thumped him in the chest. "You should have done more than shiver in the hallway. I can tell you that much. Did all your trying at The Donnybrook, leaving me to worry and fret on me own. What kind of plan is that?"

The O'Briens rose in unison, and Mr. O'Brien took a step back.

"I'll tell you this much, I almost wish you had been with another, if it would have kept me Mary-Kate out of this." She waved a hand through the air. "It would have broken me heart, but I can live with a broken heart far easier than a broken daughter."

Taking a deep breath, Mrs. O'Brien turned on her sister-in-law. A new vigour filled her as she waved the letter in the air. "This, the nerve of you. First you claim our girl, and gather her to your hard bosom with no regard for her future or our family, and then with not so much as a bye your leave, you dismiss her! You might as well have nailed her failings to the church door."

"I thought that's what you wanted? Her dismissal. Thought by now you would be celebrating, dancing on the rooftops."

"I would be, if it weren't for what you wrote in the margin." Mrs. O'Brien snapped the letter. "What is it, some kind of Latin mumbo jumbo?"

The nun snorted. "It's not mumbo jumbo, I assure you. If you were better read, or if you read at all, you'd know the difference between mumbo jumbo and Greek."

Mrs. O'Brien frowned. "So, this comment is a willy-nilly musing? A frivolous afterthought? Showing off your superior education. I don't believe that any more than you do. Me Mary-Kate's been weeping and throwing things. She's even tossed her jar of buttons."

"Let me educate you." A smile slithered onto Sister Mary-Frances's face. "It's an old word, *chlorosis*. It means love fever, the virgin disease."

Mrs. O'Brien reddened. "What are you playing at?"

"I'm not playing at anything, but I'm fairly confident that if Mary-Kate suffered from chlorosis before she came to the convent, she no longer does." Picking up a pencil, Sister Mary-Frances rolled it between her fingers. "But in nine months, if things prove different, I might consider reinstating her."

"Diseased or not," Mr. O'Brien thundered, "she's our Mary-Kate and we'll take her anyway we can have her. You'll not be getting her back."

The nun licked the lead. "Well, one can only hope."

A pyre in front of The Donnybrook was Paddy's first indication he was no longer welcome. He had slipped into the caraganas across the way and watched as they tossed his chair atop the flames. It made him ache to watch that chair burn, but nothing like the pain of seeing the effigy that had been concocted out of an ill-fitting shirt and thread-bare trousers. He would have never been caught in such mismatched attire.

Mr. O'Brien raised the stuffed imposter in the air. "Patrick Fitzpatrick, if ya are within my hearing, let it be known ya are no longer one of the lads. I can't be drinking with ya. Not again. Ya let me down, more than any other man who has walked through these hallowed doors. Not even worthy of a notch on the chair, to prove that you were ever part of us. Do ya hear me, Patrick Fitzpatrick? Ya may be out of sight but ya're not out of mind. Ya should count yourself lucky I don't have ya drawn and quartered. It'd be within me rights!"

Paddy watched, a little breathless, as the lads made the sign of the cross and Mr. O'Brien set alight the effigy. He took off his cap and said a little prayer for himself. It was the saddest thing he'd ever witnessed. He was now a man without a refuge.

"Isn't that a little harsh?" asked Father Connelly, warming his hands on the fire.

"Not at all. No one has disappointed me more. It may cost me me daughter's reputation, and 'twill cost him his place."

Paddy simmered. O'Brien had nothing to complain about. It was true things hadn't gone exactly as planned, but when do they ever? Mary-Kate wasn't going to take her vows anytime soon. Wasn't that all that mattered? He'd delivered, and O'Brien should be grateful. There was no need to burn his chair. Where was the gratitude in that? After all Paddy had done, all he'd endured, they should be pinning medals on his chest. He'd faced the Catholic Medusa and walked away with his life. And as for Mary-Kate, she wasn't any worse for wear. He could vouch for that. He rubbed his brow. The same couldn't be said for his mother.

From where Paddy sat there were few options. To free his mother, he'd need more than what he could pilfer from a few unsuspecting pockets. The pocket watch that he had in his own wouldn't be enough to satisfy the black-hearted devil. The brute would know Paddy was capable of more. The thought of leaving her where she was, was unfathomable. And the two of them running away would hasten their end. Black-Hearted John's reach was longer than that of the pope, and more feared.

As for his station, although it had never been a grand one, he doubted that without divine intervention he could ever rise to it again. And where did that leave him? Cowering in a bunch of caraganas, smelling his own demise.

He looked back towards the fire. It was pulling in more spectators, laughing and jostling as if it were some kind of celebration. Sister Mary-Frances strolled over with a can of gasoline. "With the right wind," he heard her say to her perpetual shadow,

Father Albright, "and a little help," she shook the can, "we can rid ourselves of that eyesore."

Paddy shifted in his spot. If O'Brien was so willing to be his downfall, maybe he should be O'Brien's. A little fire and effigy burning wouldn't scare him away. He'd have his Mary-Kate and free his mother. Leave O'Brien twisting in the wind. See how the lout liked them apples.

MRS. O'BRIEN

It was the despondency that bothered Mrs. O'Brien most, her husband's lack of indignation. Sitting on the front veranda, letting others pass their gateway without uttering a word of greeting? At one time, such disregard would not go unpunished. He'd find a way of grinding them down under his heel.

"Good Gawd, man," she scolded him when she found him on the veranda. "This is no way to behave. What will the neighbours think? A little run-in with your sister and you become a blithering milksop? Get on with you. Get out of that rocker and defend your daughter's honour. Knock some heads together. You can start with that Patrick Fitzpatrick."

Mr. O'Brien ground his fist into his thigh. "Don't even mention that name. I curse the day I laid eyes on the lad. He's dead to me."

"I'm weary of your moping. Cursing days will not get us anywhere. What we need is a plan. One that will get Mary-Kate back into the church." She narrowed her eyes. "I know that's against our better judgement, and everything we hold dear, but at least behind locked doors she might rid herself of any notions of that Fitzpatrick character and the wagging tongues will be put to rest. She's like a lovesick pup, and it makes my skin crawl. Those dark walls will do," she pointed towards the convent, "until you can claim her — drag her away by her hair if need be."

Shading his eyes with his hand, Mr. O'Brien looked up at his wife. "I can claim her? I faced that dragon once, woman. You can't expect me to do it again."

"It's the convent or it's Paddy. You choose."

Mr. O'Brien grumbled. "And where do you suppose we get this grand idea, the one that will chase her back and solve all our ills?"

"Well not from The Donnybrook, I'll tell you that much." She pursed her lips. "Sitting around dusty tables drinking out of that common trough of foolishness. How could you be such an idiot? We'll go to the same place Mary-Kate goes to get many of her ideas. The library."

"The library?" Mr. O'Brien bellowed. "You want to fairy-tale her to death?"

Mrs. O'Brien snatched the newspaper that lay on her husband's lap, rolled it and beat him about the head. "Don't be a fool! There are more to books than unbelievable tales. And Mr. O'Brien, you will accompany me, whether you like it or not."

"There are many things that I haven't liked since I've wed," he said, dodging her blows. "I'll add it to me list."

"You do that," she said, "and I'll add one more reason to bolt me bedroom door."

Mrs. O'Brien was sitting on the edge of Mary-Kate's bed when she woke. Her eyes were red and swollen. "I've just read a gruesome story about a man who sounded just like Paddy."

Mary-Kate stiffened. "I can't do this again. Please, I can't. Don't make me."

"Oh, yes you can. It will be fun." Mrs. O'Brien ran her finger along a page in her library book. "Here it is. It says a man just like Paddy chopped up his family and hid them in the cellar."

Mary-Kate could feel herself sinking. The more her mother talked, the smaller she felt. "I don't believe that."

"You believing it or not doesn't make it any less true."

Mrs. O'Brien flipped the page. "Here's another one here. This one is an unsavoury lout."

She placed her hand on her mother's arm. "Please don't."

Mrs. O'Brien slammed closed the book. "What do you want from me, Mary-Kate? I haven't pried, criticized, or scolded you since you've returned. I can only guess what's happened."

"I don't know what you want me to say."

"I don't want you to say anything. I want you to think." She tapped Mary-Kate on the forehead with a finger. "Don't you realize you have everything a boy like that wants? Your father is rich, and you are an only child."

"I've heard similar things about you."

"Me father was never rich, and your father wasn't an only child."

"But you married into money."

"That may well be true, but I've paid a heavy price for it. I don't want you to do the same."

―――――

HER MOTHER'S words ran through Mary-Kate's mind for most of the morning. She tried to shake them, force them to the recesses of her consciousness but it was no good. Once said, they were a bell that couldn't be unrung. So, when Paddy approached her, outside the library, with a new sense of urgency, she pulled back. He grabbed her hand and tried to whisk her off to the nearest church. "We'll be married before the dew has left the morrow's grass. Doesn't that sound grand?"

"Married!" stammered Mary-Kate. She lowered her voice. "I know unexpected things happened, but getting married doesn't seem the right thing to do."

"Not the right thing to do? What do you think I've been pursuing you for? Risking me life and reputation? "

Mary-Kate's eyes widened. "Your reputation? It was in tatters when I met you. Never held a real job. You don't even know who your father is. And your mother, well you can't even bring your-self to talk about her."

"And your set holds real jobs? Strutting around, never getting their hands dirty but willing to look down on anyone who does. Doesn't sound too respectable to me." The vein in his neck pulsed. "You've forgotten where ya've come from, grown too big for your britches."

She thumped him in the chest, the way she had seen her mother thump her father a hundred times. If she could, Mary-Kate would make it all go away. Her mother's promise, her aunt's assumptions, and her father's ineptitude — but she couldn't. They were there in her lap, squirming for her attention. And there, in the centre of it all, was Paddy. She couldn't shake free of him. There was something in his words, the way they stood sturdy, all on their own. And she wanted to believe him, but reason insisted she didn't. If there ever was a time Mary-Kate didn't know her own mind, this was it.

"It all comes down to one thing, Mary-Kate O'Brien." Paddy leaned over and brushed a strand of hair from her cheek. "Do ya love me?"

She looked at the ground.

"I thought as much. Me ma said ya wouldn't know me in the light of day."

"That's not it." Mary-Kate could feel the heat in her cheeks. "Are you sure it's me you want, Patrick Fitzpatrick?"

"What a question. 'Course 'tis ya."

"Not my father's money?"

"Money?" Paddy stammered. "Where would ya get a foolish notion like that?"

"From my mother, and Father Albright. He's of the same mind. He says you're a cad and a ruffian, and that I should never trust you. He said you'd take the pennies off a dead man's eyes."

Paddy growled. "What a little strumpet. What use does a dead man have for a couple of pennies?"

"Patrick!"

"The priest is the strumpet, Mary-Kate, not your mother." Paddy sighed and brought his hand over hers. "Don't ya trust me, Mary-Kate O'Brien?"

Mary-Kate hesitated before pulling her hand away. "Can you promise me that my father's money has nothing to do with it?"

"Not his money," Paddy said, sucking his teeth. "I can say that with an honest heart, as clear of a conscience as any man alive. But his sway, that is another story. That I would like to dip me hand into. Ya see," he continued before Mary-Kate could interrupt him. "I doubt the old man would take kindly "he paused. "How can I put this gently? To have his daughter attached to anyone who'd ply a trade like me ma's." He put a finger to the side of his nose. "'Tis frowned upon in most circles, send tongues a wagging. But your da would make short work of that. He'd see to Black-Hearted John and save me from being gutted like a fish."

Mary-Kate brought a hand to her throat and gasped. She knew getting involved with a rogue would have its disadvantages, but this was beyond the pale. A woman, a mother for that matter, plying whatever Paddy was referring to, sickened her. Being foisted upon strange men, with or without consent, was beyond Mary-Kate's imaginings. Giving up her freedom to save a lost soul was reason enough to marry Paddy — even the sisters had to admire that — but her marriage had to be more than a worthy cause.

Taking a lock of her hair in his fingertips, Paddy softened. "I can't picture me future without ya. Me nights alone and empty. I can tell ya this lass, I was only after a pocket watch until I touched ya."

"What are you talking about?"

"Sit down," he said, taking her over to a nearby bench. "It's bound to come out sooner or later, and it's best coming from me. If we are going to start a life together, I'd prefer it to be one with no surprises."

Mary-Kate listened intently to everything Paddy said. She could feel her face grow hot as he expounded on his willing

participation in her manipulation. The thought of being entertainment for The Donnybrook, for a common laugh, was the
least of her mortifications. Her world was falling away. She
closed her eyes and centred herself, and held fast to the bench
where she sat.

"Father Connelly was in on it?"

"Aye. Not at first. Thought it was akin to blasphemy."

"And now?"

"Blasphemy has no immediate family, if ya catch me
meaning."

"And my father?"

"Aye."

"My mother? Did she have anything to do with this?"

"That I don't know."

Bracing herself, Mary-Kate closed her hand into a fist and
swung at his head. She missed.

"What did you do that for?" Paddy caught her before she
toppled off the bench. "I didn't cause ya any harm."

"Any harm! You think you haven't caused me any harm?" She
was so angry that she spit as she spoke. "I can't eat, I can't sleep.
My father lumbers about muttering under his breath and my
mother is obsessed with wayward courtships."

Paddy whistled. "Ya've got an interesting lot under your roof.
But ya can't blame me for all that."

"I don't. I blame myself. The first time I laid eyes on you I
should have walked away."

"But ya didn't, Mary-Kate. Doesn't that tell ya something?"

"It tells me I'm a fool." She covered her face with her hands
and began to sob.

"None of that, now." Paddy got down on his knees and
looked up at her. She didn't protest. Instead she leaned into him.
"It tells ya that despite what was happening around ya, we were
supposed to be together. Why else would ya do what went

against all you knew? Ya were following that spark of life deep inside of ya, Mary-Kate O'Brien. The one most are deaf to. And whether he realizes it or not, it's all your da ever wanted for ya." He lifted her chin with a finger. "Like the old saying goes, we live in one another's shelter. Ya know it's true. All me life I heard it, felt it with me ma, sniffed it at The Donnybrook — but lived in it when I met ya."

"Well, it doesn't matter anymore, does it? Not when you've twisted and turned me until I don't know which way is up. None of it matters, not even marrying you." She got up and walked away.

Paddy knew better than to follow her.

Mary-Kate marched straight to the church, passed by the holy water, and approached the first person she saw. "Where's Father Connelly?"

Father Albright pointed to the confessional. "He's in there, hearing a confession. Can I help you?"

"No."

Before Father Albright could stop her, Mary-Kate drew open the confessional curtain and shoved Mrs. Donavan. Mrs. Donavan huffed an indignation as she moved over to make room.

Father Connelly slid open the small window in the confessional wall. "You're coming two by two now, are you?"

Mary-Kate burst into tears and crumpled, her face in her hands. "Father, how could you?"

Looking from the priest to Mary-Kate, Mrs. Donavan placed a hand on her goiter, as if she were drawing on something. Her eyes narrowed. "Aye. How could you Father Connelly?"

65

Considering all that had happened of late, Mary-Kate couldn't help but feel overwhelmed. Just a few months ago life was as it should be — her father and Father Connelly arguing over some ludicrous notion; her mother snickering and fussing when her father came home late tracking in mud after a spring rain; her Gran tossing toasts; the posy sisters keeping their distance. And she, herself, oblivious to Paddy's existence.

And that was the problem. She was no longer oblivious. Life would be so much simpler if she was. Now, in spite of her anger, her disappointment, and her disillusionment, she couldn't shake free of the thought of him. More than that, even if she could, she wasn't sure if she'd want to. Pulling the covers to her chin, Mary-Kate tried to find the sweet spot. The spot where she could drift off into a blissful doldrum. Anything that would give her frayed emotions a relief.

But no matter how much she tossed or fluffed her pillow, the spot eluded her, and the only thought that kept running through her mind was when she could see him again. It both frightened and exhilarated her, made her want to risk what little of her dignity was left. She pulled once more on her covers. Roll the dice, as her father would say, let things fall where they may.

Mrs. O'Brien was waiting by the sitting room window when Paddy came into sight. He turned the corner onto Germain Street as if he had the world on a string. "He thinks he's something," she said over her shoulder to her husband. "His cap is a little cockeyed, and he's swinging a walking stick. No one does that anymore." Her mouth tightened. "The things I do for me daughter." She looked back at her husband. "Are you sure the Kennedy's aren't home?"

"Aye. Sent them meself to Mutton Lane. Paid for anyone who can spy our front door to gorge themselves on whatever they fancied."

Mrs. O'Brien bit her lip. "And you're sure they went?"

"Stop your fussing, woman." Mr. O'Brien joined her at the window. "This was your idea, and I went along with it out of the goodness of me heart."

She thumped him in the chest. "It's better than anything you've come up with. You wait and see. When Mary-Kate sees Paddy in her own home, under the roof she's lived under all her life, she'll listen to reason. She'll see he has no place here, that he lacks substance." She straightened slightly and rubbed her back. She'd been stationed there all morning, waiting for this instant and she was feeling the strain of it. Despite her discomfort, she didn't take her eye off the intruder as he swung open their front gate. "And that suit he's wearing. It's ten years if it's a day. Dusty old thing, yet he struts about like he's just walked out of a haberdashery window." She snorted. "Thinks he's dapper, but all he is, is trouble in trousers."

"That's what ya used to call me."

She thumped him for good measure. "And I was right."

"Well, let's get this over with," she said. "There are other things I'd rather be doing."

The trio met Paddy at the door. Mary-Kate glared at both her parents, and Mrs. O'Brien glared back before opening the door with such vehemence the doorknob left a hollow dip where it hit the wall. She gave no formal greeting. "Mary-Kate is complaining about everything these days. She never used to, mind you. Not until she met you."

Paddy smiled. "That's me girl. If she's going to do something, she might as well do it proper."

"Aren't you too clever by half. I didn't say she did it well."

Mary-Kate narrowed her eyes and took Paddy by the arm into the parlour.

"There will be none of that in this house," Mr. O'Brien chided. "What do ya think we are? Protestants? The two of ya arm-holding and parlour-sitting, not when there is still breath in me body."

Under Mr. O'Brien's instruction, Breasal took Paddy by the scuff of the neck and frog-marched him into the kitchen. "I'll bring up the rear," he called, stepping aside for both Mary-Kate and her mother to pass in front of him. "Come Mary-Kate, there's no time for your caterwauling."

"I wasn't caterwauling."

"That may well be, but ya were thinking about it."

Mrs. O'Brien smiled as she followed Mary-Kate into the kitchen. In her mind, things were going rather well. Paddy had been put in his place and Mary-Kate hadn't even protested. Perhaps she was wrong about the affiliation. Perhaps it was a figment of the old penguin's imagination.

It was rare of late that Mrs. O'Brien entered the kitchen, but she was pleased to see it was prepared for a military inspection. Mae had done more than her duty prior to taking the morning off. Pots and pans shone on the shelves. The simplicity of it stilled her. She closed her eyes and took a breath.

"This is a fine room," Paddy said as soon as he was freed from Breasal's grasp. "Finer than that of The Donnybrook." Paddy pulled out a chair and winked.

Mr. O'Brien sniffed. "There is no place as fine as that, don't be kidding yourself, lad." He looked at his wife. "The boy has lost his marbles."

"Mr. O'Brien, I've warned you once and I won't be doing it again. We're to be putting an end to this nonsense, not digging up more."

"As I was saying," Mr. O'Brien pulled at his collar, "we O'Briens' aim to be a cut above."

"That's right," Mrs. O'Brien chimed in. "And what are the Fitzpatrick's known for? Besides thievery."

"Mother!" Mary-Kate snapped, tucking her chair closer to the table. "I only consented to this meeting because I thought it would be conciliatory. If I'd known it would be an attack, I'd have certainly not agreed."

"Conciliatory," Mr. O'Brien snorted, "that's wishful thinking. First me pocketwatch then me daughter. What will it be next? The skin off me bones?"

"No one is taking anyone's skin," Mrs. O'Brien said taking her seat. They each sat on their own side of the square table. Stiffly pouring the tea, Mrs. O'Brien filled all four teacups. After hesitating, she forced herself to ask Paddy if he'd like cream and sugar, though it was through gritted teeth.

"Don't mind if I do," said Paddy, pleased at the offer. "Won't O'Brien be having any?"

"No," said Mrs. O'Brien. "He's not planning on enjoying his tea today."

Mr. O'Brien nodded and slumped in his seat. "It would be foolish of me to enjoy anything these days."

"Yes, I hear it's a testament to a happy marriage." Mary-Kate said, adding an extra sugar to her own. "Makes me wish I'd stayed at the convent."

"That would have been lovely, dear." Mrs. O'Brien patted the back of her daughter's hand. "I'll pop by and talk to Sister Mary-Frances about it tomorrow if you like?"

"That won't be necessary." Mary-Kate dropped her teaspoon on the table before she turned to Paddy. "Don't gulp your tea."

"He can gulp his tea if he wants," Mrs. O'Brien snapped. "The sooner we get this over with the better."

Paddy smiled and looked around him. "Haven't smelt a mouse yet," he said. "And where I come from that's high praise." He put a finger to his chin and narrowed his eyes. "Are ya a shaker or a washer?"

Mrs. O'Brien choked. "I'm sorry?"

"Me ma rarely washes her sheets. She just gives them a good shake."

"That's horrible," gasped Mrs. O'Brien. "I've never heard of anything so vile."

"Oh, it's not that bad. She shakes them outside most days. They wear easier." Paddy inhaled deeply. "Now that I be looking for a wife, I think I want a washer instead of a shaker. Smells better."

Mary-Kate squeezed Paddy's arm. "Let's talk about something else."

Paddy leaned back in his chair. "Since ya've invited me over, I've been making a plan. I haven't even told me Mary-Kate about it yet. Want to show you all the good in me bones. So, after a great deal of thinking, I've decided to open a gold mine in Saskatchewan. Mary-Kate can wait for me here as my future Mrs. Fitzpatrick."

"She'll do no such thing, and as for that upstart province," scoffed Mrs. O'Brien, "there are no gold mines there."

"That's what they want you to think."

Mrs. O'Brien snapped the handle off her teacup. "Have you come here to infuriate me?"

"Do you want to be infuriated?"

"I'm not answering that."

Again Mary-Kate patted Paddy's arm. "Keep going."

Paddy brought his chair closer to the table. "I'll write to Mary-Kate every day, and when I'm rich, I'll send for her."

Paddy's talk of gold mines and boundless riches outraged Mrs. O'Brien more than anything else he'd said. "No more tea for you," she said, as she snatched the cup from his hand.

"Saskatchewan! What kind of fool can make his fortune there?" At the sound of her husband's grunt, Mrs. O'Brien turned to her daughter. "Look at him, he's hardly literate."

"Which one?" Mary-Kate's brow furrowed. "Paddy or Da?"

"Oh, I think she means me," Paddy interjected.

"For the love of god, can you just shut your mouth?" Mrs. O'Brien vibrated and pointed a finger in Paddy's direction. "Is that too difficult to ask?"

Paddy gave her no reply, and from her periphery she could feel Mary-Kate pull away. She took a breath, and after regaining a portion of her frayed nerves, Mrs. O'Brien refocused. "Mary-Kate, do you think there's a heaven for men the likes of Patrick Fitzpatrick? Do you? I'd rather go to hell if there is. After an afternoon tea with him, hell would be a godsend."

Mary-Kate gasped. "How could you say such a thing? He's sitting right here."

"I know where he's sitting. I've eyes in me head, and if you weren't being such a Molly Coddler, you'd see what a wretch he is for yourself." Mrs. O'Brien dabbed the spittle from the corners of her mouth with her napkin.

"Do you want to convince me to think that way? Like you? Hard and unforgiving?"

"Why shouldn't you, I ask you that? The lad is nothing but trouble."

"How would you know? Besides this trumped up tea party, you've never spoken to him, or spent time with him."

"I don't have to. I've met enough Patrick Fitzpatricks' in me time to know what they're all about."

"Paddy's different."

Leaning across the table, Mrs. O'Brien picked up Paddy's hand and dropped it. "See? The boy hasn't a solid bone in his body."

Mary-Kate flicked her fingers. When she spoke again, her voice was pleading and her eyes wet. "If it weren't for him, I'd still be at the convent. Is that what you want? Locked up with some dried up spinsters?"

"Don't get all dewy-eyed. You were asked to leave, which makes your behaviour more than suspect." She looked from her daughter to the intruder. "All he sees is your da's money, and don't be foolish enough to think otherwise."

"How can you say that?"

"The lad has never bent his back to anything. He's a thief. A confidence man. Someone who needs paying to go away."

Mary-Kate slammed her hand on the table. "Then pay him."

"Pay him?"

"Yes, pay him. If you can pay a man like him to go away, pay him." Mary-Kate waved her hand at her surroundings. "There's certainly enough money."

Mr. O'Brien dropped his gaze and mumbled. "We've tried. Sent Father Connelly meself with his thirty pieces of silver."

"I should've guessed. So, he isn't that type of man. The kind you can buy."

"Don't be a fool, Mary-Kate. He's just like his mother, playing the long game."

"I don't care what kind of game you think he's playing. Paddy sat at the same table as my father almost every day at The Donnybrook. They raised their glasses and wished each other well. Is there any better friend than that?"

"Paddy was not me friend." Mr. O'Brien looked at his wife from the corner of his eye. "It was a mistake if he believed it to be so. He was nothing more than a wee bit of entertainment. I should have been home where I belonged."

"That may well be," Paddy interrupted, "but how can ya hate almost-family? I'm the son ya never wanted."

Mrs. O'Brien burned. "I'd rather gouge me eyes with a spoon than call you family."

"When ya're blind and useless," Paddy said in a comforting tone, "I promise not to turn ya out in the street like a common beggar."

There was no disguise this time. No skirting around the edges or sipping from empty tea cups. Mrs. O'Brien rolled up her sleeves and bore down on the convent. There was a job to do, and she couldn't count on her husband to do it. He'd blundered about for weeks and was hardly equipped to tie his own shoes. She scowled as she mouthed his name. One humiliation after another. And he expected her to stand by when her life was barely tenable? If asked at any time during her thirty-years of marriage if she would approach her sister-in-law or employ her help, Mrs. O'Brien would have called the questioner mad. There was no way she would have considered doing such a thing. Until today.

After tea with that Fitzpatrick person, she wasn't convinced that Mary-Kate's affections towards him weren't genuine.

She would ask Sister Mary-Frances.... No, she would *cajole* Sister Mary-Frances.... No, she would *beseech* Sister Mary-Frances to reconsider. Take Mary-Kate back into the fold and ship her off to some distant place where secrets could remain secrets and the come-what-mays could disappear. The request seemed reasonable enough; Mrs. O'Brien would put the sleeping draught into Mary-Kate's evening tea herself.

Sister Bernadette opened the side door before Mrs. O'Brien knocked. *A good omen*, she thought. But no sooner had the nun stepped back to allow her entrance, than Sister Mary-Frances swooped down upon her. In the shadow of her sister-in-law, Mrs. O'Brien lost all her agency. Not a word lay on her tongue. The one thing that came to her was to throw herself at the other's feet. Weeping.

Sister Mary-Frances grunted and stepped over her. "I'm not taking her back. Didn't really want her in the first place. Live in your own misery. All these years I've lived in mine."

68

PADDY

It was a stroke of genius, and Paddy didn't know why he hadn't thought of it sooner. If he was going to take his chance in Saskatchewan, what better ally to have than his mother? The two of them could make a fortune, gold mines or no. And the best part — it would be O'Brien thwarting Black-Hearted John, not him. Paddy could stand back while O'Brien salvaged his family name, and Paddy's was elevated. None would be the wiser. A coward's escape if ever there was one.

The plan had been brewing since the nuns tossed him. At first it was to go back to the lamp post where he'd last seen his mother, follow her to Black-Hearted John's, and whisk her off to the convent. Not that she would ever take her vows, she'd never warm to such a notion. No, she could hide among the clutter in forgotten corners. There were a myriad of places he could have stashed her. But since he'd been caught vacating Mary-Kate's cell, Sister Mary-Frances had taken to packing her revolver. And even if he got Biddy past the old penguin, Father Albright was sure to sniff her out. A lifetime of lip licking couldn't alleviate the stain from that encounter. Now that Paddy weighed both options, Saskatchewan was the far better of the two.

By the time he'd run past The Donnybrook and his smoking effigy, he was feeling like his old self again. The darkness enveloped him, welcoming him back. How many times had he and his mother roamed these streets arm in arm looking for their next mark? Paddy couldn't remember. He had taken their time together for granted. He wouldn't do so again. For now though, he needed to tell her, let her know he hadn't forgotten.

Before he rounded the next corner he heard the deep voice. His heart pounded the same way it had when he was small. It made him pull up and stay well back in the shadows.

"This one's a peach," Black-Hearted John said, as he made Biddy spin in the dim light. Paddy caught a glimpse of her face and saw that there was hardly a breath of spirit left in her. "Trained her meself."

"Well if you've trained her, she'll know her place," said the stranger.

"And a pleasing place it is. Come back to me establishment and you can see for yourself." John draped his arm over the other's shoulder. "Mind you, don't mark her up though. Do what you like, just don't mark her up. Damages the merchandise."

Paddy ground his teeth. If he were a larger man, a braver man, those words would have never been spoken. He would have rushed out from where he hid and dashed their heads upon a stone. Yet, when they moved off, he followed, pacing his steps with a soft tread, unnoticed until they reached their destination. There he waited. The damp in the air went through him, and he shifted from foot to foot, biding his time, hearing Black-Hearted John's words over and over — *Do what you like, just don't mark her up.* He hated that man.

It wasn't until a slight hint of pink crossed the horizon that the stranger came out of the twisted door, buttoning his trousers. Paddy wanted to come at him from behind, strike him down in the street and leave his body for all to see, to step over, to spit upon. But that's not why he'd come.

Before the light gave too much away, Paddy took his chance. He slipped across the street and slid along the side of the ramshackle building. No paint or repair had touched its surface in Paddy's lifetime. He peered through the first window he came to — the shredded curtains did little to block his view — and there she was. She was fixing a button on her dingy blouse. He whistled through his teeth. Biddy lifted her chin. He whistled again. She turned and her face lightened. "Paddy," she mouthed.

He nodded and she was there, pushing up the window. "You shouldn't have come." She reached out and touched his cheek. Paddy leaned into her hand. "No telling what he'll do if you're caught."

"I won't get caught then, will I?"

Biddy bit her lip and her eyes grew large and wild. And Paddy knew, without looking behind him, that caught he was.

"Fancy meeting ya here." Black-Hearted John's breath fell upon Paddy's neck. "Had me man staking you out. Reporting to me on your comings and goings. Was beginning to wonder if you'd ever show." His voice dropped. "Now we can have a little chat."

"Oh, John. It's nothing, really it isn't." Biddy waved a hand in the air, and there was a brightness in her voice. "The boy just came to see how I was. Didn't you, Paddy?"

Paddy nodded but didn't turn.

"Well now that you've seen," John said, forcing Paddy's chin up with the tip of a knife, "you won't have to be troubling us again. Will you?"

Paddy shook his head. He couldn't have croaked out the words even if he wanted to. It was as if he'd swallowed a mouthful of sand. Biddy crooked a finger as she spoke to John.

"Come in, me love," she purred. "Before you catch your death of cold."

Black-Hearted John slackened, and Paddy felt the pressure of the knife lesson. "You hear that boy? She wants me in her bed. Since I've come along there's no place here for you." With a final shove Paddy hit the ground, the heel of a boot on his neck. "You remember that, and you may live to see another day."

Paddy lay in the dark, his cheek on the cold earth. It was the same as when he'd been a small boy, sent out of the house by his gran. The cold bit into him, he felt small and alone. On the other side of the window pane he could only imagine what his mother was doing.

69

FATHER CONNELLY

"Ah, there he is. Skulking around outside the church," said Father Connelly, cleaning off the window with the sleeve of his robe. "Bring him to me."

"Are you sure that be wise?"

"I wouldn't be asking if it wasn't."

Keen nodded and followed the priest's directions. Father Connelly had taken over the helm of The Donnybrook while Mr. O'Brien attended his muddle of a home life, and until now he had honoured his friend's decision to banish Paddy. But promises, like everything else in life, required moderation.

Through the window, the priest watched Keen approach Paddy. There was a short exchange before Paddy hugged Keen and made for the pub.

Paddy strode through the door as if he were O'Brien himself. "How's the men?" the interloper called, and when he got his answer, same as O'Brien's, Paddy nodded at Callum. "I've got a throat on me."

Father Connelly smiled. The place was as it should be. All it was missing was the old man, himself.

"The light in this place is a little dull without you," called

Father Connelly, standing up and waving Paddy over to their table by the window. "It made me want to give up the drink."

Keen and Keenan nodded. "I agree," said Keen. "The light has been a little dull, but I'd never been so inclined as to forego tipping a glass or two."

"'Twould be a sad day," said Keenan. "And we wouldn't want that, would we now?"

The priest pulled a chair out from the table and insisted Paddy sit. "O'Brien doesn't need to know about this, does he, lad? We're going to give ya a wake."

"A wake?"

"Aye. We won't be making it to your funeral, whether you stay or leave," said Keen. "O'Brien would never allow it." He put his hand on the back of O'Brien's chair. "So, we thought we'd drink to you now."

Father Connelly motioned to a coffin being hoisted onto the bar by some of the men. "Afraid we won't be seeing ya after you re-cross that threshold." The priest inclined his head towards the door. "Not hear from ya either, considering where ya're going."

"And where do ya think I'm going?"

"To the great war, the one to end all others." Father Connelly scowled. "Did I not tell ya lad? I enlisted ya this morning. It was your ma's idea. Claimed it would keep ya from under foot, safe and out of the mix. Snuck away from that black-hearted man just to tell me about it. Said if she didn't hurry back it could be the end of her. Don't know what ya did me boy, but ya did give that woman a fright."

Paddy dropped his gaze.

"I tried to tell her that war wasn't such a place," the priest continued. "But she insisted. Said it was the last gift a mother could give. And she made me promise to tell ya to say the words. When I asked her what words, she said you'd know." He slid a rucksack from under the table towards Paddy. "Bought ya this meself. Well, Sister Mary-Frances did. When I told her me plan she paid for it out of the church's coffers." Father Connelly leaned back on his chair. "Now the old girl can't complain I'm spending too much time with the drunks, when just this morning I spent time with" he hesitated. "Ya get me meaning."

Paddy stared at the rucksack and thought back to his mother. "Her parting gift," he repeated.

"She wants ya out of Tnúth on the next train. Said it's a matter of life and death." Father Connelly jabbed a thumb towards Keen and Keenan. "The 'boys will keep ya company until ya board the train. Make sure ya don't give them the slip."

"I don't think that's necessary."

"Your ma did."

"Doesn't that woman know that I'm not a fighter? I never shot a gun in me life. Never even held one."

"Oh, don't worry about that. Ya're not likely to get a chance. They're dropping like flies over there."

"That's not very encouraging."

"Aye. But 'tis your only option. Ya'll not gain respect with that Saskatchewan nonsense. No one's gone there and come back a rich man. But maybe as a temporary gentleman ya might."

"A temporary gentleman. The words lay heavy on me tongue." Paddy shrunk until he was the size of Father Connelly. "If I come back a hero with a chest full of medals, O'Brien couldn't deny that."

"Could be." Father Connelly tilted his head back and forth. "But I think it's wishful thinking. The man doesn't want ya around Paddy, and no amount of heroics is going to change that."

Keen stood and put his fiddle to his chin for a salute to Paddy, the soldier. Paddy rose, as did the rest of the gents. Singing was one of the things he liked best about the pub. On occasion, they all joined in on some old Irish tune, their voices rising as a choir. Paddy's clear tenor, at times, rose above them all.

His love for song fell directly between his love for women and his love for drink. *The Bold Rascal* was his favourite, a song that must have been written for Paddy himself. When it began, Paddy climbed up on his chair, spread his arms wide, and sang from the very marrow in his bones.

Come let your daughter sit 'ere on me knee,
If it don't bother you man, it won't bother me
I'll treat her the way it ought to be
And she'll never want to leave, 'ere on me knee

As it often did, one tune melted into another, and as the next began, Paddy couldn't help but let a tear roll down his cheek. There was hardly a man who didn't do the same. Songs of the famine brought them all to their knees. Although few had lived through it, all felt it deep in their Irish souls. They sang as if their stomachs were empty, and there was nothing left in life to be done.

"Ya have a soft heart," said Father Connelly, as Paddy climbed down from his chair. "'Tis good to see a true Irishman."

Paddy dried his eyes and sat down. "The same could be said about ya, Father."

The priest's head wobbled. "A soft heart doesn't bode well for those headed for war. Just ask all the lads who haven't come back."

Paddy wandered into the church, unsure of his own intentions. Succour, sanctuary, death by pistol — none appealed to him. But the communion wine, that was an entirely different matter. In short order, he'd divested the stores of the plumpest stock when Sister Mary-Frances came plodding down the nave.

She paused. "Are those Father Albright's robes?"

Paddy had two empty wine bottles stuck to the ends of two fingers on the same hand. A third bottle was well on its way to joining the others. He clicked the empty bottles merrily together. "They may be," he said, looking down at his attire. "But they suit me better."

"I think not."

"Come now, Sister Mary-Frances, ya know it's true," he returned in a come-hither tone. "And I might say ya're looking grand this fine evening."

The nun rolled her eyes. "In this light, and with the amount you've been drinking, anyone would look grand."

Paddy nodded. "Don't count yourself short. I see ya've been taking beauty tips from your brother. Now come sit with me, lass, and sing me a song."

The nun grunted, and Paddy scrambled to dodge her blow. "There's no use dallying with me, young man. I've thrown you out once and I'll do it again."

"What kind of nun would that make ya? When all a lad is doing is repenting before heading off to war." Paddy clicked the bottles once more. "It would be unpatriotic."

"What do I care for patriotism? And as for repenting, what would you know of it?"

"I heard the good Father telling the lads that ya needed to repent before partaking. I did."

Sister Mary-Frances's face reddened as she snatched the half-empty bottle from his hand. Her words popped out like bubbles. "You are a piece of work, Patrick Fitzpatrick. Communion is not something to be taken lightly. The wine is not the same as a common drink."

"Do you swallow?"

"Pardon me?"

"When ya take the holy wine, do ya swallow?"

"Of course."

"Aye. In me mind, that be common drinking." He leaned towards Sister Mary-Frances and lowered his voice. "To tell ya the truth, I've much to repent of. Abandoned me ma without even knowing, and I don't know if I have it in me to do anything about it. Too busy playing at switching grave markers to feel her need of me. And then there was Mary-Kate. Was out of me depths with that one."

"It was you." Her colour deepened. "Forcing me to run about like a fool, putting things straight only to have you un-right them again. I do hope that you have the pleasure of becoming cannon fodder."

"Oh, lass. I can promise ya that won't be a pleasure. A bit of a messy business." He stood and dropped the robe he was wearing, causing the nun to raise an eyebrow in surprise. "But this I hear has more of that desired effect." A smile flitted across his face. "Ya're welcome."

"Where are your clothes?"

"I am Adam, and this be me Garden of Eden." Paddy waved his arms about him as if he was showing her something she had never seen before.

"Your clothes," barked Sister Mary-Frances.

Paddy stumbled as he pointed with one of the bottles still attached to his finger. As soon as he was dressed, Sister Mary-Frances grabbed him by the arm and marched him to the front gate. "The only thing I can say," she said, depositing him unceremoniously on the other side, "is that — when it comes to you — the war is good news for bad rubbish."

I n the morning, Paddy made the solemn walk to the railway station. He felt it was best to make the trip of his own volition, rather than having Keen and Keenan send for dockworkers.

Mary-Kate's left hand was neatly tucked into the crook of his arm, while the rucksack hung over his shoulder. He squeezed her hand, not knowing what to say. She seemed to be equally as lost, her bottom lip in a permanent quiver. In a short period, their lives had changed so much. He, evicted from The Donnybrook, and she, passed over for a nun — more of a refusal than a pass over, but Paddy didn't feel like quibbling.

Paddy was going to make sure she wouldn't forget him. The plan was to kiss her passionately before boarding the train. It was to be a grand production. Paddy thought of every detail, right from the monogrammed handkerchief to the sorrowful tune he insisted on humming. If he was going to die in some godforsaken place, he was going to make sure Mary-Kate likened it to a biblical experience.

Mary-Kate's voice trembled. "I can't believe you're leaving. I might never see you again."

He snapped his hanky before handing it to her. "Aye. And how will that make ya feel?"

"What do you mean?"

"Not seeing me again."

Mary-Kate paused and dabbed her eyes. "Paddy, you know I'll miss you, wherever they send you."

"You'll miss me. I was hoping 'twould be more than that."

"What were you hoping for?"

"Your undying love."

"After all that's happened," she lowered her voice, "after all we've done, how can you ask me that? I'd think it was apparent."

"Once is not apparent. It could be a regrettable dalliance," he said, raising an eyebrow. "So how could I not ask?"

"I don't do dalliances." She blew out her cheeks. "Do I have your undying love?"

"Ya do until I'm dead."

"I should hope so," she whispered, closing her eyes and tilting her face towards his.

"I can kiss ya, Mary-Kate O'Brien, but I want more than a kiss." Paddy caught her around the waist and pulled her into himself. He brought his mouth down on hers and held it there until she pulled away. "Ya shouldn't be teasing me."

"I wasn't teasing you." She looked around. "We're in public."

"That may well be, but ya kissed me like your dead gran."

"Patrick Fitzpatrick! You'll bring bad luck on us speaking of the dead that way."

"Ya sound like your mother." The words seemed to irritate his intended. Paddy touched his breast pocket and hesitated. "I have something for ya," he said. "Something that can mark our time together even when we're apart." He swung the watch on its chain, narrowly missing Mary-Kate.

She furrowed her brow. "Isn't that my father's?"

"Not by choice," he said, laying the timepiece in the palm of her hand. "'Twas me great-granddad's."

Mary-Kate ran a finger along its engraved edge as Paddy told her the tale, the same as his mother had told him. The tale of a man, and what he was willing to give up for a woman.

"Besides ya, it's the only thing I have of value." He looked at her, considering if he should go on. "And me ma. Tell ya da I left like he wanted. Tell him to take care of ya, since I won't be around to do it meself."

Mary-Kate nodded, looking from Paddy to the watch. "I don't need this Paddy, I really don't."

"Maybe not," he folded her fingers around the orb. "But it's yours, just the same."

Taking a deep breath she leaned into him, kissing him in a way no mother would approve of.

When she pulled away, Paddy lowered his head and joined the line of other young men. His steps were slow and heavy, causing the dust to rise and cover his shoes as if he were walking on a dark cloud. He was almost out of sight, swallowed by the throng, when Mary-Kate called out, "I could love you, Patrick Fitzpatrick, and only you, if you could prove to me you want me for more than my father's money."

"I have loved ya for many reasons, Mary-Kate O'Brien," he yelled back. "And only a few of them have had anything to do with your da's money."

EPILOGUE

Five years passed, and there was no word from Paddy. The war ended, and young men limped home, though Paddy wasn't one of them. Mr. O'Brien pulled an ornate pocket watch from his vest pocket and checked it. It was early enough in the day. There was plenty of time. He'd leave for the pub after lunch. He tapped his pipe on the heel of his shoe before refilling it, but he didn't light it. He looked to the empty armchair across from him, unfinished handwork left in a pile on the seat. Then he flipped open the newspaper and began to read.

THIS REPORTER HAS ONCE AGAIN BEEN PROVEN right. No more than two weeks ago one of our upstanding citizens made his way, mistakenly, into a foreign side-street cafe. He was on a business trip in Saskatchewan, staying in a town named after some animal's jaw. The cafe in question was dubbed after one of our own old pubs, The Donnybrook.

It wasn't until the gentleman was seated and ordered a bowl of soup that he began to have misgivings. There was not a woman on the premises, and all the other patrons were questionable at best. Not surprisingly, when his soup arrived, it wasn't soup at all. It was a foul-smelling concoction that had been produced illegally in an unwashed bathtub. To top it off, the server was none other than Patrick Fitzpatrick, a one-time associate of the O'Brien family. Fitzpatrick is still as much of a scoundrel as ever, as it has come to light that he may have impersonated a priest.

As you can well imagine, our upstanding citizen didn't disappoint us and left the premises as quickly as he'd come. All this reporter can say is that Tnúth is a far better place since Fitzpatrick's departure. Moreover, any town named after an animal body part deserves what it gets!

MR. O'BRIEN CHUCKLED and handed the paper to the downstairs maid. "Cut that out will you," he said as he motioned to the little red-headed girl playing with cut-out dolls before the fireplace. "But don't be showing it to me wee Edna."

Thanks for reading *West of Ireland*. If you enjoyed your time with the O'Brien's, a review would be much appreciated as it helps other readers discover the story.

If you haven't joined my Readers Group please do. You'll also be notified of giveaways, new releases, and receive personal updates from between the covers of my books.

Here's how to get started:

www.blackcrowbooks.com/readersgroup

A peek at

A Town Called Forget

LONGLISTED FOR THE STEPHEN LEACOCK
MEDAL FOR HUMOUR

A Town Called Forget
C.P. Hoff

"It's not often I meet a young girl travelling alone," the older woman said as she stared hard at the girl sitting across from her. "There must be a good reason."

The girl said nothing. Instead, she frowned, looked past the stranger and tried to catch the conductor's attention. At first she thought a little wave of her hand would do; she had seen her father attract attention that way quite successfully. It didn't work; the girl cleared her throat and raised her arm a little higher. The conductor looked confused and checked his pocket watch. The older woman nattered on and flapped her arms about as she talked about God knew what. The girl felt like wadding up her ticket and beaning the conductor in the head; her mother had paid him a generous tip to keep her isolated.

"My daughter is in no mood for polite company or idle chit-chat," her mother had said, a sentiment the girl agreed with whole-heartedly. But the elderly woman with the round build, and hair the girl was sure a pixie had wrapped in frayed gauze and scattered with dandelion fuzz, seemed oblivious to her mood.

"You'll not get his attention that way," the older woman said, tapping the girl on her knee. "Lord knows I've tried. Ever since I walloped him on the backside, he gives me a wide berth." She furrowed her brow. "Perhaps he'd preferred more of a squeeze. I'll corner him in the dining car later and ask. He won't know what hit him."

The girl sighed and let her ticket drop to the floor.

"Where was I?" asked the older woman. "Oh, yes, I was appraising my overall impression of you. As I was saying, you are rather well-dressed: some might even say handsome, with your dark hair and high cheekbones. These things seem to be in fashion; even your willowy frame might draw attention. I would never say you were handsome though; it can make one vain. A vain young woman is of little use to anyone." She leaned closer. "You're not vain, are you?"

With a deep breath, the girl tried again to get the conductor's attention, but to no avail. He seemed to deliberately turn his back to her. Her only other option, as every seat in the car was taken, was to pretend to be asleep. Unclenching her fists, she closed her eyes, and let her head bob slightly with the sway of the train.

"I'm Harriet Simpson. You can call me Mrs. Simpson if you like. Although, I've never married. I've imagined what it might be like though." Harriet's voice cracked. "He was a real brute, and I was glad to be done with him."

The girl opened her eyes.

"Ah, you can hear. I thought perhaps you were deaf, and that's why you didn't respond, but now I see it's just because you're a mute. How terribly exciting! I've never met a mute before. What's it like?"

The girl's jaw dropped.

"Forgive me, dear, I forgot; mutes don't speak." She paused for a moment and pursed her lips in a most unattractive way. "I bet I can guess what it's like though; I'm awfully good at guessing. Let me see, let me see. You were born under a full moon, and the first thing you saw was a black cat. Am I right so far? Just nod if I am."

"No, you're not right."

"Oh." Harriet seemed more disappointed with her inaccurate guess than amazed at the girl's ability to speak. "If you were born under a full moon and saw a black cat, you would surely have been a mute. I can almost guarantee it."

The train lurched, causing both Harriet and the girl to shift in their seats. They watched each other for a moment before Harriet resumed the conversation. "Travelling by rail is only slightly better than by motorcar. Although I've never travelled by motorcar, but I'm sure of it. Motorcars are quite unpredictable: a little bit of bad weather and you're stranded. Can you imagine! Me and that brute of a husband standing by the side of the road in the pouring rain; what a sight that would be." Harriet dabbed her forehead with a gloved hand. "It would be my undoing." Mrs. Simpson looked out the window and sighed.

The girl thought she must be envisioning a marooned motorcar and a furious husband in his duster and goggles. Harriet in a wide brimmed hat and ripped veil. It was the only way the girl could picture Harriet Simpson: thinking she was de rigueur, but in reality being quite passé.

"It's much different on these black devils with their coal fires burning." Harriet grabbed the arm rest and yanked on it as if she were trying to rip it from its foundation. "Dependable as the day is long. From a seat, much like this one, I've spied the wonders of Saskatchewan. From the vast openness of the south, to the mid- and northerly parts where I've watched quivering aspen, birch and poplar transform into spruce and pine." Her fingers spread wide as she moved her hands like the fans of a Japanese geisha. "The soil is so full of life. I've seen places where the dirt is so dark you'd swear it's wet."

The girl wasn't sure how to respond. She too had seen changes. From the bustle of Toronto streets and Union Station to the ever-changing landscape of hills and trees dotted with farms and intermittent pockets of civilization, to the flat barren southern prairies. A place so open there was a naked vulnerability to it. It made her uncomfortable. She was sure no one could keep a secret in such a place, as there was nowhere to hide.

Mrs. Simpson hadn't been privy to all the girl's impressions, as she was only a recent travelling companion, boarding this train as she did in Saskatoon. The place where the girl and her parents parted company.

"It doesn't feel like a grand adventure anymore, not since that so-called Great War....." Harriet paused and looked past the girl as if unable to finish her thought. The girl followed the older woman's gaze to a young man sitting two rows down and across the aisle, an empty shirt sleeve pinned to his shoulder.

Nodding, the girl rubbed her arms. There was nothing grand about her adventure either.

"You haven't told me, dear," Harriet reached out and touched the girl's arm, "why are you travelling alone?"

The kind touch brought the girl to tears. Harriet pulled a hanky from her sleeve and slipped it into the girl's hand. "There, there now, it couldn't be that bad."

"Oh, yes it is. My parents abandoned me in Saskatoon."

"They must have had their reasons. No one abandons a perfectly good daughter for no reason. You must have done something."

The girl shook her head.

"How old are you, child?"

"Sixteen."

"And you can't think of anything you've done wrong?"

"No, I've done nothing wrong. My parents and I were taking a trip across the prairies and when we arrived in Saskatoon my luggage and I were transferred to another train and they went on without me."

"Without a word of explanation?"

"They said I'm to stay with my eccentric aunt. We're to get acquainted."

"Eccentric?" Harriet dismissed the comment with the wave of her hand.

"And they gave me a bundle of letters."

"What did the letters say?"

"I'm not supposed to read them yet."

"That doesn't make any sense. Start from the beginning, dear, and let's figure things out." Harriet leaned back in her seat. She looked particularly pleased with herself. "You're in good hands, dear; I'm a splendid listener you know. I nod at the most appropriate time and click my tongue in support. There has been many a weary soul that has commented on my ability. I call it my magnum opus."

Every word Harriet Simpson spoke made the girl wish she were a deaf mute. And although she had her misgivings, she ignored them; she needed to talk to someone.

"My mother has always fussed over me," she found herself saying. "She's never abrasive or demanding. All my friends envy me; they think I'm indulged. With my parents. I've been almost everywhere in Toronto that's considered fashionable. Before the war, we were supposed to go on a European tour. Have you ever been to Europe?"

"No. Saskatchewan trains don't travel that far." There was a hint of bitterness in her voice.

"When my mother packed our things she said we were going to catch a train in an hour. I was excited, but my parents weren't. They boarded the train as if it were a great misfortune. Mother feigned a headache for most of the trip, excusing herself to go lay down in the sleeping car whenever I pressed her. Father hardly looked up from the newspaper he had brought with him. He must have read it at least a half dozen times."

Harriet clicked her tongue and winked at the girl.

The girl ignored her and continued. "When I asked them where we were going, they said to Forget. 'To forget what?' I asked. My father told me that Forget was a place, and that was where I was going, not them."

Harriet sat up straight in her seat. "You are a lucky girl. I'm from Forget and it's far better than Europe. I've never been to Europe, but I'm sure it's just dreadful and expensive. It sounds expensive."

The girl shrugged and blew her nose.

"You'll love Forget; everyone does. Our slogan is, *Forget is a place you won't forget.* Very ingenious, don't you think?" Harriet didn't pause long enough for the girl to answer. "Forget is full of picaresque souls. I read that word in a book once. Didn't know what it meant until I looked it up in a dictionary. It describes our town so precisely, beguiling rogues to the core. Picaresque." Harriet's voice lowered and became almost grave. "Remember what I am telling you dear, and don't believe a word of what some townsfolk might say. We are not all related." And as if to prove the point she added, "We have a class three railway station."

The train slowed, and the girl looked out the window.

"That's our sign." Harriet pointed to a signpost flanked with pussy willows at the edge of the tracks.

"That's not how you spell *Forget*."

"Yes it is. It's the French spelling. Forgetta. Makes us sound a bit more exotic."

"That's not how the French spell *forget*."

"Oh, it is now. The town had a vote. Keep it under your hat. We haven't told the French yet. They are so persnickety." Harriet smiled, and her eyes almost pinched together. "*Persnickety.* I read that word in a book as well."

Although she tried not to, the girl furrowed her brow in frustration. "But what about your slogan, *Forget is a place you won't forget?*"

"Silly girl. Our slogan isn't French."